What the critics are saying

I read this story in one sitting and found it to be very entertaining. It was very unusual and original.
- *Laura Lane, Sensual Romance*

Ellora's Cave Publishing, Inc.
PO Box 787
Hudson, OH 44236-0787

ISBN # 1-84360-564-3

The Academy edited by Martha Punches.
Cover art by Scott Carpenter.

Warning: The following material contains strong sexual
content meant for mature readers. *THE ACADEMY* has
been rated NC-17 erotic, by a minimum of three
independent reviewers. We strongly suggest storing this
book in a place where young readers not meant to view it
are unlikely to happen upon it. That said, enjoy…

THE ACADEMY

Written by

ELIZABETH STEWART

Chapter One

"Daria! Daria!"

Pausing uncertainly, the young woman swiveled her head in the direction of the voice and peered groggily through the airport throng. Above the crowd, about thirty feet away, a raised hand waved wildly, and a head bobbed like a jumping bean at the end of a long, thin pole as the body wound its way hurriedly toward her.

Wearily, she set down her travel bag and waited the few seconds for the other woman to reach her. Almost immediately, a massive bear hug engulfed her and a rain of fond kisses began to fall.

"Oh Daria," she squealed delightedly, looking her friend up and down, "it is so good to see you even if you do look like something the *fenises* dragged in!"

"Cat, Analet," Daria corrected gently, extracting herself with some difficulty from her friend's embrace. "It's *cat*. I've told you a hundred times, if you're going to use human adages and proverbs, you've got to try not to mangle them. It's good to see you too."

"Yes, yes, 'cat,'" she repeated in mild frustration. "There are too many of your languages. And they're too hard to learn and remember. You humans should just pick one and stick with it. On Carus, everyone speaks the same language and understands one another. Perhaps that is the reason your people have had so many problems in their history."

"Perhaps, but I'm too tired to argue galactic politics with you right now."

"Ah, I understand. The luggage claim is this way. I assume that for the length of time you're probably going to be here, you brought more than that teeny travel bag." She pointed a long, pale blue finger at the small black bag at Daria's feet.

"I have two larger cases," Daria agreed, picking up the bag. "I didn't know exactly what I was getting into so I thought I should err on the side of overkill. Lead on."

"So," Analet asked as they threaded their way through the crowd, "the trip was pleasant?"

At barely five foot three, Daria gladly trailed her Amazonian friend as she parted the crowds like a huge luxury cruiser amidst a harbor of toy boats. Like all the women of Carus, Analet stood over six feet tall, board-straight hair falling like a snowy waterfall to her waist, amber eyes and blue skin the color of a sun bleached August sky back in Daria's native home of California, Earth.

"As pleasant as these things ever are," Daria answered wearily. "Except for a few short jaunts to Mars on business, I haven't traveled very much. I don't like getting into those little hibernation chambers at the start of the trip, and I always feel like I'm still half-suspended until I can get a proper night's sleep after we land."

"Well, you needn't worry. Your audience with The Sildor, Minsee, isn't until tomorrow afternoon."

"The Sildor." Daria recited aloud. "'Hereditary ruler of the planet Utan. Minsee, current ruler, the fourth in her dynasty, having been on the throne for the equivalent of twenty-six Earth years. Considered to be progressive and forward thinking, especially in comparison to her recent forebears. Seeks expanded contact with other planets and civilizations.'"

"You've done your homework well, little friend," Analet laughed, draping her huge arm around Daria's small, thin frame. With Daria's honey-colored hair falling in thick waves around her oval face and her emerald green eyes, the women made quite a sight as they traveled down the long moving sidewalk to the luggage claim area.

"But then, you always do. The proposal you wrote for Unitech to enter into an agreement for the exclusive mineral rights to Utan's north sphere was nothing short of brilliant."

"Thank you. But my position as New Projects Analyst has always been behind the scenes. I've never had any desire to be in the spotlight. To tell you the truth, I'm more than just a little frightened."

The other woman threw back her head and literally roared with laughter. Several people in the near vicinity jumped at the massive sound and turned to see where it was coming from.

"Daria Evans, afraid? I can't believe that. You, who've engineered some of the biggest deals in the history of the biggest conglomerate in the known universe? Ridiculous!"

"Those 'deals' as you so blithely refer to them, resulted from months, sometimes years of careful planning; assembling every scrap, every detail of information. Plotting every conceivable scenario and every conceivable permutation of every conceivable scenario." Daria shook her head and frowned. "There are any number of people at Unitech who could and should be making this presentation."

"Well, that's not how The Sildor does things. She is smart and she is tough and she does not care about the smooth talk and the smiling faces. She wants to see for herself, what kind of mind thought this project up. Who will be, in large part, responsible for making this thing a reality, and that, Daria my friend, is what you do best."

They arrived at the luggage claim as pieces disgorged from the transporter into their individual bins. Joining a group of others from the liner just docked, they waited while everything was unloaded.

"Analet," Daria turned cautiously to her friend as they waited, "how long have you been on Utan now?"

"Uhm…six, no, seven years as you humans measure time."

"And most of that has been with the Carusian delegation to the palace?"

"Correct."

"Well…" Daria could feel pink rising in her cheeks and she stared down at her feet. "In my preparations for coming here, I was reading up on Utan. You know, its history, culture, customs. That sort of thing."

Knowing by the slightly embarrassed tone of her friend's voice where the conversation was leading but determined to make Daria actually say what was on her mind, Analet feigned ignorance.

"A wise idea," she commented simply.

"Apparently, the planet has been in the grip of an Ice Age for some thousands of years and that thanks to geothermal energy, the civilization was able to move underground."

"That is true."

"But before the transition could be completed, most of the women and children died from the freezing weather and a plague."

"Uh-huh." Analet stifled a giggle.

"As a result, there's a tremendous shortage of women, even now, and they hold a great deal of power. Not just political, but economic and social as well." Daria cleared her throat. "I…uh…understand that many women here have…multiple husbands." She could barely get the last words out.

"Exactly," Analet agreed. "Most women who can afford it have at least four. In fact, The Sildor, being the most powerful woman on the planet, is reputed to have a harem of some one hundred mates, although the exact count is not known because no one, save The Sildor and her servants—all males—are allowed access to them."

Daria's head popped up, a look of astonished disbelief on her face. "Four?" she practically shrieked. "A harem? That's…that's…"

"That is the way of Utan," Analet laughed.

"But it's wrong," Daria insisted. "Marriage is a sacred institution. To be shared by *two* people. Not some state-sanctioned orgy. It's just not right."

"You humans have your ways," Analet shrugged. "We Carusians have ours. And the Utanians have theirs. They are not 'right' or 'wrong.' They are simply different. It is the way of the Universe."

"But…"

"A word of advice my friend," Analet told her quietly. "If the Utanians came to Earth, you would expect them to abide by your customs as well as your laws. It is the same here. And here, the matters of males and females and the pleasures of the flesh are as they are. You would do well to keep your opinions to yourself."

"Well, fortunately," Daria told her friend firmly, "I'm not going to be here long enough to find out about the Utanians and their customs. Tonight, a good soak and a long sleep at the public accommodations center, tomorrow the audience with The Sildor, a few days to get all the paperwork signed and then back to Earth on the first liner."

* * * * *

"I absolutely can't believe we're underground," Daria commented as Analet skillfully maneuvered her small vehicle through the congested city skyway. "It looks just like any city on a calm summer's day. I mean, that 'sun' is so bright, I can't even look at it. And the sky is such a beautiful shade of light green."

"The Utanians did a wonderful job, all right," Analet replied, almost sideswiping a large, public vehicle changing flight patterns in front of her. "Realizing they would probably spend about two hundred thousand years underground and with almost unlimited power and a relatively small population, they decided to do it right. That is one of the reasons there was such a loss of life among the women and children. Setting this up was a long, arduous project; many of the men spent months, years even down here actually trying to build the infrastructure and the power source. And then, just before their females and young could be moved to safety, a plague of Gul-Shad's Death swept the planet. It claimed the very young, the very old and the weak, mostly the females and offspring."

"I think that's so sad."

Analet sighed. "Daria Evans, you are too much the sleeper…"

"Dreamer," she corrected almost without thinking.

"Dreamer. For a woman of your almost," she stopped, converting her Carusian numbers to Earth figures, "thirty-five years and fine education, sometimes you sound like such a baby. The universe neither knows nor cares of such things as ice or plague or even the mating habits of some of its animals." She threw her friend an evil grin. "The universe simply is. You would do well to remember that, too."

"Perhaps the universe 'simply is,'" Daria persisted. "But that doesn't mean that we shouldn't be trying to make an impact. Change things for the better if we can. Unitech has made huge differences in people's lives. These mining operations will bring new wealth to Utan. People from all over the universe will come here. Growth. Expansion. Prosperity. And I'm proud to be even a small part of it."

"Overcrowding. Dilution of the Utan culture. And a very large slice of that newly created wealth will find its way into the insatiable maw of Unitech. In fact, I would be much surprised if some of it didn't dribble down to Unitech's newest Presidential Vice Person in Charge of Vast New Mining Projects."

"Vice-President. And I doubt seriously that will happen. I'm a very small fish in a very large pond."

Her friend's high forehead wrinkled in confusion.

"That means, I'm a very unimportant person in a very large company."

"Oh."

A few minutes later, they arrived at a large public accommodation(s-add) center. It rose above the busy flyway, two hundred slender stories of burnished copper colored windows and metal jutting into the 'sky.'

Expertly, Analet pulled her vehicle into the parking garage. As they exited the vehicle, a robot porter appeared for Daria's luggage. Fully loaded, it chugged away and the women headed for the nearest transporter. Daria punched her cubicle number and almost instantly, they found themselves in her assigned room.

Sniffing slightly, Analet frowned. "Not very big," she commented, eyeing the single bed, small table and chair and wall-mounted monitor. "I would think such a large, wealthy company as Unitech could afford better."

"It's fine," Daria told her half-heartedly, surveying the small room. A soft "ping" announced that her luggage had been deposited in the closet to her left. "Besides, I'm not going to be here very long."

Her friend shrugged. "If you are content…"

"I am, thank you."

"Very well. I must return to the consulate. Rest now. I will call for you this evening and take you to dinner. I know this marvelous place."

"That sounds wonderful." She threw her arms around her huge friend and looked up into her face. "Thank you very much for coming to meet me at the transportation port. I'm sorry to be such a grouch. I'll be fine after I've had some rest."

"I know, friend Daria," the other woman reassured her, gently patting her back with a catcher's mitt-sized hand. "Tonight we shall talk and laugh. Until then."

When Analet was gone, Daria sighed, overwhelmed with fatigue. Even the thought of a warm bath was too much of an effort. Slipping off her shoes, stockings and suit jacket, she lay down on the narrow bed. It was stiff as a board; far more uncomfortable than the cushioned pallet on which she'd spent a little more than a week in suspended animation as the superliner had made its journey from Earth. Still, she was so exhausted, Daria suspected she could have slept on a solid rock.

Just as she closed her eyes and felt herself drifting off, she heard a distinct buzzing, as if an angry insect had invaded her room. For a few moments, she pretended not to notice and tried to force herself to sleep. But the buzzing continued, insisting that she pay heed. Finally, she opened her eyes. The buzzing came from the transmitter in the bedside table, keeping time to a small red light, pulsing brightly.

With a resigned sigh, she reached out and waved her hand over the light. Immediately, a laser beam shot out and a hologram appeared.

"Good morning, Daria," the figure called cheerfully. "Or is it afternoon there?"

"Good afternoon, Trout," she smiled wearily.

"Can you see me all right?" he asked. "Damn connection stinks on this end. Either that or you're under water." He laughed at his own joke.

"You look fine," she lied. The image was actually very shaky, his tall, slender frame, wobbling in his black suit, white business shirt and plain charcoal tie like an eel, his neatly trimmed black hair like a partial circle around his long face, his beautiful black eyes barely visible. She was just too tired to discuss the shortcomings of intergalactic communication right now. Even with her fiancé.

"Did you have a good trip?"

"As well as could be expected. I was just going to lie down and see if I could catch a catnap. I'm meeting Analet tonight and she's going to give me the lowdown on Minsee, The Sildor, before our meeting tomorrow."

"That's my girl," his laugh rumbled over the light years to her. "Always do your homework. Always get the details down pat. That's what makes you so good."

She felt her eyes falling shut and it was everything she could do to keep them open.

"I just hope I don't blow it," she mumbled. "I understand this Minsee is quite a woman."

"I know you'll be fine," he insisted, reaching out a hand as if to pat her head, "just fine. I'm sure that no matter what this old battle-ax throws at you, you can handle it." His voice dropped a notch and took on a serious tone. "Don't forget how important this is, Daria, not just to the company, but to you and I personally."

"I know, Trout," she whispered wearily, "I know."

"This contract is worth billions," he kept on, "absolutely billions. When you bring home that signed contract, you're going to become the first female vice president in Unitech's history. Old Man Hennessey told me himself and he'd fire me in a hot second if he knew I'd told you. It's supposed to be a surprise for when you get back. Said he had a devil of a time selling the idea to the Board but if you swing this deal, you'll have earned your stripes. With that and the promotion I'll no doubt get for supervising this project, we can finally get married. Even my family won't be able to say anything."

"Hmmm," was all she could manage.

"Well, you better get your rest, Daria. We want you fresh and at your best for the meeting tomorrow. Call me the instant you finish and let me know how it went."

"Of course, Trout." Daria closed her eyes and leaned back in the pillow.

"Good bye. And good luck."

The image snapped off and Daria sank almost immediately into much needed sleep.

* * * * *

"I do not understand how you can marry a fish," Analet told her seriously. "I mean, you are of the primate species, far evolved beyond a trout. You do not breathe water and he does not breathe air. Where will you live? How will you mate? Or is the term 'spawn' for a fish?"

Daria rolled her eyes and nibbled on a dinner roll. "You shouldn't try to be funny, Analet," she scolded softly. "You're not very good at it."

Her friend smiled and took a long drink of red wine. "I am serious," she insisted. "Your Trout is as cold and slippery as any fish I have ever seen. All silvery and attractive on the outside and who will no doubt stay as long as the food supply is good. But throw out that hook and he is gone. How long has it been that you have been trying to land him?"

"I haven't been trying to land him," Daria answered a little defensively. "Both of us have been very busy with our careers and decided early to wait until we knew for sure marriage was what we both wanted."

"How long has it been?" Analet asked frankly, her amber eyes dark with intensity.

"Really, Analet..."

"How long?"

"About five years," Daria retorted, "not that it's any of your business. Now can we please drop this whole subject?"

"No," the other woman replied flatly, obviously not willing to be put off. "You share the same living space, the same food, the same bed. You say that you love him; you say that he loves you. Yet you do not join and you do not produce offspring. It makes no sense."

"It isn't that simple," she replied softly, lowering her head to examine her plate.

"What could be more simple? Life-forms all over the universe mate and reproduce. All seek the companionship and intimacy of their own kind."

"You're not married," Daria snapped, looking up at her friend. "You're a career diplomat. Why can't you understand how important my career is to me? It's the same thing."

"It is not the same thing," Analet told her firmly, shaking her large head. "My people have served Carus since we practiced diplomacy with a rock and a pointed stick. This life was not my choice. I was pledged to it in my mother's womb. And I have lived that life to the best of my ability. But in one more year, as humans measure time, I will be released from my vow, honorably I hope, and will return to Carus where I shall actively seek to end this life of aloneness. But you are not bound by honor or duty or family. You've chosen this barren life. I suppose even a trout is better than being always alone."

"You just don't understand," Daria sighed. "For one thing, there's Trout's family. The Erdman's are a fine old family. Very refined, very old fashioned, very old money. Socially prominent."

She stopped, biting her lip at the harsh thought.

"Compared to them," she whispered, "I'm practically nobody. Left on a church step in the middle of the night. Raised by nuns in a Catholic orphanage. No way to know who or what my people were. Trout's family has every right to be a little wary of me. After all, I hope one day to be the mother of his children."

"You sound like this herd of fish will devour you," Analet replied disdainfully. "Like those Great Black Fish of your planet that eat your kind."

"Great White Sharks," Daria corrected automatically. "And it's school of fish, not herd."

"What difference does it make to them anyway? I mean, I confess to knowing little of the fish of Earth, but I thought you would only be taking one trout to mate and not his entire pack."

"School, Analet. And wouldn't it make a difference to your family who you married?"

"On Carus, when the young mature to a point where they begin to think of mating and producing young themselves, they go out into the world and seek a compatible mate. In fact, if they stay with their family too long, they will probably be turned out anyway. We believe that only by listening to your own body, feeling the blood rise and run hot, can you know the time and person is right. Does your cold fish make your blood rise and run hot, little friend?"

"Analet," she hissed, "stop that! It's none of your business."

"I thought not," she giggled and took a bite of her dinner.

In the silence that followed, Daria became aware that the pale blue areas just under her friend's amber eyes had turned a dark, almost navy and that every few seconds, she cast a furtive glance to her left.

Cautiously, Daria let her eyes travel in the same direction. Three tables over, two men, one middle-aged and one younger, ate dinner. Their large build, pale blue skin and amber eyes, immediately identified them as Carusian, probably part of the diplomatic contingent. Between bites and conversation, the older Carusian was glancing in their direction, he and Analet making eye contact and quickly looking away. But even from this distance, Daria could see that the area under his eyes was almost black.

"That's disgusting," Daria whispered loudly to her friend.

"I don't know what you mean."

"Of course you do," she answered, feeling the blush of anger and embarrassment rising. "It's written all over your face. Or more precisely, in big black circles under your eyes. Really. You ought to be ashamed. And in a public place, too."

"Ashamed?" Analet asked dryly. "Ashamed of what? That the physiology of my people is different than yours? That sexual arousal causes the skin under our eyes to change color? You might as well ask me to be ashamed that my eyes or my hair are a different color than yours."

"That's not what I mean, and you know it."

"What then?"

"How can you just sit there and...and flirt with a perfect stranger? It's...it's undignified for a woman of your position."

"He is Benwa, a Minister with the Carusian trade delegation and hardly a stranger."

"Obviously not," Daria agreed, her words dripping acid, "especially judging by the circles under his eyes."

"I would not use the word 'judge' so lightly if I were you my little friend."

Daria opened her mouth to say something, but just then, a large shadow fell across their table.

"*Dai shan*," the tall man smiled to Analet.

"*Dai shan*," she replied and demurely lowered her eyes. Daria was shocked to catch a glimpse of her friend eyeing his crotch as she pretended to study her plate.

"I hadn't expected to find you dining here, Ambassador," he told her in a kind, warm, baritone that seemed to come from deep inside his towering body. "And certainly not in the company of such a beautiful companion." His smile focused on Daria like a spotlight.

"This is my friend," Analet answered, raising her eyes and smiling slightly. "Daria Evans. She is the one I told you about."

"Ah, yes, I remember our conversation well. But from the way you talked, I imagined some ugly, sour old hag, part computer, part Ventonian Bloodsucker. Had I known how wrong I was, I would certainly never have allowed two such desirable females to dine alone." He turned slightly and motioned for the other man to join them.

"This is Ramel," he said by way of introduction. "He is just arrived from Carus to take up his duties as my assistant. Ramel, this is Ambassador Analet Tol and her friend, Daria Evans of Earth."

"An honor, Ambassador Tol," he said in a quiet, solemn tone. "Daria Evans. I have never been to Earth, but I have heard that the females of your primate species are most attractive. If they are a fraction as lovely as you, the males of your planet are truly blessed."

"Thank you," she managed, transfixed by the darkening circles under his eyes—eyes seeming to almost glow as he looked at her.

"Perhaps you and Ramel would care to join us?" Analet smiled coyly. "We have just finished our dinner but perhaps you would be interested in some…dessert."

Horrified, it was all Daria could do to keep from kicking her friend under the table. The last thing she wanted was to be trapped at this small table with three large, sexually aroused Carusians.

The circles under Benwa's eyes pulsed a rich ebony, Analet's fast approaching the same color.

"Well, perhaps a glass of wine."

And before Daria could say anything, the two towering figures had settled themselves into the remaining chairs on either side of the table and Benwa had ordered another bottle of wine.

"So Daria Evans," Ramel turned to her, "what is it that brings you so far from your home planet?" He was perhaps her age or even a little younger with eyes the color of winter wheat and snowy hair worn like a thick mane around his face. *It was,* she thought grudgingly, *not a bad face at all.*

"I…I'm here on business," she stammered.

Analet laughed heartily. "My little friend is modest indeed. She works for Unitech and has come half-way across the galaxy to sign a contract with The Sildor for the mineral rights to the northern hemisphere."

Both men gazed at her appreciatively.

"Indeed?" commented Benwa, raising an inquisitive eyebrow. "A large task for such a small female. Obviously you must be as intelligent as you are beautiful. A most enticing combination."

My God, she thought in amazement, *he's flirting with me, too.* It was too much.

"Your mate has made the journey with you?" Ramel asked, those eyes alive now with a dark gold fire.

"Daria has no mate," Analet snickered. "She has a fish."

The two men exchanged confused glances.

"Analet is trying to be funny," Daria replied, throwing an angry look at her friend. "My fiancé's name is Trout. Trout Erdman. It's an old family name but it's also a species of fish on my planet and for some reason, the Ambassador seems to find that extremely amusing."

Several uncomfortable moments of silence passed before Ramel spoke again. "Well, if I possessed such a jewel as you, Daria Evans, I know I could not bear to have you out of my sight, much less across light years of space." He sounded so sincere, so earnest, for a moment, Daria almost forgot about those dark circles under his eyes.

"Thank you," she told him simply, hoping he'd turn his attention back to Analet.

"I was just thinking," Benwa ventured. "Ramel and I had planned to go to The Spirit Palace this evening. Being new to Utan, I thought he would enjoy it. Since you too are a visitor, Daria Evans, perhaps you and the Ambassador would care to join us? It might make for a very entertaining evening."

It was obvious to Daria that Benwa didn't think she knew about The Spirit Palace. Well, she'd show him.

"I'm sorry," she feigned, "but I really am exhausted and I have to meet with The Sildor in the morning. I'm really just not up to it." She glanced knowingly at her friend, waiting for her to make her excuses so they could be rid of these interlopers.

"A visit to The Spirit Palace would be a most welcome diversion," Analet smiled coyly. "Especially in the company of two such fine Carusian gentlemen."

Daria's mouth fell open in surprise.

The two men beamed.

"Excuse me," Daria interjected through virtually clenched teeth. "I was just going to the powder room, Analet. Perhaps you'd like to come with me and freshen up too?" She slid back her chair and got to her feet.

Sensing her friend's mood, Analet rose. "Of course, Daria," she agreed amiably, falling into step behind her friend as they wound their way between the tables and to the ladies' room.

As soon as the door swung closed, Daria turned and pounced.

"My God, Analet," she snarled, "how could you! I mean, The Spirit Palace!"

"I don't know what you are talking about."

"Of course you know what I'm talking about," Daria responded, growing angrier that her friend was trying to pretend with her. "I've read quite a bit about Utan and I know about The Spirit Palace."

"Then you know," Analet replied quietly, "that it is a place of music, dining and amusement."

"It's a sex club!"

"So?"

"So!" Daria could hardly believe her friend's nonchalance. "So those two men out there want to take us to a *sex club*. And judging by the circles under their eyes, it's not to listen to music!"

"Fine. You know that people can go to The Spirit Palace and indulge in the pleasures of the flesh. Simply because you do not wish to go does not mean I have to turn down their invitation."

"To have sex with *two* men?" she shot back acidly.

"Unless Ramel finds a more companionable female at The Spirit Palace," Analet replied calmly. "In which case Carusian hospitality would demand that she be invited to join us also."

"Unbelievable!" Daria cried, clutching her head with both hands and turning her back. "Absolutely unbelievable! You're just going to waltz off into the night with two men, one of whom you just met, and have an orgy with them. What's gotten into you? I've known you a long time and I never thought you were…"

"Were what, my friend?" Analet pinned her with those huge golden eyes.

"Nothing," she breathed, turning her sorry face to her friend. "I'm tired, that's all."

"No, I think it is very much 'something.' I wish to know what."

"Analet, please…"

"You never thought I was what?" she prodded, taking a step closer to Daria so that she towered over her. "My knowledge of your language is not great so I cannot tell what word you meant. But I know that tone of voice and on Carus the word is '*petuh.*' It means a woman of very bad character who takes many men for casual, meaningless mating. Since that is what you meant, you might as well tell me. I am always anxious to learn another of your words."

"I'm sorry, Analet," Daria tried to beg off, "forgive me."

"The word." There was a layer of steel under the calm words.

"Slut," she whispered, closing her eyes and turning her back again to hide the tears stinging in her eyes.

"Slut," the Ambassador repeated slowly, rolling the word around in her mouth and her brain for a moment. "It has a mean, hard sound. Most unpleasant. Hurled like a stone it would hurt very much."

"Oh Analet," Daria wailed turning quickly back and throwing her arms around her large friend. "You're right. It was a horrible thing to say and I'm so terribly sorry. Please forgive me. Please." She buried her face in Analet's thin, pale gold dress and cried.

"It is all right," she murmured, stroking the top of Daria's head softly. "In my years I have been called many things, this certainly not among the worst. I was truly unaware that the invitation would distress you so. On Carus, as on Utan, sex is considered a social pleasure like sharing food or drink or any other form of entertainment."

"I know," Daria whimpered, raising her tear-streaked face. "It's just that on my planet, we take it as a very solemn thing. To be shared between a man and a woman in a deeply committed relationship. A special gift. Sacred almost."

"The Carusians and the Utanians also understand this relationship. The joining of a male and female to one life and offspring. It is as special to us as to your kind. But the body can enjoy the pleasures of mating without joining just as it can enjoy a meal at a restaurant as it does in the privacy of home."

Daria nodded and wiped at her face with her hand.

"I will not go to The Spirit Palace if it will distress you."

"No, no Analet, you go on. I insist. I really do need to go back to the accommodations center and get some sleep."

"I will drop you then."

"That isn't necessary. I'll get a car back. I saw a port just up the street when we came in. You run along and enjoy yourself."

"You are sure?"

"Yes. Now go on. I'll be fine."

The large woman folded Daria in her arms and gave her a bear hug. "The fish is not worth it," she whispered.

* * * * *

The Spirit Palace was a large, multi-story building that took up one entire city block on the outskirts of town. A wide expanse of lawn and gardens, washed with artificial 'moonlight' surrounded the building, which in turn was surrounded by a tall, lovely brick wall. A large man in a dark burgundy uniform stood at the gate, admitting people and helping others exit.

"Good evening, Ambassador Tol," he smiled respectfully as he pushed open the black metallic gate for her party.

"Good evening, Gee," she replied, flashing a shy smile of her own.

"I see you're well known here," Benwa teased gently as they made their way along the wide, well-lit path toward the front entrance.

"Alas yes," Analet sighed. "Having to entertain visiting dignitaries is one of the chores of my profession. The Spirit Palace is always a much sought after attraction."

His smile widened. "Especially, I'm sure, in the company of such a lovely female as yourself."

Inside, they found themselves in what at first glance seemed to be the lobby of a large, busy public accommodations center. People strolled leisurely through wide-open archways on either side of the room. As they moved, the trio could see people dining in one area and dancing to soft music in another. A hallway branched off toward the rear of the building.

She lead them through the crowd to a long desk, behind which stood several men, all dressed in matching burgundy outfits. Immediately, one of them came to where the three of them stood.

"Ambassador Tol," the little gray haired man beamed, "it is always a pleasure to see you at the Palace, especially with guests. In what way may we be of service tonight?"

"These gentlemen are part of my planet's diplomatic mission to Utan," she explained. "I ran into them at dinner and since Ramel," she pointed a graceful blue hand to her left, "is new to the planet, I thought The Spirit Palace the perfect place to introduce him to your beautiful planet and its many delights."

The beam intensified. "You are too kind, Ambassador. We hope that the Palace lives up to your expectations."

"It always does." Her voice took on a more serious tone. "I know that it's very late and you're obviously very busy and I should have called ahead, but would it be possible to have the Vendar?"

"Your wish is my command, Ambassador. And you are very fortunate indeed. The Vendar is one of our most popular suites but for some reason, it went unclaimed this evening. Obviously the Creator knew that you would be gracing us with your presence this evening and left it vacant for you and your party. I shall have your usual bottle of wine and a platter of delicacies sent up."

Reaching behind him, he removed a small dark metal circle from a pigeonhole. Smiling, he placed it in her outstretched palm. "I hope everything is to your satisfaction, Ambassador, but if you need anything, please call. I shall attend you personally."

"Thank you, Zel."

They moved to a bank of transporters and were whisked immediately to a long hall with doors on either side. Following Analet a short distance, they stopped while she placed the disk in a small round opening just above the door handle. There was a *click,* and the door swung silently open.

As they entered, the light came on automatically, bathing the room in a soft candlelight, the ceiling and the walls glowing warmly. A huge bed, nothing more than a fat mattress on a raised platform, dominated one end of the room, pillows and cushions of all sizes scattered on the deep, thick pile carpet. An aroma drifted to them, something silken and musky, wrapping itself gently around them.

"A most hospitable room," Benwa observed as he looked around.

"I hope you approve," Analet whispered, bringing her mouth close to his ear.

"I shall give you my opinion later," he sighed, feeling a tingle below his belly.

A soft hiss announced the arrival of the wine and the food, almost at Benwa's elbow.

"Would you care for something to drink?" His lips brushed the side of her neck and she trembled slightly.

"Yes, please." She closed her eyes and drenched herself in his scent, his touch, his presence.

"Ramel," he called out behind him, "if you would be so kind as to pour?"

"Of course." He moved to the bottle.

"I hope you like it," she murmured, a little rasp at the edge of her voice. "It's Utanian. Sweet. And warm."

In a moment, the young man appeared in front of her, three small glasses balanced in his hands. Reaching over her shoulder, he gave one to Benwa, one to her and held his up. "To the beautiful and desirable Analet Tol."

They emptied their glasses, dropping them heedlessly on the carpet where they landed without a sound.

Wordlessly, Benwa reached up, gently taking a handful of her long, white hair and moving it to the side. Tenderly, he placed his lips at the base of her skull, knowing it to be one of the most sensitive places on the body of a Carusian woman. Instantly, she shivered in reaction to him and he began running the tip of his tongue in slow circles.

"Oh…oh…" she murmured.

Carefully, he grasped the slide at the top of her long, flowing dress. As it slid down her back, it revealed more and more of her skin to him, finally stopping just above her tailbone.

Putting both hands lightly on her shoulders, Ramel gently pulled the dress down her arms and watched it form a golden puddle around her ankles. Moving as close as he could to her, he took her breasts in his hands, amazed at the beautiful, pale blue sacs, full and bulging, the black tips of her nipples erect. Below her belly, a triangle of soft white curls pointed the way to her treasure.

"You are the most beautiful female I have ever seen," he breathed. "More beautiful than I ever dreamed a female could be."

Without opening her eyes, Analet smiled a little and reached down, her fingers immediately finding the bulge of his cock straining against the fabric of his pants. At her touch, it seemed to expand further, wiggling to escape its confines. Seeing the effect she had on the young man excited her even more.

"Haven't you ever been with a woman?" she asked, bringing her body against his and moving in slow, tantalizing rotations. With skillful quickness she undid the buttons of his shirt, pulling it out of his pants and pushing it off his shoulders to the floor.

"None I've wanted as much as you," he growled, leaning down and taking a nipple in his mouth.

"Oh," she moaned, fumbling for the slide on his pants, eager to take him in her hands.

"Aw," she heard the older man laugh lightly, "I knew when I saw your eyes in the dining place that your...interest had been aroused. When you agreed to come here, I knew your willingness. Now that you have a fat cock in your hand, I find you anxious as well. Fortunately, I would never leave a woman, especially as beautiful as you, to wait."

Analet felt a movement behind her as the older man released his dick from its cloth prison and pushed it upright between her cheeks. Putting both arms around her, he flattened himself against her, rubbing slowly, continuing his nuzzling at her neck and ears.

Finally, she managed to get the slide open on Ramel's pants and as they fell to the floor, she felt his dick, full and hot against the little swell of her belly. Being careful not to pull too hard, she gently guided it down between her legs to the welcoming wetness of her pussy.

She heard him make a sound between a moan and a growl as she pressed herself to him and began rocking gently back and forth on his cock. Behind her, Benwa had joined in the rhythm, keeping himself tight against her as she moved. Sandwiched between them, Benwa's arms around her waist, Ramel's hands gripping her shoulders, the heat of their bodies joining together almost overcame her.

"I've never felt any female like you," Ramel told her between ragged breaths. "Soft and warm yet holding me in you like another hand. Running yourself along me like warm, moist lips, caressing and tender."

"And the feel of you inside me is like a shaft of fire, filling me to bursting with pleasure and desire."

"Don't forget me," Benwa chuckled, moving his fingers to her breasts and nipping at the back of her neck as he continued to ride between her cheeks.

"How could I?" she breathed. "Your cock against my skin makes my body cry out for you. Why do you not venture inside?"

"Because I don't want to distract you or Ramel. There'll be time enough for everything. And everyone."

Analet closed her eyes and melted into the rising heat. Inside, she could feel the entire length of Ramel, hot and hard, pounding into her, grinding and trying to force himself as deeply into her as he could. His breath felt hot and ragged on her skin as he brushed his lips over her neck and face, and small moans of pleasure mixed with soft sighs and mumbled sounds.

Moving over her hot, engorged clit like a rippled iron bar, she could feel herself building toward release. Caught between reveling in the exquisite pleasure of her mounting excitement and the need to explode, she hung like a dancing star between ache and fulfillment.

A cry filled the heated space between their bodies, as the dizzying whirlpool pulled her toward climax. Perhaps her, perhaps one or both of the men had made the cry of passion. For a moment, she hovered on the brink, feeling Ramel thrusting inside her and then she was swept up like a leaf into molten ecstasy, fountaining out in a million droplets of red-hot pleasure.

Sagging back in exhausted satisfaction, Analet felt Benwa behind her, still rock hard, seeming to hold her up by the sheer force of his erection. Even the added weight of the sated young man in front of her didn't seem to matter to his steel rod.

As Ramel removed himself gently, she felt Benwa moving her slowly, tenderly backwards, his hands, arms and cock never leaving her. Carefully, softly, he helped her onto the bed, rolling her to her stomach and allowing her to sink into the thick mattress.

"You have the most beautiful body," he whispered as he stretched out over her back. His tongue made small, short passes over her neck and she shivered with the feel of him. He knew exactly how to arouse her and keep her on the knife's edge, even though she had just been satisfied. "I wish to know every piece, every secret place of it. I wish to possess it completely, if only for a little while."

His lips and tongue wandered leisurely down her spine as she squirmed under his attentions, part of her drifting at the edge of exhaustion, part of her drifting back toward excitement. The erotic tension between the two different sensations charged through her like high voltage electricity.

As he worked along her back, she felt his hands under her, pulling slowly upwards and back to him. Ramel, almost forgotten, slid a fat pillow under her head, cradling it as her hips rose toward Benwa. An instant later, she felt Ramel's head nudge under her slightly raised chest, his soft mane of white hair against her skin as his lips closed around the dark nipple of her full, dangling breast.

The unexpected sensation raced through her like a jet of fire, causing her to quiver in startled pleasure. Benwa raised her a bit more, and she felt his erection behind her, seeking her pussy, warm and wet and waiting.

She felt him slip in, hot and hard as Ramel had been, but with a different feeling. He filled her, pulsing with energy and life. Immediately, she felt as if she'd stepped onto a moving stairway, lifting her effortlessly toward another release of building passion.

Opening her eyes, she saw Ramel's cock, hard and erect as it had been when it entered her. A single drop of his fluid clung to the tip like a small, perfect diamond. Balancing herself on one elbow, she reached down to her dripping pussy, wetting her hand with her juice and then taking his shaft in hand. It wiggled and seemed to expand even more as she began running her hand over its length, his heat coursing through her closed fingers, up her arm and into her racing blood.

She could hardly bear the feel of him in her hand, his lips on her sensitive, full nipple, and Benwa in her pussy. Sparklers danced in her veins, filling her body with rushing rivulets of lava waiting to erupt.

Naked flesh slapping against naked flesh and moans and purrs and grumbles ran together, indistinguishable from each other. The scent of aroused bodies hung in the air like heady perfume. And the growing passion rose like super-heated water, pushing up from the depths of the earth to burst forth like a wild geyser.

She felt Ramel in her fist as she worked him in time to the furious tempo of her own pounding heart. Inside her, Benwa raced headlong to his goal. Analet felt the first small tremors of the young man's climax but everything was erased in the fireball that whistled through her, crashing through her body and exploding into tiny fragments of crystal pleasure. Even Benwa, grabbing handfuls of her ass and bellowing his own release disappeared, lost in the spiral of her own splendid coming.

They lay in a tangled heap, panting and wheezing for breath, sated and exhausted. Analet managed to lift herself enough so that Ramel could ease himself out from under her and Benwa slid out only to collapse by her side, wrapping himself around her and pulling her round, warm ass to his now satisfied dick.

* * * * *

"More wine?"

"Mmm, yes please," she purred, snuggling her head deeper into his lap, feeling his downy, white pubic curls and flaccid cock brush lightly against her cheek.

Benwa twisted his upper body a little and reached for the amber bottle at his left elbow. They'd rested for several minutes on the bed and then quietly slipped away to a pile of large cushions scattered in a round depression in the thickly carpeted floor.

As he poured, he glanced over at the bed where Ramel lay sprawled, the rhythmic cadence of his breathing marking his satisfied slumber.

Chuckling softly, Benwa handed her the glass, marveling as he did so at her long, feline body, stretched out among the pillows, her fine white hair spilling over his skin, making a perfect frame for her beautiful, contented face gazing up at him, a dreamy half-smile on her lips.

"What?" she asked, taking the glass.

"As I looked at Ramel, I thought about the impatience of youth."

Analet giggled as she raised her head to sip the wine.

"Indeed," she agreed amiably. "He needs to learn maturity...to pace himself."

"That comes only with long years of study and practice, Ambassador. It is a skill not learned in a day. Or a night."

"Is that why Ramel's family sent him to you?" she teased. "I know they are merchants, not diplomats. His life is commerce, not service."

"The Ambassador is perceptive as well as beautiful," he grinned. "Ramel has come to assist me in the trade mission that he may better understand the universe in which he lives and will do business. Utan has much to show a young man."

Picking up a handful of ripe, red berries, he popped a few in his mouth, savoring their slight tartness in contrast to the sweet wine. Carefully, he placed one between his lips and bent forward to hers.

Pursing her lips, she accepted the offering, pushing it to the side of her cheek as she accepted his tongue as well.

"Do you remember the afternoon we spent on Velus II?" he whispered.

"We took food and drink and wandered into the vast woods," she replied softly. "We found that spot by the large pond."

"The day was warm and we sat in the sun and you stood up, declared you needed a swim and before I could say a word, you'd stepped out of your dress and ran across the grass into the pond with a mighty splash."

Analet closed her eyes and smiled at the memory. "Your rings were black with desire," she teased, "and my whole body burned from the want of you. Had I not gone into that cool water, I would almost certainly have burst into flame."

Benwa laughed, the rumble of it shaking Analet like a small earthquake. "As I remember, you did. Twice. Once in the water behind a fallen log and again on the shore lying in the tall grass."

"Mmmm...." she purred again without opening her eyes. "I remember. I also remember the singe marks around certain parts of your body as well."

They laughed and sipped their wine, the fire banked but not forgotten. Now they could bask in the warmth of their companionship.

"Have you ever shared a woman with another man?" Analet asked, sitting up a little, finishing her wine and holding out her glass.

"No," he replied refilling it. "Why? Have you ever had two men before?"

"No." She settled back into his lap, turning the glass slowly in her fingers. "Why tonight, then? With me?"

"Because I wanted you and I could not think of a polite way to get rid of Ramel. Especially when I saw the color of his rings. I feared he might try and take you there on the table."

"A female of my years is flattered."

"He's a child," Benwa sniffed dismissively. "A female such as yourself needs a grown male. I had hoped perhaps that your little friend, the human female might join us. I think Ramel would have been most content with her. Now, of course, you've spoiled him for any other female in the universe. More's the pity as I've heard that primate females are capable of great passion. It would have been most interesting to have seen if the promise of her clothes had been fulfilled by her nakedness."

"Daria hesitated for many reasons."

"Yes," he nodded thoughtfully. "Ramel and I are strangers. Not even of her kind. I'm sure the sheer bulk of our bodies must have seemed...intimidating to such a small creature."

"Your size does not intimidate Daria," Analet laughed. "In fact, I think there is little in the universe that intimidates her. Except perhaps her feeling of...difference, her aloneness."

Benwa looked down at her, confusion plain on his face. "Difference? Aloneness?"

"It is difficult to explain," Analet murmured. "Daria was abandoned as an infant. Left outside a religious place with nothing. Not even, as she says so bitterly, a name. The religious women with whom she lived consulted a list and chose a first and last name for her. These they gave to the government which issued her the identity she has."

"It is not unusual for groups of animals to take in young of their own kind. I do not understand what is different about the humans."

"Because they are descended from troop animals, for a primate to be different...to be alone and not belong, is a great shame. Other primates feel that they are...are somehow less because of it. The young are cruel, the elders suspicious. If the pain I have seen in my small friend's eyes when she speaks of it is any measure, it must be truly awful."

"And your friend feels that she is 'less' than others of her kind because she has no troop of her own?" Benwa cocked his head to one side, trying to comprehend Analet's story.

Analet nodded. "She has been hurt very badly, I think. I know that no one gets truly close to Daria. Even me, after all our years of friendship. So to 'belong,' she has made a nest for herself with the great galactic mega-troop, Unitech. There, she is one of their 'family.' And to no longer be alone, she has chosen a fish."

She sighed, those amber eyes filled with sorrow. "Sometimes I think it is not because he makes her blood run hot that she chose him, but because he has much family. Family which Daria covets above all things."

"I feel pity for your little friend," he told her earnestly. "Now I wish even more that she would have come with us. I guarantee that Ramel could have made her blood run hot." He grinned broadly. "Hot enough even to boil away the stench of fish."

They shared a hearty laugh and lapsed back into a comfortable silence. Nothing but the sound of Ramel's steady breathing and occasional shift of position disturbed the quiet.

"I'm afraid," Benwa whispered at length, "that it's time to rouse Ramel and leave. The hour grows very late. We have early appointments and you are to make the introduction of your friend to The Sildor."

"Another moment," Analet told him, turning her lips to the soft flesh of his resting cock. "I wish to give you a proper good-night kiss while we are still alone." She moved her lips along his shaft, barely touching it, until she reached the head. Carefully, lovingly, she took it in her mouth, sucking slightly and making quick circles around the tip with her tongue.

Instantly, she felt his body and his dick stiffen.

"As the Ambassador wishes," he moaned. "I am at your command."

Chapter **Two**

The audience line in which they stood snaked from the official receiving room where The Sildor received people, down the long hall, around the corner where they stood and as far behind them as Daria could see. Analet had told her that because they had an appointment, they would be near the head of the line and that those who wished to see The Sildor without an appointment would have to stand in line and hope for the best.

Out of the corner of her eye, Daria studied her friend. When she'd come to pick Daria up at the public accommodations center, she'd said nothing of the night before. But she seemed unusually happy, giddy almost. And the dark rings under her eyes had disappeared, the skin now so pale as to be almost white. She seemed rested and well. In fact, standing there, she looked as if she might suddenly burst into laughter at any moment.

She, on the other hand, had spent a restless night. The strange, uncomfortable bed, not being used to sleeping alone and her mind filled with today's meeting had all conspired against sleep. She'd planned her presentation carefully, stressing all of the positive features and trying to predict and defuse any of The Sildor's possible questions or objections. Sleep had come finally but in shallow, fitful bursts.

They moved a few steps forward.

"Now remember, Daria," Analet whispered to her, "keep your head down at all times. Don't speak or even look up until The Sildor acknowledges you, by name. When she does, look straight at her and make a small bow." She bent at the waist about forty-five degrees in demonstration. "And she is to be addressed at all time as 'Sildor.'"

"I know, Analet, I know," she snapped. "I've studied all the protocols. I know exactly how to handle this."

"Very well," Analet conceded cheerfully, "but you may find that books on protocol are not the same thing as having a friend who has actually stood in The Sildor's presence. If you need help, I will be there."

"I won't need any help." Daria set her briefcase down on the floor beside her. It felt heavy and seemed to be getting more so by the minute.

This was, she thought sourly, *a most stupid, inefficient method of doing business.* She'd made an appointment specifically so that she wouldn't have to waste her time standing in line. It was ridiculous that the ruler of an entire planet still saw people in such an antiquated and awkward fashion. Thankfully, Unitech would be able to bring modern time management to this chaos.

Yes. Get an appointment secretary to sift through all of these silly requests for an audience. The Sildor's time would be reserved and rationed for only the most important visitors and business. All these nobodies with their trivial problems would be disposed of by people at much lower levels.

After Unitech's efficiency people got through here, audiences would probably be a thing of the past anyway.

Good riddance!

As they turned the corner, Daria saw wide corridors running off on either side of the main hall. Guards stood on either side of the openings, the four of them standing at rigid attention mirroring each other. Dressed in what Daria recognized as the traditional palace guard uniform of black pants and shirts with red sashes and broad brimmed hats, they each carried a large, lethal looking sword at their side.

Inching closer, Daria craned her neck but could see nothing but massive barred doors, chained and padlocked shut and an empty hall beyond.

"What are those?" Daria asked, keeping her voice low.

"The passage to the right," Analet answered, "is the way to The Sildor's *karavat*…what you would call, harem."

"Harem!" Daria repeated loudly, drawing the stares of those around her. Blushing slightly, she again lowered her voice. "What do you mean, harem?"

"Do you not remember? I told you of The Sildor's mates."

"I know," Daria replied slowly, "but...but I didn't think you meant it. I mean...I mean how would one woman...a hundred...oh..."

Analet nodded in that direction. "When The Sildor takes a mate, he goes to live in the *karavat* and stays there always. It is said that the *karavat* is the most beautiful place on Utan where all desires are fulfilled. No one comes or goes through that door except The Sildor, and the males who attend her mates."

"And the other passage?"

"That is The Academy," Analet told her, the tone of her voice almost reverent with awe. "It is a place of great learning and knowledge. There are many academies throughout Utan, but none so great as here, in the palace. Many wait years for the chance to attend and learn the lessons inside."

Daria wracked her brains but couldn't remember any mention of an Academy in all her studies of the planet. It unnerved her that she didn't know anything about something obviously so important.

"What sort of school is it?" she asked.

"One of mystery. Those outside Utan are not permitted to know its secrets."

"Oh...I see."

Of course she didn't see at all, but she didn't want Analet to think she didn't understand.

The doors of the reception room loomed in front of them as they made their way to the front of the line.

"As soon as we reach the doors," Analet continued in a hushed voice, "look down and do not look up again until The Sildor speaks to you. Watch my feet. And the same when you are dismissed. Look down immediately and back away from her presence."

Side by side, they went through the huge portal and immediately looked down. In the thick, sapphire carpet, Daria could make out a design of twisted gold vines that seemed to be wending their way toward the other end of the room. She watched them and her friend's basketball player-sized feet as they moved slowly forward.

Abruptly, the vines in the carpet twisted together creating a fat barrier across their path. Analet's feet stopped just short of it. Daria made sure to do likewise.

Somewhere in front of her, Daria could hear the hum of low voices but she couldn't hear the words or even the sex of the voices. Her right shoulder was beginning to complain about the weight of her briefcase, but she didn't want to put it down or even shift to her left hand for fear of inadvertently doing something wrong. And now the tiny translation unit in right ear had begun to itch as well.

"Good morning, Ambassador Tol," she heard a mellow, authoritative, alto female voice intone solemnly.

"Good morning, Sildor," Analet replied just as somberly.

"You are well I trust?"

"Yes, Sildor, thank you. I trust you are the same?"

"I am as always."

Why, Daria wondered, *couldn't they just get on with it*? Why did they have to go through all this needless, pointless ceremony? She had a lot of ground to cover and valuable time ticked away.

"And I hope you remain so for many solar revolutions to come."

"I see by your petition for audience that you wish to make an introduction."

"If it pleases The Sildor, yes."

"You may proceed."

"Thank you. Sildor Minsee, ruler of all Utan, I wish now to present my friend, Daria Evans. She is a human from the planet Earth who comes at The Sildor's pleasure to discuss the mining contract between your planet and her company, Unitech."

Seconds dragged by in silence while Daria waited for The Sildor to speak. The itch had become a spreading fire and the briefcase was now filled with boulders.

"On behalf of all the people of Utan," she said at last in the same solemn monotone, "I bid you welcome, Daria Evans."

With an inaudible sigh, Daria raised her head, bowed and looked up to get her first glimpse of The Sildor Minsee of Utan.

She sat about ten feet in front of Daria, not in a grand throne as she'd expected, but in a large, comfortable looking wooden chair with a high back and upholstered in some kind of dark, wine-colored fabric. Raised about three feet off the main floor, Daria imagined it was to give the small woman a better view of the reception room than for any illusion of grandeur.

Older than Daria had expected, perhaps in her middle sixties, The Sildor had a smallish body and head, dark brown hair now flecked with silver, worn in a top knot. Her skin had a sort of light brown, cream-in-coffee color, highlighting large, slightly almond-shaped black eyes that watched her carefully from an impassive face.

Beside her sat a man of about her own age, same salt and pepper hair, brown skin and black eyes. But he seemed somehow taller with a bigger body than The Sildor and he did not seem as intent on Daria. She noticed also that his chair sat slightly lower than The Sildor's, bringing the top of his head to just about her chin.

"There is no need for your translation unit," The Sildor told her. "I am familiar enough with your language to converse with you. While the translation unit can be of great value, I believe that it is important also to hear the tone of a person's voice, their manner of speech. I have found in my many years that there is often more to what is being said than mere words. You will remove it please?"

Not quite understanding but anxious to make a good first impression, Daria dutifully reached into her right ear and removed the molded plasteen, taking an extra instant to casually rub the itch.

Only a nod from the older woman acknowledged the gesture.

"On behalf of the people of Earth and especially my company Unitech, I thank The Sildor for the opportunity to come to your beautiful planet and speak with its ruler. I hope that our talks will result in lasting friendship and mutual advantage. If I may, Sildor?" She held up her briefcase.

The old woman nodded every so slightly.

"Thank you." Turning to a small table a step away, she set the briefcase on it and flipped it open.

"As a small token of Unitech's warm regard for The Sildor and all the people of Utan," Daria continued, still keeping her voice serious, "we would like to present you with this globe." She took out a golden object about six inches around and held it up.

"This is a representation of our planet," Daria explained. "It is handmade of a metal we call gold, a very precious and rare commodity on Earth." She turned it slightly and pointed to a raised red dot. "This is New York City, in the part of our planet called America. It's where Unitech has its headquarters. This is a genuine ruby, a gemstone of great value to my people, shaped by laser in Unitech's own laboratories. We hope it will serve as a reminder of the goodwill between our two planets and peoples."

A guard appeared at her elbow and took the small metal object to The Sildor who examined it carefully and apparently with great interest. Even the man leaned over to get a better look at it.

"I accept this kind token," she said finally, "on behalf of my people. I shall see that it is put on public display so that they too may enjoy it and see something of your home."

"The Sildor's kindness and generosity are indeed great and I shall take pleasure in reporting your satisfaction to my superiors."

Again, the older woman nodded and Daria thought for a moment she might even smile.

Waiting a heartbeat longer, Daria reached into her briefcase and pulled out a thick, neatly bound report, clear plastic cover, charcoal gray backing and black plastic binding holding the pages together.

"At this time, I thought I might give The Sildor an overview of the proposed project and see if there are any questions I might answer."

"I regret Daria Evans, but that will not be possible at this time."

Daria felt as if she'd run full speed into a brick wall. "Excuse me? I don't understand. I mean, I thought we had an appointment to discuss this…"

"That is so," she replied simply, "but there has come a grave matter of state which requires my immediate and total attention. However, I desire greatly to speak of this matter with you in some detail. We will begin at tonight's evening meal. I have taken the liberty of having your things taken from the public accommodations center and brought here. Quarters have been prepared and I will send an attendant for you. That way, you may be close at hand so that the discussions of this great project may proceed."

"But…"

The Sildor held up her hand. "The audience is concluded. You will be shown to your quarters. Whatever you desire, make known to your attendant and it will be provided. Until tonight."

"I don't…"

"Until tonight," Analet interrupted, putting her hand on her friend's arm. Daria saw the Ambassador's head move ever so slightly from side to side as she bowed.

"Uh...yes, Sildor," Daria stammered uncertainly, "until tonight."

And as carefully as they'd come in, the women backed from the room.

Holding up the globe again, The Sildor turned it slowly, running her fingertip along its surface, finally stopping over the dark gemstone.

"So, Minsee," the man beside her chuckled, "what is this 'grave matter of state' that has so suddenly arisen and must take precedence over your meeting with the Unitech female? Especially after she comes bearing such unusual and interesting gifts."

The old woman tapped a long, unpainted fingernail on the ruby for several moments, studying it intently. At last, she held it out to the man. "It is truly a most interesting gift. Telling, perhaps, also."

"Telling?"

"I wonder if the human primates believe that somehow the Earth is the center of all things." She tapped the stone again. "And I wonder especially if this female believes that Unitech is the center of Earth?"

"And this is the grave matter of state you spoke of?" he teased.

"Yes, Albre, it is," she responded slowly, her voice deadly serious. "It is the opening gambit in this game we are entering into. She came here prepared with nothing but a trinket and a pile of paper, no doubt believing that we would conclude our business and she could return quickly and triumphantly back to her home planet and Unitech. She thinks because I am old and have spent my life underground on a small, ordinary planet in the far reaches of the galaxy, that I am no match for her worldly, sophisticated wiles. But I have learned much from this short meeting which may yet be useful and for which I gave away nothing."

"Such as?"

"I know now that she does not deal well with the unexpected. This is a useful piece of information. I shall remember it."

"And I'm sure you will waste no time in showing this young female primate the error of her ways."

* * * * *

"Do you believe that?" Daria fumed as she and the Ambassador exited the reception room and found themselves in another hallway, this one deserted. "I have *never* been so insulted in my whole life. I travel halfway across the galaxy and that...that woman sends me away like a street peddler."

"Lower your voice, Daria," Analet warned sternly, glancing nervously up and down the corridor. "Remember where you are."

"I am painfully aware of where I am," she shot back angrily. "I am in an empty hallway having just been dismissed by the rudest person I have ever had the misfortune to meet."

"No," her friend hissed, leaning down into Daria's face, "you are in the house of the absolute ruler of Utan. Her word, literally, is law. And she has little patience with foreigners who wave their tongues in a loud and disrespectful manner."

"Wag, Analet."

"Wave? Wag? It will make little difference if it is cut from your head with a dull knife."

Daria's eyes grew wide, blinking with surprise. Immediately, she closed her mouth and swallowed.

"That's...that's barbaric," she managed to get out. "Surely there must be laws...courts. On Earth..."

"You are not on Earth," Analet reminded her harshly. "You are on Utan and as I've said before, you would do well to remember that. And you would do well to remember also that here, The Sildor is all-powerful and answerable to no one. She is judge, jury and executioner."

Before Daria could answer, a tall, middle-aged man appeared from the reception room behind them.

"Ambassador Tol, Daria Evans, I am Voh, First Attendant to The Sildor." He bowed slightly in their direction. "She wishes me to escort you to your quarters. If you will follow, please?"

Knowing she had no choice, Daria smiled limply.

"Thank you," she told him as they started down the hall.

* * * * *

"The Sildor hopes you will find the hospitality of her humble home to be adequate to your needs and instructs that all measures be taken to insure you are comfortable during your stay." They paused in front of a pair of huge double doors, a light colored wood with intricate carvings and handles like golden sword hilts stuck in the wood. Grabbing them, he pushed open the doors and stood aside for them to enter.

Daria gasped as she stepped inside, stunned into unaccustomed silence by the size and elegance that suddenly surrounded her.

"This is the outer room," Voh told her matter-of-factly, "for your working, dining and leisure.

Pale rose-colored walls soared to a cathedral arched ceiling at least two stories above her. A wall entirely of glass, covered by sheer panels, filled the space with a warm, soft light. Thick carpet the same color as the walls appeared to be littered with cushions and pillows of all colors, shapes and sizes. A couple of what looked like small settees and tables of every description, from large ones with chairs like dining suites to tiny, low ones, had been scattered haphazardly among the cushions.

Everywhere she looked, rich, gaily colored fabrics, gold, silver, bronze and marble-looking stone, showed an understated, quiet quality.

"Through here is your sleeping chamber," Voh continued, crossing the room and opening a second set of doors as big as the first.

In the sleeping chamber, as enormous as the outer room, a large bed on a slightly raised platform took up a good portion of one wall and dominated the room. Slowly, she sat down, sinking instantly into a thick, velvet-like gold spread and a feather-soft mattress.

"Bathing facilities are through those doors." He motioned toward yet another set of doors in the left wall on the other side of the barn-sized room.

"Your belongings have been arranged in the clothes keeper, beside your vanity mirror, just there."

Daria's eyes followed his finger to a wall of large cupboards surrounding a mirrored table and small stool.

"Your attendant will arrive shortly. Relay your desires and they will be seen to. If there is anything else, you may call on me at any time. Now if there is nothing else, I must return to my duties with The Sildor."

"No, thank you," Daria murmured. "Everything is just fine."

He bowed a little and departed.

"Isn't this the most beautiful place you've ever seen?" Daria asked turning her head in all directions.

"It is the palace of The Sildor," Analet replied simply. "What did you expect?"

"I...I honestly hadn't thought about it," she admitted. "I mean, I know that The Sildor is rich. I read several articles about her in preparing for my trip here. But this..." her voice melted away, no words seeming adequate.

Analet plopped down beside her. "But this is very grand and elegant for such a pitiful place as Utan," she teased. "You thought, no doubt, in this distant, backward place, we would all be living in caves, eating raw meat and wild plants with our bare hands."

"I certainly did not," Daria tried to protest. "I've read extensively about Utan. Moving the entire population underground was a momentous technical achievement and…"

"And worthy even of the respect of humans," Analet finished, the teasing taking on a mocking tone. "But truly, you had not expected to find such luxury, such splendor here. Even in the palace of The Sildor."

"I hadn't thought about it one way or the other," Daria insisted. "I never expected to be here except in some official capacity. The Sildor's office. A conference room. Perhaps even a room for the formal contract signing."

"Very well, little friend," Analet relented as she raised herself from the bed. "Have it your own way. I have work to do and I must return to the consulate. Call me tomorrow and tell me how your dinner with The Sildor goes tonight. I will be very interested."

"Aren't…aren't you coming?" Daria asked uneasily.

"I was not invited. Only you. Besides, I have every faith that by the end of the evening, you will have The Sildor eating out of your fingers."

"The palm of my hand. And I wish I had as much faith in me as you do."

"Relax. Enjoy this. How many times in your life will you get to live as an absolute monarch? Good-by, Daria. I will expect to hear from you bright and early."

"Good-by, Analet. And thank you for everything."

They walked to the outside door and after a final round of farewell hugs, Analet departed and Daria found herself alone in the huge suite. She had just gone back into the sleeping chamber to see about her clothes, when she heard the front door open and close quietly.

"Daria Evans?" a male voice called out.

Going to the open chamber door, she looked out and saw a man standing just inside the doors, peering around as if looking for something. Or someone.

"Yes?" she answered uncertainly, peeking out.

Crossing the large room in a few long strides, he stopped just outside the chamber door, his tall, well-built body towering over her. Straight black hair, worn a little long and slightly shaggy, fell over his forehead toward piercing black eyes, a rugged, square face and full lips. A lean body, muscular with broad shoulders and a big chest, tapered down to a flat stomach and long legs. His dress, not the uniform of a guard, but a simple white garment that covered his shoulders and chest and fell in a kind of toga-like drape to his knees, tied by a gold cord at his slim waist. On his feet he wore plain, leather-looking sandals.

"I am Ston," he announced quietly his voice deep and melodic. "I have been sent by The Sildor to attend you."

He smiled then, his face lighting up and those dark eyes almost disappearing in merry crinkles at the outside corners. His whole being seemed to light up with warmth and welcome.

"That's...that's very kind of The Sildor," Daria replied slowly, finding herself staring a bit too long at those wonderful eyes and strong face.

"The honor is mine to attend such an important guest," he told her, making a small bow. "I hope that I may serve you well during your stay."

Those eyes beamed steadily down at her and Daria had a momentary but distinct feeling of lightheadedness and a fleeting thought of her fingers moving slowly through that dark hair.

"Yes...well," she continued, trying to shake off the lapse, "I think I really will be all right. I'm very independent and used to doing for myself."

Immediately, the light went dark and anxiety appeared in those dark eyes. "But it is my duty to serve you," he explained anxiously, moving a bit closer to her. "I am here at her command. If...if you turn me away, The Sildor will be most upset. I will lose favor with her and probably be sent away."

The realization hit her like cold water. She hadn't considered that in this monarchal society, there would be no protection for workers, especially not servants in the house of the ruler. She could certainly understand that he would probably lose his job, and Analet's words about her tongue still rang fresh in her ears. *Judge, jury and executioner.* And he had those anxious, beautiful eyes...

"I...I, uh, didn't mean that I would send you away," Daria backtracked hurriedly. "It's just that I've never had anyone...attend me before and I'm really not sure how it's done."

Sunshine reappeared in his face. "I am here to make sure all your needs and desires are fulfilled. You have but to make them known."

"Well...uh...I don't even know where to start."

"Then perhaps I might suggest food and drink? I was chosen for this duty because I have some knowledge of the customs of your planet and believe that primates often stop their activity in mid-day for nourishment." He looked at her, obviously hopeful that he'd got it right.

"Yes, we do," she reassured him with a smile. "In America, my part of Earth, we call it 'lunch.'"

"Lunch," he repeated, pleased no doubt that he'd made a good suggestion. "With your permission, I will depart and return as quickly as possible."

"Of course. And take your time."

Well, she thought when he left, *this is going to be awkward.* She had no experience with servants. Servants smacked of antiquated, outdated class systems. Even dealing with her administrative assistant or the young man who saw to her computer made her uneasy, leaving her feeling as if she were trying to be something she wasn't. Asking for anything had always been hard for her. Probably going back to her fear of the nuns and the strict, impoverished circumstances of her upbringing in the orphanage.

Another familiar wave of anxiety, this one bordering on panic, swept over her. If she couldn't ask her assistant to stay late because of a looming deadline, how then could she possibly stand before the absolute ruler of an entire planet and ask for the mining rights to a whole hemisphere? If only Trout had come with her.

Trout exuded the confidence she didn't have, and would never have. He'd been born with it, learning early how to deal with servants — his family had several — and subordinates. Never truly sharp or arrogant, he knew how to get things done. Get people moving. True, he could be single-minded and even abrupt, but he always got the project finished, the goal reached.

It all rested on her small shoulders, in her incompetent hands. Not just the future of this planet but her own personal future as well. Both stood at a critical crossroads and only she could determine which road would be taken. Failure towered above her, black and overwhelming.

Sinking into a chair at one of the tables, she put her head in her hands and tried not to cry. Her attendant would be back any second and he mustn't see her like this.

Of course, she thought, her head suddenly raised in inspiration. Ston had been assigned to her by The Sildor. He was absolutely at her mercy. While she would certainly not be cruel and would try to maintain as egalitarian a relationship as she could with him, she would give him concise instructions, make sure that he followed through and practice her confidence building on him.

The door opened again and Ston appeared with a large silver-colored tray, which he set on the table before her.

"These are *shata*," he told her, pointing to the contents of an amethyst bowl about twelve inches across. "What you call 'fruit,' in your language. There are several different kinds, all, I trust to your palate. And this," he picked up a slender pitcher of clear glass and gold-colored metal trim, "is *Fal-Trank*. 'Amber Bliss'."

"Oh, no," Daria told him as he tipped the pitcher to pour some of it into a matching goblet, "please, don't."

The servant looked at her quizzically.

"I'm sorry," she said, more quietly, "but I don't drink."

"All creatures must consume liquids to live," he responded, confusion written in his face. "Except, of course the Donnans of Cretor but they absorb moisture through their scales."

"No, that's not what I mean." Taking a breath, she tried again. "Of course I consume liquids to live. All humans do. On Earth, we normally drink 'water' for that purpose. What I mean is, I don't drink liquor. Of any kind." She giggled nervously. "Alcohol, even a little bit, makes me tipsy."

"Tip...sy?" he repeated.

She searched for an explanation. "Intoxicated. Giddy. Silly. I do things I wouldn't normally do and I certainly wouldn't want to do anything to embarrass myself, especially in the palace of The Sildor."

"Ah," he grinned, the light of understanding clearing his face. "*Beedshan*. A very undesirable state. But you need not worry about Amber Bliss. It is made from the nectar of a very rare flower. Once, it grew only in the high mountains of our surface. Now it is grown only in the plant houses of The Sildor. She does you great honor to send it. She does not do this for all of her visitors. Only those she considers very special. And do not worry. It does not make *beedshan*. It only warms and relaxes the body. Soothes the mind and senses."

"Well," Daria relented, eyeing the beautiful golden liquid shining through the glass, "I suppose one goblet couldn't hurt anything. And I certainly wouldn't want to offend The Sildor."

The smile widened and he filled the goblet almost to the brim, handing it to her and watching her expectantly.

A faint aroma came to her nose and she took a deep sniff. The delicate scent of some fragile, exotic, jungle plant, blooming in a tranquil, moonlit mountain glade. Something that made her think of warm breezes and soft...

Good heavens, she thought with a start. This wasn't like her. She didn't think in such idiotic terms. This was ridiculous. Ston had told her the drink came from the nectar of flowers. The smell of some unfamiliar flower. Nothing more.

Slowly, she put it to her lips and took a sip. Room temperature and slightly thicker than she'd expected, but it tasted delicious...a little sweet but with an after-taste she couldn't quite identify as she rolled it around on her tongue and swallowed. Like berries and cinnamon and that...that other thing. Daria took another swallow, this one bigger than the first. Glancing up, she saw Ston, still clutching the pitcher and obviously waiting for her verdict.

"It's very good," she told him, smiling. "Like a fruit juice only...only different. I like it. I like it very much in fact."

"Good. Now if you require nothing further, I will leave you to finish your *shata* and will return in a little while."

"I'm fine, Ston, thank you."

Without taking his eyes off her, he backed out of the room and softly closed the door.

Daria drained the remaining goblet, poured herself another one and began picking through the bowl of *shata*, trying to decide which one she'd try first. Judging by this, her stay on Utan might be very enjoyable indeed.

* * * * *

"Trout? It's Daria."

The image wobbled slightly but was much clearer than it had been with the first communication. Sitting at his big desk, the skyline of Manhattan a blur through the bank of windows behind him, Daria felt reassured just to see him smiling at her, even across all these light years of space.

"Daria," he greeted cheerfully. "It's good to see you."

"It's good to see you, too."

"So, how did the meeting go with The Sildor?" He laughed out loud. "Knowing my girl, I'll bet you dazzled her with projections, charmed her with your number crunching and enchanted her with your bottom line. In fact, I wouldn't be the least bit surprised if you had the signed contracts in your briefcase right now."

"It didn't go quite the way I'd hoped," she told him quietly.

He leaned forward, the smile erased, replaced by something hard. "What do you mean by that?" She didn't need to see his face clearly; she could hear the irritation in his voice.

"Don't get upset, Trout, please," she soothed. "There's nothing wrong. It's just that we had to cut the meeting short this morning. Before I had a chance to present the overall project. Some kind of 'grave matter of state' came up. But I'm having dinner with her tonight in her private dining room. She told me herself that she's very anxious to speak to me about the project. It's just a little glitch that's all. You aren't mad at me, are you?"

"No," he answered reluctantly, leaning back in his big chair. "It's just that there's so much riding on this. For all of us. I guess I'm just getting antsy to have the thing signed, sealed and delivered. Sometimes I feel like we've been working on this forever." He paused and looked at her. "I'm sure you're doing your best. By the way, where are you? That doesn't look like the public accommodations center."

"It isn't," she brightened. "It's The Sildor's palace. She said that she wants me close at hand so that we can discuss the project, so she moved me in, lock, stock and barrel. It's very luxurious. I wish you were here, though."

"You know I'm with you in spirit, Daria. Look, my other line's ringing and I've got a meeting with Hennessey in a couple of minutes. Keep on it and let me know how it goes."

"Trout?"

"Uh-huh?"

"I...miss you."

"Miss you too. Gotta run. Call me when you hear something."

A loud click and his image disappeared.

* * * * *

A single, quiet rap sounded on her door and Analet looked up from her desk just in time to see Benwa closing it behind him. As he quickly strode across the thick carpet, she leaned back in her large chair and smiled.

"*Dai shan*," she purred.

"Where have you been?" he asked anxiously, settling himself on the corner of her desk.

Analet raised a pure white eyebrow. "I've been to the palace," she explained, eyeing him, "to make the introduction of my friend Daria to The Sildor. Not that the comings and goings of the Ambassador of Carus are any concern of the Trade Consul."

Benwa glanced at the huge, multi-colored floral display in the crystal vase sitting on the other side of her desk.

"Ramel?" he asked curtly, jerking his head toward the flowers but keeping his eyes on her.

Analet smiled knowingly. "Yes."

"For last night?" he growled.

"A very thoughtful gesture."

"And he wants to see you again, no doubt."

"Actually, the card did mention dinner and a concert. Why do you ask?" Of course she knew exactly why he asked, but it flattered her to think of him jealous, even a little bit.

But Benwa seemed to change the subject.

"I have a very important meeting this afternoon," he announced seriously, leaning toward her. "One in which I must present the projections for the coming solar revolution's trade balance with the trade representative of the planet Kenso."

"And why would that concern me?" she chuckled, seeing the circles under his eyes growing darker with each heartbeat.

"Because I cannot read, cannot grasp, cannot think," he replied, his voice taking on a raspy quality. "It is your fault and yours alone."

She leaned forward and turned her face up to his. "What could I possibly have done?" Her own voice grew lower and rawer than usual. "I have not even been here."

"A major part of the problem," he told her, inching closer to her face. "But now that you are here, I'm sure you can remedy the situation and return my thoughts to more mundane business."

"What did you have in mind?"

Their lips met…softly, tenderly, both feeling the rising fire.

"I thought you might like to come over to the bookcase," he growled when they separated enough to talk. "Away from all these large, bright windows."

Gently taking her hand, Benwa helped her up and guided her slightly unsteady feet to a small space of blank wall between the floor to ceiling bookcases that took up one wall and the entry doors to her office. Carefully, he pushed her back against the wall, pinning her there with his own massive body.

"I have much to do," she mumbled. "The communication device may come on. My assistant may enter unexpectedly. What if…?"

Benwa put his lips on hers and pressed, forcing them open to admit his searching tongue. He slowly ended the kiss but held his lips close to hers.

"I have sent your assistant to my office to help Ramel gather the needed information for the meeting while I meet privately with you. I told her we must not be disturbed for any reason."

"But…"

"Shhhh," he said softly, putting his lips on her mouth again. "I see your answer plainly."

He was right. She didn't need to see her own circles. The heat running through her body told her that she wanted him as much as he wanted her.

"Perhaps we should go to the couch," she whispered between kisses. "Or even the rug."

"There is no need," he assured her.

"I don't…"

"You know," he began, pulling away a little and gazing at her, "I have always wondered how a female can be so sensual in a mere white blouse and black business suit." His fingers found the first of the two large buttons on her jacket.

"You have no idea how many meetings I have sat through, watching you move or even just sit at a conference table and marveled at the beauty of your body, even covered from neck to feet in this male attire." The buttons popped open and he pushed it out of the way, revealing her white blouse with small gold buttons running down the front.

His thumb and index finger moved to the top button at her throat.

"When the light is just right," he breathed, his large fingers fumbling with the tiny closures, "or when you move just so, the pale blue of your skin, especially the fullness of your breasts, throws a small shadow on the white cloth, like a hint of treasure." Another button and another.

"Even when you wear a garment to cover them, I can still imagine your nipples, black and hard, rubbing on that soft, giving material."

Carefully, he finished opening the buttons, pulling her shirt tail out of the waistband of her tailored slacks. Kissing her tenderly, he reached up and unfastened the small closure at the front of her undergarment, releasing her breasts to him.

Analet reached for his shirt buttons but he pushed her hand away. "Not yet," he whispered. "Not yet."

As they kissed, she felt his hands on her shoulders as he slowly pushed her jacket, blouse, and bra back and down her arms as if to remove them. Instinctively, she brought her body to him a little so that her clothes could slide off behind her. But about mid-way down, Benwa suddenly stopped and pressed her back against the wall.

"Benwa," she asked uncertainly, "what are you doing? I can't remove my clothes. I can't even move my arms like this."

He grinned and took her hard right nipple in his hand, sending a pulse of fire through her blood. "Oh?" he asked cheerfully.

Analet tried to push herself forward and shake free, but she found herself unable to move against Benwa's larger body. And as one hand played with her nipples, she realized that he'd started unbuckling her belt and pulling it off with his other hand. Using his body to keep her pinned, he reached around to her back, bringing her wrists together and looping the belt tightly around them.

"Benwa," she yelped in surprise and growing alarm, "what are you doing? I demand…"

"You are in no position to demand anything, Analet," he responded, still grinning.

"But…"

"But nothing. You are trapped and helpless. And I intend to press my advantage."

Quickly, he undid the waistband button and the slide of her trousers and pulled them down to her ankles. Rising, he stood back to survey her, satisfaction radiating from him like heat from a roaring fireplace.

As he let his eyes move up and down her body, he began unbuttoning his own shirt, taking his time and allowing her to feast on the sight of him.

"What are you going to do?" she asked, now no longer apprehensive but curious and even more aroused by his game.

In answer, he finished with his clothes and came to her again. Putting one hand behind her neck and kissing her passionately, he fondled her breast with the other. Slowly, he moved his mouth down until he took her other breast, alternately sucking and nipping at her hard, hot flesh. His reward came in a speeding up of her heartbeat and in soft, low moans.

After a last playful nip, he continued down, lowering himself to his knees so that he could see her pale, damp curls and her pussy. Breathing deeply, he reveled in the sweet, hot scent of her arousal, causing his cock to twitch with anticipation. Leisurely, he bent closer, parting her lips to give him access to her full, wet clit. One quick tickle with the tip of his tongue made her gasp in surprise.

"Oh," she squealed, her body jumping as if touched by electricity and almost squirming out of his grasp.

"You like that, huh?" he growled.

"Yes," she murmured.

Gently, he pushed her legs as far apart as her trouser-hobbled ankles would allow and grabbing her hips firmly, he attacked her in earnest, flicking his tongue lightly over her swollen mound and then wiping it slowly, putting his lips together to form a little vacuum.

He kept this sweet torture up for several more moments, his tongue swinging between quick, frenzied lapping and agonizingly slow, soft tickling. And all the while Analet wiggled and moaned, her eyes closed, struggling against her bonds.

"Do you want me inside you?" he asked, finally taking a break from his pleasant exercise.

"Yes, oh yes," she sighed, squirming with the building pleasure.

"Tell me how much," he demanded gruffly. "Tell me how hot you are and how much you want me inside you." His cock danced harder, faster, her hot wetness spiking his own fire.

"I want you," she moaned softly, "I want you now. Please...please..."

Instead, he suckled her pussy again, feeling her body moving and writhing under him. "Tell me how much you want me."

"I want you so much...oh please, I want you."

Standing up, he adjusted his body slightly and felt himself slip up inside her, wet and pulsing, immediately feeling her grip him like a velvet glove.

Analet began to grind herself against him, standing on her tiptoes in an attempt to take as much of him as possible. The feel of him driving into her, pulling his thick, flaming, molded steel cock back and forth over her own fiery, sensitive clit sent shock waves of pleasure pounding through her.

Grabbing her bare shoulders, Benwa thrust as deeply as he could, pressing his naked chest against her tender breasts and bringing his tongue to her open, waiting mouth. The small ripples and shivers of pleasure running like a fast tide through her body transferred to him as she clenched and squeezed and squirmed around his cock.

He buried his face in her silken white hair, gently biting and sucking the soft blue flesh of her neck and shoulders, feeling her tremble as he did so. Her low moans and sighs rapidly give way to cries of passion as she raced toward climax.

Tenderly, he put his mouth on hers again, as much to muffle her mounting noise as to taste her sweet, hot lips and feel her ragged breath. The thick walls of the virtually soundproof room would probably hide their noise, but he knew from experience the howls of ecstasy she could be capable of, and even in his own frenzy, he didn't want someone, alarmed by her screams, to burst in on them.

Beneath him, the first shudders of her release shook her, stiffening her body and arching her back from the wall as she pushed herself against him, every molecule of her being fighting to take more of him.

Moans like stifled thunder accompanied the lightning flashing through them as they crashed to climax together, welded in body and spirit by the exquisite joy of their passion. It seemed to go on and on, little aftershocks rolling through their limp bodies.

Still trembling, Benwa eased himself out and gently helped Analet crumple to the carpet. Quickly, he undid her belt, bringing her wrists to her heaving chest. Settling himself, he pulled her to him, pulling her jacket and blouse up to her shoulders and cradling her in his arms.

"Are you all right, my love?" he asked anxiously, examining the red marks and massaging them tenderly. "I did not hurt you, did I?"

She looked up, her amber eyes mere dreamy slits. "With you there is only bliss."

He brought her wrists to his lips and kissed them gently. "Many times during the long solar revolutions that we have worked together, I have sat in my office, aching with the need of you. Even before we had our first joining, I remember wondering how it would be to simply steal into your office on some pretext of business and have you."

"Then why did you wait so long?" she teased.

"In the beginning, before our first joining, our relationship existed only on a professional level and in the consulate; you, always my superior, dignified and official. Aloof and attentive to business. Only after I discovered you to be a passionate and playful partner, willing to explore all the realms of the flesh, whatever form they might take at the moment, did I begin seriously to consider actually taking you here, in your own office. But always the doubt lingered."

"Doubt? About what?"

"That you would not consent and surrender yourself in this most public, official place."

"And what made you finally decide on today?"

"Last night, when I saw how you embraced the excitement of two men, one a virtual stranger, I knew that the wells of your curiosity, your adventure, ran as deep as your sexual need. I have often dreamed of taking you, pinned against your office wall, half-naked, wet and hot, the knowledge that we could be interrupted, discovered at any moment, edging the act with a tinge of danger. Hobbling you with your own clothes and binding you with your own belt came as a spur of the moment thing."

"Looking at you, no longer my superior but a hungry, helpless female burning for me as I did for her, pushed me past sanity. If the President and Council of Carus, The Sildor herself had opened the door and found us, it would not have stopped...even slowed me. You excite my mind and my heart as well as my body."

"As you do mine," she replied, pulling him down to her so that they could share a passionate kiss.

"Perhaps..." he began but the communication buzzer sounding on Analet's desk cut him off.

She stirred and started to pull away, but he pulled her back. "Let it go," he breathed, pressing her lips against his again.

"But...but it may be important," she murmured, opening her mouth so that their tongues could dance. "You...you said you told my...assistant not to ring unless...unless..." Her thoughts and words faded as the passion heightened.

The buzzer went quiet and she felt his cock brush her leg as it hardened. Even though they had just finished, she could feel the heat rising again.

A knock sounded at the locked doors.

"Ambassador Tol?" came the timid voice of her assistant Shenrak from the other side.

"Yes?" Analet managed, reluctantly pulling her mouth from Benwa just enough to answer.

"I am sorry to disturb you and the Trade Minister, but there is an urgent communication from Consul Tavkeru. He says it is most important that he speak with you. Now."

"Tell the Consul I will be right with him," Analet replied. "I am just finishing my meeting with Minister Benwa."

"Yes, Ambassador."

"I must get up now," she sighed. "Tavkeru is not known for his patience and I think I should at least pull up my trousers and button my blouse before I speak to him on the holophone."

Benwa sighed, kissed her lightly and grinned. "Who knows?" he chuckled. "Maybe if you answered his call as you are, he would be more agreeable to your proposal concerning the new fleet of trade vessels."

Analet giggled and they shared a last kiss. Standing, he helped her to her feet, watching as she hurriedly buttoned her blouse, tucked in the shirttail, pulled up her pants and slid them closed.

"You may need this also," he smiled, reaching down and retrieving her belt.

"Thank you, Benwa. But I think you'd do well to take your clothes into the bathing chamber and remain there until I'm finished with my call."

"Do you think my cock would make him feel inferior?" Benwa joked, moving his hips slightly so that his re-awakened cock danced at its full length.

"I think your cock would make a full-grown Lithorian bull feel inferior," she answered lightly. "Now, leave, please."

"Only if you promise to get rid of those ugly flowers and your schoolboy admirer."

"Benwa, please…"

"Promise."

"All right. All right," she agreed in exasperation. "Anything you wish if you go now."

Grinning, he gave her cheek a quick peck.

She waited while he picked up his clothes and with a sweep of his arm, disappeared behind her bathing chamber door. With a last nervous run of her hands over her hair, Analet settled back into her desk chair and hit the blinking communicator button. Instantly, a holographic image appeared just beyond the front edge of her desk.

"*Dai shan*, Consul Tavkeru," she said respectfully. "I'm sorry to have kept you waiting, but I was…engaged with Trade Minister Benwa."

* * * * *

"Your bath is ready," he smiled.

"Thank you, Ston. Did you find out what time dinner is and where I'm supposed to go?"

"Yes, Daria Evans. You will be dining with The Sildor in her private dining room in the hour after dusk. I will escort you personally."

"Ston, you don't need to use my full name when talking to me. You may call me Miss Evans."

"I do not understand."

Daria sighed. Having to explain even the simplest things to these people had passed mildly irritating and arrived at full-blown annoying. When Ston had told her of his familiarity with her customs, she'd thought that at least she might feel more comfortable with him. It had become obvious very quickly, though, that his "knowledge" perched next to non-existent.

"On my planet, most humans have at least two names. Their first name is normally used to denote them personally. I'm 'Daria.' The last one is generally the name of their family. You know...their clan. My family name is 'Evans,' hence, I'm Daria Evans."

"Did I not pronounce it correctly?" Those deep, gorgeous eyes immediately filled with an anxious, child-like, eager to please look.

"No, you pronounced it very well. But you don't need to use both names when speaking to me. You may call me Miss Evans."

Total confusion appeared in his face.

She tried again. "Among my people, 'Miss' is a term of respect for adult, unmarried females. 'Missus' is for married females and 'Mister' is for males, married or unmarried. It's used with the last name by people who don't know you well enough to call you by your first name alone."

"Married. This is when humans mate?"

"No," she snapped.

Ston flinched in surprise at the curtness of her answer.

Daria took a deep breath. "I'm sorry, Ston. I didn't mean to be so short with you. It's just that humans don't 'mate' as you call it. We humans take great care to find a compatible person, someone with whom we wish to spend our entire lives. We call it, 'being in love.' When we find that person, we stand before a minister or a rabbi or a priest or even a judge and go through a very special, very beautiful ceremony, called marriage, and then settle down and have children. We call that 'living happily ever after.'"

"I see now," he nodded thoughtfully. "On Utan, the ritual of taking a mate is called, '*Fahn-jul.*' There is no word in your language that means the same thing, but your marriage is probably very close. It is the time when a female chooses her first mate and leaves the house of her clan to have offspring and make a place of her own. Her clan usually has a great celebration afterwards. As she takes more mates, the ritual is done very simply. Unless, of course, she is very rich and important like The Sildor. Then all the *Fahn-jul* rituals are as the first one."

"Well we don't take multiple mates. At least not all at once. I mean, we believe that marriage is something special...sacred...that is only for one male and one female. We understand that things don't always work out and so people get 'divorced.' Go to court and a judge dissolves their marriage and then it's like it never happened and the people are free to marry again if they wish."

"On your planet each male has a female of his own?" Wonder and envy sounded in his voice. She thought of a small child discovering a candy store for the first time.

"Yes, that's pretty much how we do it."

"Then there is an abundance of females?"

"Well, I'm not sure that I'd use the word 'abundance' but yes, there are a lot of us. In fact, the Earth's population is about fifty-one percent female."

Those beautiful eyes grew wide with surprise. "On Utan, a male could never hope to possess a female of his own. Females are few and precious and must be shared to keep our planet alive until we can return to the surface. Surely the males of Earth must give thanks to the Creator for living in a world where such a treasure may be obtained."

Daria had to laugh. "Females may be treasured on Utan, but not so on Earth. I suppose it's the law of supply and demand."

"I do not understand." He lowered his head and shifted his weight uneasily. "I am sorry to be so stupid and to ask so many questions. I realize that to such a female as yourself who is both beautiful and intelligent, a mere attendant taking up your valuable time must be both burdensome and troubling. It is just that you know so much and I so little and the sound of your voice…your words… You will forgive me?"

For one of the few times in her life, words failed her. No one had ever called her beautiful before. The nuns had used the word 'pretty' but always added, 'tended to be overweight.' Trout had said 'nice looking' and even 'attractive' on occasion, but never actually used the word 'beautiful.' It made her a little giddy.

"There's nothing to forgive," she assured him, reaching out and putting her fingers on his muscular arm. "I'm complemented that you think I'm beautiful, although that's probably because I'm the only human female you've ever seen. If you could see other human women, you'd know that I'm very plain by comparison. And you must never be ashamed to ask questions. Asking them shows that you are anything but stupid. It shows you're inquisitive and interested in the universe around you. You go right ahead and ask me whatever questions you'd like, whenever you'd like for as long as I'm here. I'll do my best to answer them."

Gently, he put his hand on top of hers, pinning it for a moment against his arm. A warm sensation shot from her hand, up her arm and burst into her solar plexus. The room wobbled slightly and everything but those huge black eyes shining down at her got a little fuzzy around the edges.

"Excuse me," she mumbled, pulling back her hand. "I really have to get to my bath. I don't want the water to get cold and I don't want to be late for The Sildor's dinner." With that, she almost ran across the sleeping chamber and into the bathing facilities.

The tub, actually about an eight by eight-foot pool, was sunken into the marble-like pale green and gold veined floor. Quickly, Daria got undressed, dropping her clothes on a nearby stone bench and going down the steps. Ston had prepared the water just the way she liked it; very warm but not hot. A bottle of blue liquid and a round, slightly roughened ball sat on the lip beside the steps. Opening the top, she was met with a fragrant, musky smell.

On the other side of the pool from the steps, Daria found that the bench dipped, forming a sort of reclining area. Lying back brought the water to her chin. Blissfully, she closed her eyes and let herself drift. She enjoyed this much more than the shower in the apartment she and Trout shared. Trout enjoyed the 'invigorating, scrubbed' feeling of a good shower. And she did, too. But nothing compared to warm water and a closed room for giving you a sense of peace like nothing else. When she'd suggested to Trout that she'd like to have a place with a tub, he'd made a face, sort of wrinkled his nose and grumbled something about lying in dirty water.

The gentle sound of lapping and a few small waves of disturbed water washing over her caused Daria to open her eyes.

Ston stood naked on the steps of the pool, the tip of his relaxed dick just barely touching the water as he leaned over to retrieve the bottle and the ball.

Reflexively, Daria screamed and turned her breasts to the wall of the tub.

Instantly, Ston stood over her, fear and concern in his eyes, voice and touch.

"Miss Evans," he said frantically. "What is the matter? Are you ill? Injured? What has happened?" As he reached out to touch her, she flailed behind her with one hand.

"Ston!" she screamed again. "Touch me and I'll scream so loud The Sildor will be down here herself. What are you doing in here naked?"

He blinked helplessly. "Doing? I came to help you with your bath. To do that, I must get into the bathing pool with you. And to do that, I removed my clothes."

"I don't need any help with my bath," she yelled. "I've been bathing by myself since early childhood. Just get out! Now! And for Heaven's sake, put your clothes back on!"

"But it is part of my duties as your attendant to help with your bath," he continued plaintively, obviously still not understanding what had upset her so badly. "Wash your body. Your hair. Whatever you desire."

"Well, my desire is to have you out of my bath tub…my bathing room. Now!"

He stood a moment more, so close she could almost feel his cock at her back and then she heard a deep sigh as he retreated across the pool and back up the stairs. Hesitantly, she ventured a peek.

Standing just on the top step, his hard, flat ass faced her, a ridiculous creamy white between the tan of his strong back and long legs. As she watched, he paused and turned back to her, his cock stretched to its fully aroused length, water droplets clinging to it like diamonds. But the look of pain, confusion and misery in those deep eyes made her quickly turn her head. She didn't turn back until she heard the door click quietly shut behind him.

Thankful to be alone again, Daria sank back onto the recliner but did not close her eyes. Her heart pounded, her blood raced and she felt as if she might explode at any second.

My God, she'd seen him naked. And he'd seen her.

He'd startled her, she told herself firmly. She'd had a perfectly normal reaction to that fright and nothing more.

That wet, erect cock glistening and hard.

Stop it! There was nothing sexual to a total stranger barging in on her bath.

Her fingers remembered the feel of his skin and her heart sped up a little more.

Perhaps he'd misinterpreted the touch, the whole conversation about marriage. After all, these people took an entirely different view of relations between the sexes. He might even have believed his attentions would be welcome.

She would just have to get rid of him. Politely but firmly.

Ah, but…

He'd been personally sent here by The Sildor. Perhaps in her twisted logic, she'd believed that making this handsome, sexual man available to her would be taken as a complement. Like the *Fal-Trank*. And refusing this gift might be suicide, negotiation-wise. Or she might believe that Daria had not found her choice suitable. In that case, she would probably send another man with even less decency. And what would happen to Ston, personally, if she refused him?

Judge, jury and executioner.

Daria frowned. She could not afford to offend The Sildor, nor could she risk having a man big enough to overpower her at any second so close at hand.

What they needed, she decided finally, were rules. A working agenda. After her bath, she would simply lay out the ground rules. He seemed intelligent enough and certainly eager to please her. She'd simply explain the differences in their culture and once he understood what she found acceptable and what she didn't, there wouldn't be any further incidents.

Yes, she thought closing her eyes again, it was a simple matter to deal with.

* * * * *

Finishing her bath, Daria put on the thick warm robe she found hanging on a hook and went into her sleeping chamber. Ston stood quietly by her wardrobe cubicle. Well, she might as well start here and now.

Walking over to him, she looked up into those eyes.

"Ston..." she began.

"I am truly sorry to have offended you, Miss Daria Evans," he stammered like a schoolboy apologizing to a teacher. "Here it is my duty to attend a guest in all functions, no matter how small. I did not realize that appearing in your bath unannounced would so disturb you."

"You surprised me, Ston, that's all." She'd been prepared to lay down the law to him but he seemed so upset, so contrite, she didn't have the heart. After all, he simply didn't know any better. "On Earth, only the very young, the very old and the infirm have help with their bathing. It's a very…private sort of thing. And on my planet, we don't expose our naked bodies to just anyone, especially males and females."

She could tell from his expression that she was rapidly losing him again. Why couldn't these people understand something as simple as modesty?

"Only males and females who are very close…bonded, as in marriage, show their naked bodies to one another. It's considered…" she looked for a word he would understand. "It's considered very offensive."

"Why?"

"Well…because…it's…" her voice faded in exasperation.

"I personally have seen pictures of human primates without clothes, male and female. They look much as Utanian bodies do even though our evolution was different." He shrugged. "They seemed pleasant enough to look on. Are humans ashamed of their form?"

The honesty and openness of the question took her completely by surprise.

"No," she told him emphatically, "we humans are not ashamed of our forms. Some of the greatest artwork of our history has centered on the unclothed human body. Simply because we don't go around flaunting it, doesn't mean we're ashamed of it."

"Oh," he nodded again. "Then humans believe their bodies are good to look at?"

"Under the proper circumstances, of course."

"Such as when you are mated?"

"Married," she corrected, relieved that he seemed finally to be getting the gist of situation.

"Then you are afraid that the sight of your bodies will arouse you and cause disruption to your matings?"

My God, she thought in amazement, *no matter what we talk about, somehow the conversation always comes back to sex. Didn't these people ever think about anything else?*

"I'm sorry, Ston," Daria smiled thinly, trying to turn the conversation to a new course but feeling as if she was maneuvering a battle cruiser. "I really must see about something to wear to dinner tonight. Perhaps we can talk…"

"I looked through your clothes," he told her simply.

"Yes, well Ston, that's one of the things I wanted to talk to you about. You can't just go around…"

"I wanted to see what I should lay out for you to wear for The Sildor."

"That's very nice, but…"

"I did not find anything suitable."

"What do you mean, you didn't find anything suitable?" She didn't know whether to be insulted or embarrassed.

"The Sildor dines each evening in her finest gowns and jewels," he told her patiently. "Whether she dines alone or with guests. Tonight, because you will be there, she will be dressed especially well. She will expect you to do likewise."

"But…but I didn't expect that I would be dining with The Sildor," Daria replied, a trace of panic edging her voice. "I mean, I only have one good dress to my name and I didn't bring it because…well because I just didn't think I'd need it."

"It is all right," he assured her quietly. "As your attendant, it is my duty to see that you have all that you require."

Turning around, he opened the wardrobe cubicle and stepped to one side. On a hook just inside the door hung the most beautiful dress Daria had ever seen, long and simple, the color of her eyes, made of some kind of material that seemed to shimmer and sparkle with its own light with a high, round neck and long, slender sleeves. The sight of it made her gasp.

"It's…it's gorgeous," she breathed, taking a step and reaching out to run tentative fingertips along the front. It felt as soft as a cloud. "Simply gorgeous."

"I'm honored that you are pleased with the choice," he said quietly. "I have had little experience with female's clothes but I thought it would look well with your eyes and fit well on your body."

"But…but where did it come from? I mean…this is far too elegant and expensive…"

"It is the wish of The Sildor that you have all that you require. Such a garment is required. If this is not suitable, simply describe to me what it is you wish and it will be provided."

"But, I can't…"

"There are coverings for your feet," he continued, bending down and producing a pair of evening slippers that matched the dress exactly. "I took the liberty of looking at the clothes and foot coverings you had to determine your size. I think everything will be to your satisfaction but if not, any changes can be made."

"Ston, I can't accept these presents."

"It is the will of The Sildor that you have them," he insisted calmly.

"But my company doesn't allow me to take gifts. They have very specific, very strict rules. Especially concerning gifts from people that we may do business with. And most especially, such extravagant, expensive gifts."

"Before you reject The Sildor's generosity," Ston told her firmly, "perhaps you should consider that you will offend and insult her by not being dressed as one should be in her presence. Even if your company has a rule against gifts, it would not want you to be dressed incorrectly for such an important occasion."

He was right, of course. If she ruined this deal by slighting the old woman, it wouldn't matter about the dress and shoes. She'd lose her job anyway. Not to mention The Sildor's possible reaction.

Judge, jury and executioner.

"Of course it would be rude not to accept these gracious gifts from The Sildor," Daria smiled sweetly. "And I certainly wouldn't want to dress inappropriately for such a grand occasion as a royal dinner."

"A wise decision." She could tell by the gleam in his eyes that he wasn't surprised by her change of mind.

"Well, if you'll excuse me now, I'll get dressed. I still have my hair and makeup to do and I want to be on time."

Ston brightened. "I will help you to prepare. I have attended many female guests of The Sildor with their dressing, hair and facial rituals." He cocked his head to one side and surveyed her critically. "I will put your hair on the top of your head. It will show your lovely neck and ears, and with the elevated foot coverings, will make you look taller, more imposing. I think, though, not too much on your face. Only a little color on your cheeks and mouth. And something to show the beauty of your eyes."

"That really isn't necessary, Ston."

"It is necessary if you wish to look well for The Sildor."

And she could see by the determined look in those dark eyes, she would give in with this as she had everything else.

"Very well," she conceded. "You may help me with my hair and make up. *After* I've finished getting dressed. Now out."

His face fell. "But it is my duty…"

"It is your duty to do as I desire. And right now, I desire that you leave me alone. I will summon you when I'm ready for you."

Dejected, shoulders stooped, Ston dragged his feet toward the large doors. Pausing with his hand on the knob, he turned back to her, a faint hopeful smile at his lips.

"I'll call you," she repeated sternly and waved her hand away from her.

"As you desire."

* * * * *

"You will excuse our humble fare," The Sildor told her gravely, "but living underground as we do is not conducive to the production of livestock, so we live a primarily...primarily..." Her face darkened and she turned to the man on her right, the same man who'd been seated next to her when they'd met in the reception room. Leaning over, she whispered something in his ear and a moment later he whispered back to her. She nodded once.

"A primarily vegetarian lifestyle." The Sildor glanced at the man who moved his head a little up and down and smiled.

Satisfied, she continued. "You will forgive me, please. My knowledge of your language is adequate but not extensive. I hope our conversations may enlighten and enrich me. Albre is my Chief Counselor. He is much more familiar with your language than I am, and has agreed to help me, should I falter."

"You're doing very well," Daria lied smoothly. "Ours can be a difficult tongue even for those of us who are born to it. I hope to learn some of your language during my stay as well."

"Perhaps. But as I was saying, we grow our grain and vegetable products indoors, hydroponically with artificial sunlight. They provide us with everything we need for a balanced diet, including protein. Our clever scientists have come up with methods for making the protein into forms resembling meat. The look and taste is remarkable. If you did not know, you would be certain you were indeed consuming animal flesh."

At this point, Daria thought wearily, *I'd be glad to consume anything, animal or vegetable, no matter how it looked or tasted.* She'd arrived at the appointed hour and been ushered into the small room, perhaps not even half as large as her sleeping chamber. But her rooms paled in comparison to the opulence of this one.

The walls shimmered like the tiny drops of petrified tree sap on Earth they called amber. Panels of it, perhaps four feet wide and running from ceiling to floor alternated with equal panels of what looked like gold. A crystal chandelier hung above the table, warm light spilling down over rows of perfectly matched ribbons of glass. On the smallish round table sat three place settings, pure white dinnerware with a thin gold band around the rims—bowls set on small plates set on larger plates. Heavy gold flatware arrayed on both sides, more utensils than Daria had ever seen. Four exquisite, crystal glasses of different sizes and shapes sat above each place setting. Daria made a mental note to watch The Sildor and do exactly as she did.

Catching herself in the mirror, Daria paused to check her reflection.

She had to admit, even to herself, that if nothing else, Ston was certainly a fine hairdresser and makeup artist. He hadn't allowed her to sit where she could watch as he worked, placing her in a dining chair at one of the tables on which he put a box with drawers, rather like the one the man who fixed the computers at Unitech carried. Turning her away from the table, he had set to work for the better part of an hour, first on her hair and then on her face. Finally satisfied, he'd allowed her to go to the mirror in her sleeping chamber.

The difference had been so great, she literally almost hadn't recognized herself, doing a double take just like in the videos.

He'd pulled her honey colored hair flat, meeting in a mass of curls piled atop her head and spilling over slightly like a little fountain and sprinkled with a confetti of small, glittering glass beads that matched her dress. Ston, true to his word, had spread some kind of ruby-colored gel on her lips with his fingers, making them shine like wet cherries, a little glow on her cheeks and something that sparkled like tiny emeralds on her eyelids. To finish the picture, he'd added a simple necklace of smooth, milky white beads—they reminded her of pearls—and tiny gold threads for her ears, from which hung clusters of the same beads only in miniature.

"This is satisfactory?" he'd asked anxiously, standing just behind and to the side of her.

"It's beautiful, Ston. Just beautiful."

"It is you who are beautiful," he'd replied quietly.

Grinning, she'd turned, stood on her tiptoes and planted a quick kiss on his cheek. "Thank you, Ston." She giggled and turned back to the mirror. "I feel positively giddy. Like Cinderella going to Prince Charming's ball."

But that had been almost an hour ago and there was still no sign of food. Like everything else, dinner seemed bogged down in ritual. *If I'd known this*, she thought dryly, *I would have packed a lunch.*

"Perhaps while you are here," The Sildor was saying, "you might like to visit one of our hydroponics farms. We obtained the original technology from one of Unitech's many companies. Of course, that was long ago and I'm sure much has changed but perhaps since Unitech may be here mining, they might be interested in updating and upgrading our food supply as well."

At this point, I'd do just about anything for some food.

"If time permits," Daria answered, "I would be honored to see how you manage to feed an entire population on hydroponics alone. It might be a model for other planets to emulate."

"Good. We shall plan on it."

Terrific. "I shall look forward to it."

A door opened and three men in starched white uniforms with shiny gold buttons down the front appeared, one of them pushing a sort of silver cart, the other two bringing up the rear. He stopped the cart just to the left of The Sildor. Raising the domed silver cover, he displayed a filled soup tureen. She glanced down and nodded. Immediately he took her soup bowl and served her as the two men scurried for the other bowls.

As they settled the filled bowl in front of her, a whiff of something tangy drifted to Daria's nose. Pretending to open and spread her napkin, Daria stole a glance to see which spoon The Sildor and her companion picked up. A large, round shallow one at the very left side of the arrangement. Making sure that the older woman had started, Daria picked up her spoon and took a sip.

"This is delicious," she said, a note of astonishment creeping into her voice. A note not lost on either of the other people at the table who exchanged quick glances.

"I'm glad you approve," The Sildor answered without emotion. "It is a simple mixture of…of…" she looked at the man and mumbled something.

"Ah, yes, tomatoes, a wonderful plant brought to Utan from your own planet long ago when we first began growing our food underground. They grow especially well on our hydroponics farms and are favored by all the cooks on the planet from the poorest to the chefs of the palace."

"Tomato soup has always been one of my favorites," Daria grinned. "Since I was a small child."

"Your clan must take great pride that you have accomplished so much in such a short span of life," Albre commented casually between spoonfuls of soup.

Daria's spoon stopped midway to her mouth, a tremble causing the soup to jiggle a tiny bit. As always when the uncomfortable subject came up, she lowered her head and took a deep breath.

"I'm afraid I have no family…no clan," she replied softly. "I'm what my kind call an orphan. I was found on the steps of a Catholic church, lying in a box and wrapped in an old towel. I was about two months old. Being sickly and skinny and ugly, I was never adopted — placed with another family who wanted a child — so I grew up in the orphanage. I studied very hard and when I finished my schooling, what we call high school, I won a scholarship so that I could go to college and further my education. Unitech hired me right out of college as a Junior Analyst and I've worked my way up to my present position."

"Then you can be proud of your own accomplishments."

She looked up and saw the old woman gazing at her thoughtfully, as if turning something over in her mind. A few more moments and the look disappeared, replaced again by the impassive mask.

"As I was saying about the tomatoes…"

Dinner wound leisurely past soup, a large salad of vegetables Daria had never seen before, a main course of something that tasted faintly of beef, a grain that reminded her of rice, a blue side vegetable resembling mold which Daria couldn't even bring herself to try and a dessert of light sponge cake with a cream filling and some kind of berries on top. Each course was lavishly accompanied by sauces, gravies, rolls, spreads and of course, different beverages which Daria suspected were some kind of liquor. She sipped them enough to assure The Sildor that she enjoyed them but not enough to allow them to impair her judgment.

At last, the waiters cleared the table, leaving only three small glasses, a decanter of some kind of dark, smoky liquid and a bowl of what looked like dinner mints. Albre poured out the liquid and handed The Sildor a glass as she leaned back in her large burgundy colored chair.

"The meal was to your satisfaction?" she asked.

"Everything was excellent," Daria replied. "I don't believe I've eaten more tasteful food or enjoyed better dinner companions." She was stuffed and ready for bed. The meal had gone on and on and there'd still not been a single word about the project. Only formality and ritual.

"I am pleased you are content. It is my wish that you take a positive report back to your company."

Daria's ears pricked up. Perhaps this was a subtle signal that The Sildor was at last ready to discuss business. But she must still keep a low profile.

"The Sildor can be assured that there will be nothing but praise for yourself and your planet when I return to Earth. The extent of your generosity and hospitality has been overwhelming. Unitech would indeed be fortunate to establish a branch here."

"And Utan would most certainly benefit from the increased wealth and prestige among other planets," The Sildor agreed.

Now we're finally getting somewhere, Daria thought eagerly.

"You have not tried your drink," Albre observed, nodding toward her glass still on the table.

"Oh, I'm sorry," she muttered, reaching for the drink and taking a sip. It was like charcoal flavored syrup and it was everything Daria could do not to spit it out. Instead, she swallowed and smiled. "What an interesting dessert wine. I don't think I've ever had anything quite like it."

"It is made from a special fruit which grows only for The Sildor," he told her. "It is buried in stone pots for the length of several solar revolutions...about ten of your Earth years."

Yuck! "It certainly has an unusual taste."

"I'm pleased that enjoy it," The Sildor responded. "Many who try it find it too thick and sweet. I shall make sure you have a bottle to take back to your planet."

Oh goodie. "Thank you, Sildor."

"You have said you have no clan," Albre picked up the thread of conversation. "Does this also mean you have no mates?"

Uh oh.

A simple enough question but Daria had already had a glimpse of Utan's sexual views and felt there might be more to it than mere curiosity. After all, The Sildor herself had a hundred mates. Utanian women mated and reproduced for the good of the civilization. A woman who'd reached her age and hadn't yet married and had children might very well be regarded with suspicion. And even on Earth there still lingered those who felt that marriage and family contributed to a person's stability and somehow made them better business risks.

"No," she replied carefully. "I'm not married yet. I am engaged though...promised to a wonderful man named Trout Erdman. He works for Unitech too, and we're planning to set the date…get married, in the near future. Probably as soon as I get back from Utan."

The Sildor leaned over to the man and there was more whispering. She made noises that sounded to Daria like nothing more than squeaks and clicks and she couldn't make out what Albre's replies.

"I have studied with great interest your proposal for the mining of the northern hemisphere," The Sildor began, straightening herself in her chair and focusing those dark eyes on Daria. "I have spoken to those whom I trust," she glanced at Albre and back, "and I have calculated the amounts of wealth that you project will come to my planet. I have also considered the influx of new people, new ideas, new ways of doing things. They are very impressive."

"Well, we've tried to be as realistic as possible," Daria told her trying not to break into giddy laughter. "The projections are based on the relatively small sampling our robot explorer did. We believe though that the deposits may be much larger than we've stated, especially of *pluronium* and *dimethetrioxium.* And who's to say what other minerals we may find when we actually begin the mining process? Utan will become the financial, commercial, industrial and political hub of this part of the galaxy. You'll no doubt be invited to join the Galactic Confederation and Utan will take its place among the great planets."

"You paint a most enticing portrait."

Whip out your digital signature instruments, Daria thought merrily, *'cause we're signing on the dotted line.* She would get The Sildor to sign the preliminary binding document tonight, probably right here at this very table. In a few days there would be the official contract signing with lots of publicity and pictures and she would be on a liner for home by week's end. Wouldn't Trout be proud of her? The image of his satisfied smile came to her across the void.

"However, I have not yet made my final decision."

Thud!

Daria came crashing back to reality.

"The hour grows late and I must retire," The Sildor announced. "Ston is waiting outside to escort you back to your apartment. I trust you will sleep well and we will speak of this again."

Immediately, a door behind Daria opened and Ston appeared.

"Good night, Miss Evans," Albre said as he rose from the table.

"Good night," she mumbled as she got to her feet.

"Good night, Miss Evans."

"Good night, Sildor."

When Daria had departed, Albre sat down and poured them both another glass of wine.

"So, what do you think now, Minsee?"

The old woman's shoulders moved up and down fractionally as she sipped her drink. "I knew she was intelligent and thoughtful when I read her proposal. It is the work of a clever mind and a clear thinker. And she believes most sincerely that this project will benefit not only our people but others as well. The division of wealth is fair although from what I have learned, perhaps a shade more favorable to Unitech than us. As she says, we would go almost overnight from a small, ordinary planet, to a very wealthy, very influential one. It is a very tempting offer."

"Then why are you not tempted sufficiently to stop toying with this young female and sign the document?"

"Because she asks me...asks all the people of Utan, to trust her when she does not trust herself."

Albre raised a questioning eyebrow.

"She seems greatly shamed by the circumstances of her youth. Of having no clan of her own and being physically imperfect and not being chosen to be part of some other clan.

She has risen far and achieved much and yet only this...this orphanness seems to matter to her."

Minsee took another sip of wine and continued thoughtfully.

"She's also ambitious and greedy."

"And how do you know this?"

"Because instead of mating and producing offspring, she works and struggles for this Unitech thing. Even the mate she will take is provided by Unitech."

He laughed. "A most thorough employer. Perhaps they will provide her with offspring as well."

"Don't be so quick to dismiss them. I have studied them and they seem to survive and grow by swallowing and absorbing smaller, lesser entities. I have no desire to become Utanitech."

"Then say that we will continue as we have and send the female away."

Those dark eyes closed to thoughtful slits and she considered the dark liquid in her glass for several moments. Finally, she turned to him.

"Perhaps," she answered cryptically, "there may be another choice."

* * * * *

Daria closed the door, leaned against it and sighed heavily.

"I take it that Voh's news was not welcome." Ston stood across the wide outer room in the doorway to her sleeping chamber.

"He says that The Sildor regrets that she still cannot grant me an audience, even a short one. 'Matters of state,' he says." She sighed again, this one in growing frustration.

"It's been three days since we had dinner and not a word. Nothing! Trout calls me morning and night and if I don't have some word for him pretty soon..."

"There is no use to become angry over that which you have no control," he told her calmly. "The Sildor will give you her answer when she is ready. Until then, there is nothing you can do. Disturbing your body and mind will do nothing to make the answer come sooner."

Of course he could take that attitude, she thought cynically. He's a servant. His life and job remained secure as long as he behaved himself. He had no deadlines, no decisions, no projects that could make or break his career. Everything that she'd planned and worked for, hoped and dreamed for, hung on this old woman's whim and she was powerless to intervene.

"I have prepared your bath."

"Not now, Ston..."

"It is a special bath, filled with herbs and scents to calm and relax you. Make the waiting easier. Also, I have put out *Fal-Trank* and *shata* for your lunch." He grinned. "It would be more pleasant to pass the time that way than standing at the doors waiting for word."

How could she refuse, especially when he crinkled up his eyes and smiled like that?

In a few moments, she'd stripped out of her clothes and entered the tub, unworried that Ston would appear uninvited. Pouring herself a goblet of *Fal-Trank*, she settled back in the tub, letting the warm water and the faint bouquet of unfamiliar aromas leach the tension and worry from her body and mind.

By the time she'd finished two more goblets of the amber liquid, Minsee and Trout and Unitech seemed far away. There was no place in the universe but here.

She heard a soft knock on the door and Ston's head appeared. For some reason she couldn't quite understand, the sight of him there didn't upset her.

"Yes, Ston?" she smiled.

"After your bath, I will rub your body with scented oils," he announced calmly. "It will help relax you further."

"A massage?" She considered the possibility for a moment. "That sounds like a wonderful idea. Especially if you're as good a masseur as you are a hairdresser."

He grinned back at her. "An attendant must have many skills if he is to perform his duties. When you are finished, dry yourself, wrap the towel around you and come into the sleeping chamber. I will have everything ready."

"I'm finished now. I'll be right there."

When she came into the sleeping chamber, she saw that Ston had set up a long, narrow table near the bed. Walking over to it, she saw it had a thick pad on top, covered with some kind of dark blue, soft, napped material that felt plush under her fingers. Ston retrieved an extra sheet from the linen cubicle. Folding it twice, he laid it down, smoothing out the wrinkles.

With a little help from Ston, Daria laid down on her stomach and pillowed her head on her folded arms. The pad seemed to give and shape itself to the contours of her body.

"Mmmmm," she purred, closing her eyes, "this is wonderful."

Tugging a little on the sheet, Daria raised herself and felt the towel disappear. A part of her mind raised the objection that she was now naked, but the rest of her didn't seem to care. After all, to get a body massage, one usually had to be naked.

Something thick and warm poured over her shoulders and upper back. A moment later, Ston's large, powerful hands began to move slowly and gently over her skin. His touch felt rhythmic, peaceful. Daria melted like warm wax.

"Your body has the feel of the finest fabric," he told her, leaning down slightly. "Never have I known such rare, silken softness."

"It's probably the lovely potion you put in my bath," she chuckled. "It makes me feel positively limp."

"I may be permitted a question?" he breathed in her ear, his lightly oiled hands continuing to move over her skin in a soft, lazy, random pattern.

"What is it?" she murmured, never opening her eyes.

"Do all human females smell as you do," he whispered as he leaned his face down, almost touching her back and breathing deeply, "or is that rich...sweet...sensual musk your scent alone?"

The feel of his breath on her naked flesh raised goosebumps of excitement and she shivered with the pleasure of his nearness.

"I...I don't know," she managed to stammer. "I never thought about it."

"Never have I known such a scent," he continued, moving his lips slowly up and down her back, feeling the peaks and valleys of her spine and tasting the slight tang of the massage oil. "All of The Sildor's rarest, costliest perfumes pale before it."

"On Earth," Daria mumbled, "humans are taught that body odor is a bad thing. We bathe frequently so that we don't offend others of our species."

"On Utan, the musk of another body is most desirable to males and females alike. Especially when that scent is aroused." His lips brushed the back of her neck and she shivered again. "If you belonged to me, I would never allow you to rid yourself of your scent."

The tip of his tongue danced across her neck, filling her warming blood with small, icy prickles of pleasure.

"Relax," he whispered, his breath hot and slightly ragged. "Let me feel your body in my hands. Feel my flesh on yours."

A distant alarm sounded somewhere at the far edge of her brain. Something about massage and seduction. But trying to think, listen to it even, just took too much effort so she shut it off and gave herself over to the feel of him.

His hands slid gently down her back and rested lightly on her cheeks, kneading them tenderly. "You have the most perfect ass. Round and firm yet with such softness."

"I have a fat ass," she replied dreamily. "Always have had. Everything I eat, I end up sitting on."

"You are the most beautiful female I have ever seen," he told her, brushing his cheek along her back and bringing his lips to her ass. "To spend even an hour with you, any male of Utan, myself included, would submit to your every wish, every whim. That a human male could possess you for himself…"

A loud knock on the door interrupted them.

"Tell whoever it is to go away," she told him regally, opening one eye and grinning. "Say I'm occupied with grave matters of state and cannot be disturbed. I will give audience later. Then come back and finish what you've started."

Returning her grin, he bowed slightly. "As you command."

She closed her eyes again and settled more deeply into the mat. Beyond the closed sleeping chamber door she could hear the murmur of voices but could not make out anything but the sound. In a moment, Ston appeared at her side again.

"It is Voh," he said anxiously. "The Sildor sends for you immediately."

Chapter Three

Daria glanced at her watch for what seemed the hundredth time and sighed. She'd been sitting here for almost half an hour. From the tone of Voh's voice and manner, she'd expected to be ushered into The Sildor's presence immediately. Even the few moments it had taken her to dress seemed to weigh heavily on him.

And instead of the grand reception hall, she'd been escorted to this small room where Voh had left her, saying only that The Sildor wished to see her most anxiously and that she would be summoned shortly. Then he'd scurried away through another door.

If the old biddy is playing another game with me, she thought angrily…

A door opened across the room and Albre appeared. "You will come with me, please? The Sildor will see you." He stepped aside for Daria to enter.

The old woman sat behind a large, dark wood desk, the outer edge on the top and two sides heavily carved and inlaid with what looked, to her cursory glance, like precious stones and gold. The edge where her body met the desk was unadorned. And that same impassive mask she always wore did not betray her reason for the unexpected and hurried summons.

A cold chill of panic shivered through Daria as she realized the desktop was bare of papers, contracts. Whatever the summons, it wasn't to give Daria good news.

"The Sildor sent for me?" she asked, trying not to sound as apprehensive as she felt.

"You will sit, please?" The Sildor pointed to a chair across the desk. Obediently, Daria sat down.

"I have given much thought and consideration to your proposal for the mining rights to our northern hemisphere," she began solemnly.

Daria felt her whole body tighten. Trying to act casual, she folded her hands in her lap to keep from balling them into fists and concentrated on the old woman's face.

"It is a matter of the gravest importance to my people and I am much aware that the decisions I make now will determine Utan's fate for many generations. Therefore, this is not a decision to be made lightly or in haste."

"I can certainly understand The Sildor's desire to weigh all the facts," Daria nodded in agreement.

"So, after much discussion with my counselor Albre and much thought and deliberation, I have decided to accept Unitech's offer and enter into a contract for the mining rights."

Yippppeeee!!! Daria shouted in her mind. She'd done it! She'd got the contract and the vice presidency and Trout and a wedding and a family! Ecstatic, she could have gotten up and danced with Albre. Kissed The Sildor right on the mouth! It was wonderful! It was better than wonderful. It was all her dreams come true in one glorious, fell swoop.

"I'm glad The Sildor has made such a wise decision," Daria replied in measured tones of her own, barely able to conceal her own helium-filled joy. "I know that the joining of our two people in this great enterprise will be to both our benefit."

Something flickered in those dark eyes.

"It is odd," she remarked, "that you would use the word, 'joining.' After all, it is almost as if Unitech and Utan were about to enter into *Fahn-jul* and that there will be a joining, a mating of our two people to produce offspring. In this case, wealth and prestige and security."

It was as stupid an analogy as Daria could think of, but apparently these people only thought in sexual terms.

"Yes, I suppose it is sort of like a marriage."

"Then you would agree that as in any joining, there must be absolute faith; trust that the other party wishes you no harm but goodness only?"

"Of course, Sildor," she replied, not quite certain what the other woman was driving at.

"That is very good. Because before I sign this contract as the representative of my people, I must know, in my heart, that Unitech is to be trusted. That they will keep the word they have given."

"Sildor," Daria told her earnestly, "you can be certain that whatever Unitech promises, they will deliver. They're known throughout the universe as a company to trust. In fact, I could return to my suite right now and compile a list of references for The Sildor to contact..."

"I am not interested in references," she answered flatly. "I am not interested in Unitech. I am interested only in those people of Unitech who will deal with my planet and myself." She leaned across the desk a little and those eyes narrowed again. "People such as yourself."

"Me? I...I don't understand."

"This project. You conceived and fashioned it, did you not?"

"Well, yes. New project feasibility and analysis is my specialty."

"You have worked with this plan, lived with it? Know it better than anyone else? This is correct?"

"Yes. But I still don't see..."

"That is why I wished for you to come here and not someone else. I wished to see not only the mind of this project but the heart and the soul as well. I have, for the most part, been very satisfied."

"Thank you, Sildor."

"I said, 'for the most part.' But my satisfaction must be complete before I commit my people and my planet to this undertaking."

"I'll certainly do whatever I can to set The Sildor's mind at ease."

For the first time, The Sildor smiled. A wide, knowing grin that immediately heightened Daria's renewed sense of apprehension.

"I am glad you feel that way because I have a small task...a test if you will. When...and if, you complete this test, we will have a contract."

"What kind of test?"

"I wish you to attend The Academy here at the palace. A short term only."

Daria breathed a silent sigh of relief. She'd always been an excellent student. As long as she could take her translation unit for verbal and written materials, it was a fair bet she could get through anything these people might throw at her. Even something fairly technical.

"Of course Sildor. I've heard it is a great honor to attend your Academy."

The smile widened a fraction. "Perhaps you should know something of The Academy before you agree."

"Well, I'm sure I can handle it. I was Phi Beta Kappa and Summa Cum Laude at college."

The Sildor did not seem impressed. "I wish you to learn submission and domination."

Daria blinked several times, not quite sure she'd understood correctly. "Excuse me?"

"I wish you to learn submission and domination," the old woman repeated slowly. "It is not a long process and if you are as adept at learning as you say, it should not take you very long to complete the lessons."

"By...by..." Daria could barely choke out the words, "submission and domination... you aren't speaking in the...in the sexual context, are you?"

"Certainly."

Her gaze ping-ponged between Albre and The Sildor, desperately trying to make sense of this. If it was a joke, it was in very poor taste, even for these sexual animals. If it wasn't...well, the whole idea was too horrible even to contemplate. But the two of them maintained their calm demeanor, behaving as if it was the most normal request in the world.

"You...you can't be serious," Daria offered, trying to feel her way out of this dark pit she seemed to have suddenly fallen into.

"I am most serious."

"But...but...that's ridiculous. Why would you even suggest such a thing?"

"You have asked me and my people to trust you. Not just your great company, but you personally. Your judgment, your knowledge, your ability to predict and deal with any manner of problem. You have asked me to be your mate and to join with you.

"While I do not know the ways of your kind, on Utan, before a male or female can take a mate, they must undergo certain training in The Academy. Training that will show quite clearly who they are. The results can be most enlightening to all concerned, even the person undergoing the lessons."

"When you enter, you will be given a 'safe-word.' This is a word that you may utter at any time and end the lessons but as long as you do what is required, no harm will come to you."

"And if I refuse?"

"That is your decision. But I cannot join without trust."

"Well, I won't do it," Daria told her defiantly, standing up to make her point. "I will not degrade myself, especially in such a...such a personal manner, to prove to you that my company and I are worthy to do business with you. There are a great many planets in the universe with natural resources as valuable as Utan's who would welcome us."

"Then," The Sildor told her quietly, "I suggest you seek them out. But before you dismiss my test so lightly, I would consult with those above you at Unitech. They may not share your views. I will give you one solar rotation to deliver their answer. But for now, I have spoken and the audience is concluded."

* * * * *

"Daria, what's the matter?" Trout asked. "My assistant said it was an emergency."

"Oh Trout, it was awful!" The tears that Daria had been holding until she could get back to the privacy of her sleeping chamber spilled out.

"God, Daria," concern drenched his voice, "what happened? Did...did you lose the contract?"

She mumbled something but he couldn't understand her. All he could see of her holographic image was a large wad of white that practically covered her face.

"Look, Daria, pull yourself together," he told her firmly. "I can't hear what you're saying through the tears and the hanky. Blow your nose and tell me what's going on."

Daria honked into the white wad and he waited while she stopped sniffling enough to talk.

"The Sildor told me she was ready to sign the contract..." she began between hiccupping sobs.

"Oh, Jeez, Daria, that's great! I knew you could pull it off! That's my girl. Wait 'til I tell Old Man Hennessey."

"Listen to me, Trout," she wailed.

"Okay, okay. I'm listening. I just wanted you to know how happy I am."

"Well, you won't be when I tell you the rest."

"Rest? What do you mean 'rest?' What happened? What did you do?"

"I didn't do anything. She kept me cooling my heels for three whole days. Then she suddenly calls me and tells me that she'll sign the contract but only if I'll...I'll..." She dissolved in another fit of tears.

"Only if you'll what?" he demanded across the light years. "What?"

"Only if I go through The Academy here at the palace," she told him.

"I don't have a clue what you're babbling about, Daria." Impatience and annoyance sounded in his voice.

"She wants me to...to take...take a course in...submission and domination..."

The astonishment on his face wasn't dimmed by all the distance between them.

"She wants you to do *what?*"

"Just what I said. The Sildor says that the contract is like a marriage and that anyone who wants to get married on Utan...they call it taking a mate...has to go through this...this sex university they call The Academy. It's right here in the palace but considering that she's got a harem of a hundred husbands, I'm not surprised."

"But why does she want you to do this?"

"To prove that we...Unitech and I can be trusted to keep our word and so that she can see what the person who dreamed up this project, namely me, is made of."

"And...what did you tell her?" His voice had become noticeably calmer and more thoughtful.

"What did I tell her?" Daria couldn't believe he even had to ask. "I told her no, of course! She gave me another day and told me that I should talk to my superiors at Unitech, but I told her no one in the company would even consider such a disgusting and perverted suggestion."

Dead silence.

"Trout?" she asked nervously. "Did you hear what I said?"

His eyes had wandered from her off to the side, his fingers drumming absently on the top of his desk.

"Yes, Daria, of course I heard what you said."

A tiny speck of uncertainty appeared on the horizon of her mind.

"Trout. I want to come home. Now. As soon as I can get a liner. And I'm moving out of here and back to the public accommodations center."

Another silence.

"Trout?"

"Yes?"

"You aren't upset with me, are you?" The speck had become a small dark cloud that had spawned a cold shower of fear.

"No, of course not," he replied but not very convincingly. "Look, Daria, what exactly did she say? I mean about these 'lessons?'" More than just idle curiosity surfaced in his voice and image.

"I told you what she said about the 'lessons.' She said she wanted me to take submission and domination. You're a grown man, Trout. For God's sake, do I have to draw you a diagram?" Daria felt her voice rising along with her panic level.

"That's not what I meant, Daria, and you know it. Of course I understand the terms. What did she say specifically about you taking these lessons?"

"What difference does it make, Trout? I'm not going to do it."

"I'm just trying to understand the situation, Daria. Work with me here."

"She said that the lessons wouldn't take very long and that if I did what 'was required' no harm would come to me and that they'd give me a 'safe-word' to say and I could get out of it whenever I wanted."

Another silence drew out between them.

"So," he ventured cautiously, "you wouldn't actually be in any real, physical danger?"

"Not if you don't count being tied up and raped and who knows what," she shouted, feeling the tears stinging again.

"Well I'm sure that even if there is…sex involved, The Sildor would never allow anything to happen to you. I mean, you're a human, an Earthling. An American, for God's sake. And Unitech's got a lot of pull with the government. Even the Confederation. They wouldn't dare try anything funny with one of our employees."

"I'm sure it isn't meant to be funny, Trout."

"Well, you know what I mean. And besides, this might be the test itself."

"I don't understand."

"There's probably nothing to this whole Academy thing. The test is whether you're willing to do what she wants. See how far you'd be willing to go to get her to sign on the dotted line."

"Well, you can bet I won't go that far." Daria stuck out her chin slightly to make sure he understood her position.

"Look, Daria," he cajoled, smiling across the void at her, "if you feel that strongly about this, then of course, you don't have to do it."

She smiled back, relieved that he didn't seem angry with her. "I knew once I told you what that horrible woman said you'd understand and agree with me."

"Of course I do," he soothed. "It's just that…well…"

The hesitation in his voice wiped the smile from her face.

"Well what?"

He looked away then, as if afraid to face her.

"It's just that you know how important this contract is. Not just to Unitech and for all the good we can do for that little planet but to you and me personally. Promotions. Prestige. Titles. More money."

"There'll be other projects," she insisted, feeling her heart sink a little. "Other promotions."

Turning back, she saw his face had changed to a set mask. Hard and cold. "No, Daria, there won't be. Not for either of us. You'll be labeling yourself a quitter, a failure. Someone who couldn't deliver in the tight spot. You'll go back to your old job but you can bet there won't be any more plum assignments like this. You'll be parked on a siding somewhere and left to rot until you quit or pension out. And it won't just be your career either. It will be mine too."

"Trout…"

"No," he stopped her, putting up his hands and shaking his head. "It's true. I'm your supervisor. I went to bat for you when everyone, including Hennessey, thought you couldn't cut it. I sold them on giving you this chance. By backing a losing horse, my judgment, my management skills, will be called into question. I'll be tarred with your 'loser' brush as well.

"And marriage would be out of the question."

This last statement hit her like a blow to the stomach. Tears started to flow again.

"I'm sorry to have to be so blunt, Daria," he said without remorse, "but it's the truth. You know my family's never been too keen on you as it is. I mean with your…murky background. But I told them you had the right stuff; that just because you weren't born to quality didn't mean you couldn't be quality. And even they wouldn't have been able to say anything about the first female vice-president of Unitech. But now, especially with the damage you'd undoubtedly do to my career as well as your own…well…"

"You don't know what you're asking," she whimpered. "Whips and chains and having to do whatever disgusting, perverted things they wanted. Except for you, I've only ever been with two other men in my life. How could you...how could you even look at me, much less touch me, make love to me again if you knew that...that I'd..." Tears overwhelmed her.

"If I knew you loved me so much, cared so much about our careers and our lives together, that you'd...you'd put yourself through this to get something as important as this contract, how could I help but love you, too?" A tinge of excitement appeared in his voice. "No matter what...what happened, I'd still think you were the most wonderful woman in the universe. I'd never ask, never condemn what you might do, might go through. We'd just pretend that it never happened and we'd have everything we ever wanted. Together."

She saw him then, through her tears. He stood up, his arms reaching out to her, a look of love and hunger in his eyes that she could never remember being there before.

Her mind seemed to be spinning out of control. The Academy meant sexual violation, tortures beyond her imagination, pain, humiliation. But all that paled beside the unthinkable prospect of life without Unitech. Without Trout Erdman. And he'd promised his forgiveness. His love.

"All...all right," she murmured finally. "I'll do it. For you. For us."

Chapter Four

"Well, I think that's everything," she sighed, looking around the sleeping chamber a last time.

"When you return," Ston told her quietly, "all will be as you left it."

If I return, she thought fearfully.

"I'm sure you'll take very good care of everything," she answered, trying to smile. "Just please be sure and do what I asked. Without telling anyone, including The Sildor."

He held up the small envelope. "I will deliver this into the hand of Ambassador Tol before the sun is at mid-sky and no one will know of it."

"Thank you, Ston. You've been very kind and a faithful attendant."

"I am honored to attend you, Miss Evans. I look forward to continuing my duties when you return."

A knock sounded at the front door.

"That will be Voh," Daria sighed. "I'll go with him now. As soon as we leave, please take my letter to the Ambassador."

"It is done."

"Good-bye, Ston."

"Good-bye, Miss Evans."

Voh waited just outside the door.

"You are prepared?" he asked gently.

"As prepared as I'm ever going to be," she replied wearily.

"Then you will come with me?"

She fell into step and they walked briskly toward The Academy entrance. Daria felt like a condemned prisoner walking the last mile, each footfall closing the noose tighter.

It seemed like they flew through the empty palace halls and arrived in a moment at the guarded gate.

"I will leave you now, Miss Evans," he told her, still using that gentle tone. "I look forward to seeing you upon your return."

"Thank you, Voh," she whispered, barely able to catch her breath, her heart pounded so fast.

A hooded figure moved behind the gate and a moment later it opened just enough to admit her. Once inside, the sound of it slamming shut felt like the clank of a metal coffin lid over her frightened body. A pale hand appeared from the megaphone-sized sleeve of the figure's loose garment and motioned for her to follow. Then it turned and began the trek to The Academy.

Just as they turned the corner, she peeked back but Voh had disappeared. She really was all alone now.

* * * * *

The huge, old-fashioned wooden door swung slowly open and Daria, terrified, stepped inside. Black and cavernous, the room appeared lit only by fat white candles burning in large, black sconces along the walls. Underfoot, she felt a thick, dark, deep pile carpet, and against the far wall, the biggest bed she'd ever seen.

Trembling, she stood rooted to the spot. She didn't have to go through with this. The Sildor herself had said so. Trout couldn't make her. He couldn't threaten her or hold her job hostage. There were laws...she could sue. Certainly even a company as big as Unitech wouldn't want to face that kind of expensive galactic humiliation.

"Daria Evans?"

The voice seemed to boom out of the walls, baritone and authoritative. Jumping at the unexpected sound, she suddenly felt lightheaded as her pounding heart tried desperately to rush oxygen to her spinning brain and clutching lungs.

"Daria Evans?" the voice repeated sternly.

"Y...yes," she croaked, turning her head in all directions but seeing nothing.

"You have come to The Academy to learn the ways of domination and submission. You will find nothing here beyond your consent. This is a place of learning and enlightenment, not of torture and rape. But once the lessons begin, you are committed. The fantasy becomes reality. Only your safe-word will bring you back. Do you understand fully and enter into this willingly?"

Of course she wasn't entering into this willingly. But between The Sildor and Unitech, she had no choice.

"Yes," she whispered hoarsely.

"Your safe-words are 'yellow" and 'red.' We selected these from your planet's use of yellow for caution and red for stop. When you wish to slow down, say 'yellow,' and we will pause. Say 'red,' and the lessons are finished. Once 'red' is used, it cannot be undone. All instruction will end and you will be returned to the palace. If, however, the lessons end before you have completed all of them, your agreement with The Sildor and the people of Utan is broken. Do you understand?"

"Yes."

"Then we will begin. Go to the center of the room."

Fearfully, Daria did as the voice commanded. As she stopped, a beam of brilliant white light flashed down from the darkness above, completely encircling her. She had to squint and put her hand up as a shield against the brightness.

"Disrobe," the voice ordered.

"What?" Daria couldn't believe her ears.

"Disrobe."

"I...I can't," she stammered, trying to peer beyond the ring of light.

"Can't is not a word for submissives," the voice shot back, a hard edge now appearing. "You will do as you are told or face the consequences." The single word seemed to drip menace.

She reached up and began fumbling with the button on her blouse, fear causing her hands to shake violently.

"Begin with your shoes."

Not understanding but 'consequences' still ringing in her ears, Daria raised her left foot to her knee and slid off her low-heeled black pump and then reached for its mate.

"More slowly. Disrobe more slowly."

Her shoe slid off in slow motion. It seemed to her hours before she finally stepped out of her panties and stood naked and shivering.

The voice remained silent for several moments and she could almost feel cold hands running over her body...testing, feeling as one would do with a prize horse or slave. Fearful shivers became shudders as she instinctively tried to cover herself.

"Keep you hands at your sides," the voice barked sharply.

Instantly, she dropped her hands.

A large male figure, wearing nothing but a kind of short leather apron and a hood covering everything but his eyes, nose and mouth, appeared at the edge of the bright circle. Squatting down, he quickly gathered up her clothes and vanished, never even glancing at her.

Abruptly, the light went out and she found herself once more in the soft candle glow.

"Go to the bed."

Timidly, Daria moved to the bed. A new wave of terror engulfed her as she saw the item lying on it. A leather harness, obviously for her, lay near the foot.

"Put it on," the voice ordered coldly.

Again, the large man appeared, towering over her. Reaching out, he picked up the harness and held it out for her.

Smooth, thick, wide straps crossed, forming shoulder straps, front straps chest and waist high, running horizontally, two leg holes and one hanging strap running front to back from the waist strap.

Carefully, she raised one leg and stepped into it and then the other. The man pulled it up tightly against her inner thighs. The other strap wedged itself against her pussy and she realized with a start that the inside was slightly rough.

Pulling the harness straps to her shoulders, he adjusted the front strap so it formed a narrow bra, just covering her nipples and squashing her breasts slightly. The inside of this strap was slightly roughened, too.

Expertly, he quickly buckled the shoulder straps, checking to make sure that it fit tightly but not painfully binding her. Satisfied, he left, disappearing into the blackness.

"Go to the mirror. It is on the wall to your right."

Taking a step, Daria froze.

"Go to the mirror, submissive." The voice took on that hard edge again.

She took another faltering step. As she did so, the rough leather rubbed against her nipples and pussy like the fingers of an anxious lover, the sensation totally unexpected.

As she moved slowly across the room, the sensation intensified with each step, sending small ripples and shivers radiating from between her legs.

Like everything else about the huge room, the mirror stood ten feet tall and half again as wide. Standing in front of it, Daria could see the black of the leather against the paleness of her skin. Even the brass buckles and connecting circlets seemed to gleam in the soft glow of the candles.

"Arouse yourself. Move your body so that the harness may work its charms."

"You...you want me to..." The implication horrified Daria.

"I'm growing weary of this, submissive." Real anger, real threats sounded in the voice now. "If you do not wish to go on, say the safe-word and we are finished. Otherwise, submit and continue. But be assured. This is your *final* warning. Another outburst or act of disobedience and *there will be punishment.*"

The threat in the voice outweighed the disgust of pleasuring herself. Slowly, Daria began to move her hips in small, uncertain circles, feeling even this slight movement bring a tingle to her breasts, a wetness between her legs.

She shut her eyes, making fists of her hands hanging at her sides. This was wrong! Not something nice girls did. Even in her teens when she'd first confronted her growing sexuality, and in the sometimes lengthy periods between partners, she'd never allowed herself to sink to this. And she wouldn't now.

With every ounce of her strength, she fought back the mounting excitement inside.

Something snapped across her ass; a short, sharp sting like a rubber band hitting bare skin.

"Ouch!" she yelped as her eyes flew open and she spun around, grabbing her butt and rubbing the small red streak.

The man stood just behind her, a little smirk at the corners of his mouth, a short, thin piece of leather dangling from his hand.

"Submission means body and mind," the voice boomed ominously. "To truly learn the lessons of The Academy, you must experience everything fully. Watching your arousal is as important to the experience as feeling it. Since you persist in disobedience, you will be reminded in a fashion basic enough even for you to understand."

"But…"

The whip snapped out again and flicked across her ass, a little harder this time it seemed to her.

"There are no 'buts,' submissive. Continue."

Reluctantly, Daria resumed her movements, now under the watchful scrutiny of her mysterious guard. If doing this alone had been humiliating, doing it in front of him mortified her. And she didn't need to see his face to know how much he enjoyed the show.

"Move front to back," the voice told her. "Feel the roughness on your pussy like the callused, experienced fingers of your lover."

As she did so, the pleasure increased dramatically. The sensation seemed to be flowing out of her pussy in hot waves, threatening to swamp her very being. Her body seemed to be moving by itself and she had the fleeting thought that she probably couldn't stop the tidal wave now, even if she'd wanted to.

In front of her, the figure in the mirror now writhed in tempo to the eternal dance of passion. Straining against the harness, Daria's passion grew, her eyes dreamy and half-closed, making small mewling noises as the pleasure surrounded and engulfed her.

Like a fragile, rainbow-hued bubble being slowly filled to the bursting point, Daria felt herself building to release, her breath coming in short, shallow gasps, the leather seeming to cut farther and farther into her. Any second now…

"Enough!"

The word hit like a bucket of cold water thrown on a raging fire. Even as she stopped moving and looked up in confusion, she could feel the exquisite fire rapidly fading away.

An angry, frustrated, "*What!*" leapt to Daria's lips but the hard glance of her Keeper and the leather whip hanging by his side squelched it.

"Go to the bed and lie down quietly."

Daria re-crossed the room, the leather playing tantalizingly on her tender, engorged nipples and pussy.

Silently, she lay down, sinking into a soft, downy cloud. Before she could get comfortable, the guard followed, gently but firmly raising her arm toward the corner of the bed. In a twinkling, she lay spread eagle, her wrists and ankles secured in padded, black leather manacles attached by stout leather thongs to the bed frame. She could feel herself stretched, but not painfully so.

Satisfied with her secure restraint, he reached over and slid a black blindfold over her eyes.

"Yellow!" Daria screamed, terrified and struggling once more as she slipped into total blackness.

"What is it?" The tone was neutral again.

"What's going on?" she yelled frantically. "What are you doing? I can't see."

"You have no need of sight," the voice explained calmly. "You are about to embark on a journey of discovery which requires your other senses be heightened."

"But I don't want to be tied down!" she insisted, panic covering her words.

"You are a submissive. You must give yourself up, to trust, even in unfamiliar and helpless circumstances. The decision is yours. Say the safe-word and you will be released."

Even in her agitated state, Daria knew she detected a faint note of reproof in the otherwise neutral voice.

Taking a deep breath, she forced herself to relax. She'd made a commitment...not just to The Sildor and Trout, but most importantly, to herself.

"I'm all right," she replied, trying to sound more convinced than she really felt.

"Continue."

Several long, agonizing moments went by as Daria listened to the blood pounding in her ears in time to the thudding of her heart. *With any luck*, she thought bitterly, *maybe I'll just pass out.*

A momentary shift of weight on the bed and Daria felt naked skin brush her thigh as a naked body settled itself between her outstretched legs.

She held her breath as strong fingers unbuckled the strap at the harness waist and felt the cool rush of air on her wet pussy as the leather fell away, exposing her.

Fear washed over her in a nauseous wave and she shuddered uncontrollably.

Something soft and luxurious as the pelt of an exotic animal brushed delicately across her instep like gossamer wings. As it traveled over her skin, the unbelievably sensual sensation melted the shivers of terror into tremors of pleasure.

The sensation wasn't like anything she'd ever experienced. Delicate and gentle, it barely touched her as it floated, snail-like, up her foot, ankle, leg. Just as it floated up her inner thigh and kissed her pussy, the progress stopped and the journey started over at her other instep. Daria felt the heat of her aborted passion rising again, stronger now than before. In response to the sweet torture of the soft fur, her body began twisting and turning, drawing the harness over her sensitive nipples.

The sensual pelt drifted slowly up her body, gently covering every inch of her exposed front, moving lightly up her arms and shoulders. At her neck, it seemed to curl around, and then vanished.

A moment later, something silken and smooth drifted across her face and began retracing, in reverse, the path of the sensual, furry pelt.

Daria began to moan again, the passion becoming almost unbearable. But the silky creature continued its agonizingly slow progression. She felt it being pulled ever so slowly under the harness between her breasts and down across her belly, her inner thigh, leg, ankle, foot. As it moved lightly down her instep, the sensation became too much.

"Oh God," she whimpered, "please…please…"

But her pleas for release went unanswered as the silky creature returned to the top of her other thigh and traveled leisurely down to her foot again. "I can't stand…" she moaned. "I need…please…"

Daria heard a buzzing sound, like a swarm of bees, then felt something warm and solid sliding easily into her, and suddenly, she felt the vibration of a thousand hummingbird wings beating inside.

"Oh!" she squealed as the full brunt of the pleasure took control of her.

"That's right," the voice coaxed, "feel the pleasure. Struggle against the manacles and the harness. Give yourself over to it."

The vibrator eased up and down, twisting slightly, alternately burying itself and then sliding almost out to kiss her pink clit.

Unable to free herself, Daria could only moan as her body writhed and contorted in the escalating excitement. She could never remember feeling this intense, this explosive.

"Please, oh God, please, I can't stand it anymore," she cried as the beginning of the end rolled over her. Screaming, her back arched, her body caught in a firestorm of ecstasy, she felt as her body was literally exploding, cascading into tiny shards of red and gold crystal enchantment.

Coming down was like a gentle cloud drifting from Mt. Everest. Daria lay back, gasping for air, feeling every muscle, every nerve, every molecule exhilarated. She was exhausted. As she floated peacefully back to earth, the swarm of bees fell silent and the hummingbirds flew away.

"Rest now," she heard the voice through a veil of on-rushing sleep. "The lessons will continue."

* * * * *

Daria blinked open her eyes and stretched herself as tall as she could, the feel of the bed soft beneath her. It took a moment for her to realize she was free of the manacles and harness, leaving her naked and, except for the red streaks on her ass, no worse for the wear. Her arms and legs felt tired but surprisingly not sore from the restraints. In fact, after her deep, dreamless sleep, she felt very good.

A quick glance around the room confirmed she was alone. Idly, she wondered if she'd been down for a ten-minute catnap or eight hours of genuine sleep.

"You are rested, submissive?" The voice showed no interest, no curiosity.

"Yes, thank you, sir," she replied deferentially. The title seemed to slip out on its own.

"The lessons will continue."

"Excuse me, sir," Daria said hastily, "but...I need to...freshen up. Please. It's *very* important."

"Very well," the voice agreed grudgingly. "You are granted three of your Earth minutes. Go to your right. Down the corridor you'll see a door. But remember. If you abuse this privilege, not only will you be punished, but the privilege will be revoked as well. You are dismissed."

"Thank you, sir," Daria called as she ran out of the room.

It took longer than she'd hoped to find the door, not just down a long corridor but almost hidden in a shadow shrouded alcove. By the time she did reach it, her physical and mental anxiety had both escalated almost to panic.

Going as quickly as she could, Daria took care of only the more essential necessities and then ran back. It wasn't the fear of punishment that spurred her but the thought of losing this precious privilege. And with no way to measure time, the fear that she would be late and lose this, grew a hundred times in her mind.

"I'm back," she announced breathlessly, coming to a stop in the middle of the room. "I hope I'm not late."

"You are within the designated time limit. The lessons will now continue. Turn around and put your hands behind your back, wrists touching."

Slowly, Daria did as the voice instructed. Immediately, she felt a large hand grab both of her wrists. A moment later she felt padded manacles, holding her wrists together tightly, but not uncomfortably so. A blindfold slid over her eyes and she plunged into darkness once more.

A strong fist closed around her upper arm and she felt a tug. Helplessly, she followed, thinking the walk would only be a few steps back to the bed. Instead, they continued for several more moments.

At last, the hand released her, shoving her firmly in the back so that she fell forward, landing with a *whump* amidst what felt like large, soft pillows. The hand reached down, turned her on her back and propped her into a sitting position, her legs straight out in front of her.

Close by, she heard the clinking of glass and the faint sound of liquid being poured. She felt the man, her guard's presence, as he settled himself beside her.

The rim of a small glass pressed against her lips. When she opened them, a sip of something very close to the white wine, Chardonnay that she'd known at home, trickled into her mouth, rolling on her tongue and splashing into her empty stomach. Without her sight, the flavors seemed to jump out at her, crisper, and more distinct.

It disappeared and something crunchy with a taste like oat bread replaced it. It tasted like a large cracker, but slightly sweet instead of salty. As she bit into it, she felt the bits and pieces falling onto her bare skin like ragged confetti. Because her fear had robbed her of her appetite before she'd come to The Academy and she'd been occupied since arriving, she hadn't thought about food. But now that it was presented, even in this odd fashion, her hungry body readily accepted the offering.

A glob of something sticky and tart pushed itself into her mouth and instinctively, she sucked at it. The guard's finger, dipped in some kind of soft, cheese-like substance. Hungrily, she licked it clean twice more, feeling the digit move over her tongue and teeth as she worked on it.

Something round and firm, about the size of a tennis ball she guessed, rubbed gently over her lips, leaving a tang and the sharp scent of peppermint. Opening her mouth as widely as she could, Daria bit into it, her teeth coming together in the flesh of some sweet fruit, sending a trickle of juice down her chin, neck and across her left breast.

Out of the darkness, a tongue gently caressed her flesh, slowly tracing the sticky track from her mouth downward, also catching the cracker debris as it went. The feel of his tongue sent pleasant little shivers through her. In fact, the whole experience of being fed blindfolded made eating highly erotic and sensual in a way she hadn't believed possible. Taste. Smell. Hearing. Touch. All her senses seemed super heightened, super sensitive.

He licked the last remnants of the juice from her breast, dragging his tongue slowly across her nipple. Her shudders and moans of delight seemed to inspire him and he gripped her, suckling and feeling her squirm.

Releasing her finally, he silently continued the feeding, alternating different tastes and textures, stopping to lick up crumbs and juice from her body, feeling her growing excitement.

Comfortably full at last, she turned her head to indicate she was finished. A moment later, she felt her guard reach behind her and unfasten her manacles. As she rubbed her wrists, Daria put her fingers around the edge of the mask to remove it. Immediately, a large hand took them away. Apparently, she would be freed but still in the dark.

She felt his body behind her again, pushing lightly on her back. Dutifully, she scooted forward a little. The guard settled himself behind her, his strong, lean legs holding her like a vice. Skillfully, he began massaging her shoulders, his hands gripping her flesh gently but firmly. His hands moved slowly, rhythmically back and forth from the tips of her shoulder blades to her neck, releasing her body's tension and easing her fear.

Instinctively, her eyes closed and her head lolled, rolling leisurely from side to side in time to his movements. Fingers brushed away the hair covering her neck, the edges of front teeth nibbled on her soft flesh.

Startled by the jolt of pleasure, Daria's body jumped a little, but his hands held her in place as his tongue began making lazy circles around the top knob of her spine. Goosebumps rose across her body and she shivered with the pleasure. Behind her, his hot, rock hard cock pressed into her back. But instead of fear, the sensation only added to her growing excitement.

His hands moved down her back slightly and around to her breasts, cupping them like a living bra as his mouth and tongue continued their dance across the sensitive skin of her neck. Waves of building heat collided with icy prickles of pleasure in her blood, making her a little dizzy.

Splayed fingers gently massaged her breasts as his palms rubbed over her inflamed nipples, now as hard and erect as his cock pressed hotly at the small of her back.

As his legs spread out a little, Daria felt her own move too, a breath of cool air on her moist, engorged pussy. But instead of relieving her heat, it only seemed to increase it.

His lips traveled around to her cheek and she swiveled her head to meet them, her lips parting by themselves to welcome his seeking tongue.

Without her sight hogging the stage of her brain, all her other senses seemed to be more acute, more alive. The feel of his hot flesh against hers. His earthy, aroused musk surrounding her. A sort of salty tang to his lips and tongue. Two hearts pounding, their beats slightly off tempo of each other. Breath, perhaps his, perhaps hers, coming in jagged, uneven pants between passionate kisses.

Carefully, he raised her ass a little, her legs dropping outside his and exposing her pussy. She felt his cock slip in from behind, a gasp escaping her at the feeling. He adjusted himself downward and her body up a little until their bodies came together comfortably. Strangely, she did not feel captured or overwhelmed by him, but cared for and…and safe in his strong arms.

Almost without thought, Daria began to rub her ass against his flat body, moving up and down along the length of his cock, squeezing gently and reveling in his rippled hardness. As she did so, her partner's mouth continued on her neck, his hands ranging over her nipples and stomach. Again, Daria felt slightly disoriented and awash in a sea of foreign pleasure.

Abruptly, he wrapped his arms around her and pressed her to him, stopping their motion and pausing her escalating excitement. Instinctively, she opened her mouth to question, to complain, but she shut it again, knowing that while she was in her submissive role, she had no say except her safe-word.

A few short moments went by and she felt the edge of her passion starting to dissipate. And then, as suddenly as he'd stopped, she felt him loosen his grip and begin to move again. Her excitement returned, stronger, she thought, than before.

They continued, his cock and his hands and his mouth and tongue all working together seamlessly to raise her closer and closer to release. A moan dribbled from her lips and her movements sped up a little. Again he stopped their motion, staying perfectly still, his heart thudding against her back, his raspy breathing in her ear, his cock pulsing inside her.

Now what, she wondered frantically? She didn't need to see his face to know he wanted her as badly as she wanted him. Didn't he understand that stopping, even for a moment, tortured him as much as her?

The seconds seem to drag out. She tried moving but he pressed her harder until she stopped. Once again, she felt the edge dulling. As they resumed, Daria felt another burst of energy and immediately stepped to a new plateau, the pleasure stronger, more intense than before they'd paused.

Their movements quickened, harder now and she could tell from the feel of his cock, the sound of his breathing, the pressure of his arms around her that the end was near for both of them.

Feeling the heat of him, she tightened herself around his cock, desperate now to climax.

A third time, he stopped and Daria couldn't believe it. She knew he wanted—needed—to come as badly as she did. How could he possibly play such a mean game? It didn't make any sense.

One last time he started again, and almost instantly the surge of her orgasm rushed through her, so potent, so unbelievably powerful that it shook the foundations of her being. And as the tremors of her release came, they melted in the heat and passion of his coming, as well. It was like a booster rocket, propelling her even further into brilliant, weightless, limitless space.

Collapsing together, she tried to catch her breath, lost to everything but the warmth of his embrace, his cock coming to rest still inside her and the breathtaking pleasure she'd just known.

Growing up in a Catholic orphanage, sex education had been limited to a brief explanation of the menstrual cycle and human reproduction in science. High school dates had consisted mostly of heavily chaperoned dances. Her first sexual experience had come literally when she lost her virginity to a wise and understanding older professor in college. Instead of making fun of her or taking advantage, he'd been patient and careful and she'd even believed for a while that she loved him. Then there'd been a young man she met in her junior year of college but that had only lasted a few months. After that, she'd dated some, but essentially, she'd been alone until Trout.

With sex, as with virtually everything else, Trout had been conservative. He enjoyed having her perform oral sex on him occasionally and a couple of times, she'd even been on top. But beyond that, sex stayed confined pretty much to the bedroom, in the dark, at his initiation. He wasn't what she would have termed 'skilled' even before she'd come to this place, but then, she hadn't been either and they both came fairly regularly and while there hadn't been anything to rival what she'd experienced here, there hadn't been any complaints, either.

After all, she thought, *he would never have been so thoughtless as to stop in the middle of sex.* Of course, she had to admit, that as unnerving as pausing had been, resuming had seemed to be more forceful, more explosive. And the climax...*whew!*

The thought rattled around in her mind for a few more seconds until full understanding came to her. Pausing had increased and intensified not only his pleasure, but hers as well. The blindfolded feeding had not been done just to provide food, but an opportunity to experience the ordinary in an extraordinary way. Like the sex, it had given her a very different view of something very familiar. A sampling of possibilities she hadn't even realized existed.

She felt him rise and a moment later, he gripped her elbow and helped her to her feet. Gently, he placed her hands behind her back, wrists together, and replaced her manacles. They walked a short distance and Daria heard the quiet gurgle of running water, like a peaceful brook.

Tightening his grip slightly, he led her to something that felt to her bare foot like the rim of some kind of pool. She heard a small splash as he changed his position to her front. Tugging lightly, she put out her foot and stepped down, her foot and ankle dropping unsteadily into water, warm as a bath. Two more steps and the gently rolling water was waist deep.

Suddenly, the strong, reassuring hand released her, and she heard the splashing of water as her guard got out.

"Move to the other side of the pool," the voice ordered sternly.

"I...I can't," Daria shouted back, the fear rushing back. "I'm blindfolded! I can't see where I'm going. What if I trip, fall? I could drown!"

"Do as you're told, submissive."

"No!"

"It is not for a submissive to disobey." The voice raised slightly. "Submit. Now."

"I won't," she responded defiantly.

The lash cracked out of the darkness, striking her twice, hard, across her upper back. It stung much worse than the previous lashes.

Surprised and in pain, Daria stumbled and fell face first into the water. Sputtering and choking, she managed to get back on her feet.

"See!" she screamed. "I told you I couldn't do it! I've had enough of your sick, twisted, sadistic games. I went along with this vile idea to please The Sildor and save a worthwhile project that will benefit both our worlds. But by God, I won't let some depraved maniac kill me for sport! I'm finished!"

"If the lessons are over," the voice told her coolly, "you have only to say the safe-word. The decision is yours alone."

He was taunting her. Calling her a coward. Daring her to call it quits. Instead of submitting to him and his whip and games, he was inviting her to submit to her own inadequacies. Her own worst fears.

Daria stood absolutely still as the realization struck her, as real and sharp as her guard's whip. A small flash of lightning illuminated the truth, not just in her mind, but in her soul, too.

"Well?"

Holding her head up, she stuck her chin out slightly. "Continue," she told him firmly.

"Go to the other side of the pool."

All right, she calculated silently, the two lashes told her that her guard still stood nearby, close at hand so the probability of drowning, even if she did fall, was remote. She could feel a slight downward slope under her feet. With her arms manacled behind her, she couldn't swim, even dog paddle. What little hope she had for survival was that the water wasn't too deep or the pool too wide. And the hope that her Keeper might rescue her if she faltered was even smaller.

Carefully, slowly, Daria put out her foot and edged forward. Another tentative step and she felt the water under her ribs. As she continued inching forward, the bottom continued its downward slant and the water continued to rise, eroding her faltering confidence and firing a growing panic inside.

The water reached her neck and she raised her chin, moving forward more slowly, the buoyancy of the water threatening to scuttle her tenuous footing. And still the slope went down.

As the water reached her mouth, she leaned her head back and stopped. One more step would put her nose under water. Two more and she would be completely submerged.

"Submit," the voice told her, the word barely audible through the water lapping her ears and the blood pounding in her brain. "Turn loose of that which you know and embrace that which you do not. Only then can the truth of these lessons be learned. Will the enlightenment come. Continue."

She couldn't continue. Perhaps too late, Daria realized that simply because the guard might still be near, didn't mean he could, or would, help her. Perhaps he too was a submissive; as powerless to help her as he was to help himself.

"Continue or quit."

With a last deep breath, Daria took a small step and then another. For a moment, the frightening blackness and the water submerged her, rendering her completely helpless. Almost overcome with terror, she forced herself to keep moving.

Two more steps but the surface seemed to her a bit more level now. She felt as if her lungs would burst any moment, the panic crushing down on her more heavily than the water.

Another step.

Just as Daria began to feel faint, her foot felt the slope rise a little. Heart racing with excitement and lack of oxygen, she managed to stumble forward, her head suddenly breaking the surface.

A mixture of air and water poured into her mouth as her starved lungs screamed for oxygen. Coughing and unsteady, she stumbled up the remaining distance, the water receding with each step forward. Abruptly, she banged her knee into a ledge, which she knew must be a seat.

Exhausted, she gratefully dropped down, leaning her head back and trying to get hold of herself. With the fear dissipating, the warm water swirling around her was actually soothing, calming. Little by little, she felt herself relaxing, her heart and breathing slowing down.

"It is time to proceed, submissive."

"Please," she answered hoarsely, "let me rest a minute. I almost drowned, for Christ's sake."

"The lessons must continue."

Those same strong hands of her guard grabbed her, turning her and then pulling her along the smooth bench. Too tired to resist and knowing it was pointless to try anyway, Daria submitted meekly.

The hands released her for a moment and she heard movement in the water. Before she could move, however, she felt the hands again, this time lifting her up and setting her down.

Instantly, she felt naked skin on her inner thigh and a thick, hard cock rubbing on her pussy. She was straddling a naked man!

"Yellow!" she shrieked.

"What is it, submissive?" Anger filled the voice but Daria was beyond caring.

"What is this?" she demanded. "What's going on?"

"You have received pleasure," the voice replied dispassionately. "You must now give it."

"But I didn't have anything to say about that," she insisted desperately.

"You had much to say," it corrected like a schoolteacher with a particularly dense student. "You had only to utter the safe-word and you would not have experienced the pleasure. Since you accepted the gift, you must repay."

Daria squirmed and tried to slide off, but she found her knee and lower leg pinned between the wall of the pool and the stranger's muscular leg. With one hand, he gripped her shoulder and with the other, he fondled her breast, apparently unaware or unconcerned with the voice.

"I don't want to 'repay' as you call it! I am not a prostitute or an Utanian woman who takes mates like a careless chimpanzee!"

The silence was deafening and more ominous than anything that had gone before. Even the guard's hands fell away. Daria knew that she'd crossed some invisible boundary, separating the acceptable from the unacceptable and that for the first time since she'd entered The Academy, she was in real trouble.

An eternity passed with no sound but the bubbling water. A tremor of fear shuddered through Daria's body. She wanted more than anything else to speak, apologize perhaps, but the fear seemed to have dried her throat and sealed her lips. And still the agonizing quiet dragged on.

"You...are...a...greedy...selfish...animal," the voice replied finally, each word covered with disdain, broken off and spit out. "You come to Utan in all the splendor of your ape arrogance, convinced that mere beings not blessed with your divine humanness are innately inferior."

"You did not come to this sacred place to learn. There is nothing that we puny Utanians could possibly teach a mighty human. No. You came here because there is great wealth to be gained and you thought to fool us with your feigned sincerity to truly know our ways."

Disgust soaked his words as he continued.

"Well, you fool no one, human. Your kind is consumed with itself and its things. You are not capable of knowing any truth but your own."

"Why do you not just utter the safe-word that this charade may be ended and I can wash my hands of you? You may then slink, mewling, back to your stupid kind, lick your wounded vanity and consider this more proof of your superiority."

'Red' welled up in Daria's mind, demanding to be said so that she could escape this place. Only a single, intransigent thought kept it down. The voice was right about this as it had been about everything else.

Shame engulfed her as the water had, choking and smothering her with a heavy burden of reality.

"I'm…I'm sorry," she managed in a hoarse whisper. "That was a stupid and thoughtless thing for me to say and I regret it sincerely. After everything, I would certainly understand if you didn't wish to bother with me anymore, but please, if you could, I really do want to continue."

Another long, agonizing silence.

"There will be no more disobedience or outbursts." A stated fact and not a question.

"No, sir," she agreed.

"You will submit." Again, a statement.

"Yes, sir."

A final interminable silence.

"Take her," the voice snapped.

Immediately, a large hand grabbed the back of her head, fingers twining in her hair, pulling hard and yanking her forward.

He cut short her startled cry, pressing his lips into hers, grinding and forcing her mouth open. A tongue, thick and strong, invaded her mouth, exploring and examining every millimeter of it. Daria could feel his erect cock as it began working itself against her pussy once more.

Pulling out of her mouth, he sucked her lower lip fiercely, taking it into his mouth and biting the soft flesh a little as he retreated.

Swiftly, he moved down her neck, stopping just where it joined her shoulders. She felt the sharp edges of his front teeth sink into her skin a bit, at the same time making a vacuum with his mouth.

She felt a twinge as there'd been with her lip and instinctively she tried to pull away. Fastened firmly though, her movements only pressed his shaft harder against her.

The twinge merged with the shivers from his mouth on her sensitive flesh and his cock rubbing on her seemed to heighten the pleasure.

It was a different sexual experience than she'd ever known...rougher, more physical. But its very difference seemed to arouse her.

He pulled her closer and she felt lips on her right nipple...hungry, urgent lips suckling as if she could produce milk and a tongue dancing a hard tango over and around it. The fingers of his other hand tweaked and twisted and massaged her left nipple, feeling it harden and swell just as the cock underneath her did.

Something pinched her tit as if caught between his fingers. At almost the same moment, she felt a short, sharp nip on the bulge of her right breast.

"Uh...oh!" she yelped at the momentary pain, feeling the same pinch on her left nipple. As his fingers played over her sensitive nipples, she felt a touch of metal on her skin and she could feel the pinch of clamps or clips of some kind.

She opened her mouth to call out a quick 'yellow', but instantly his tongue filled her mouth again. The movement of his cock against her increased its tempo.

Sensations whirled and eddied and flooded through her. Not real pain but small bursts of a different kind of sensation jolted her, bringing an increased excitement to her, moving her rapidly toward a much needed release.

Beneath her, the body changed position slightly, raising her and sliding inside effortlessly. Pulled all the way forward, Daria found herself laying almost flat against the man, feeling his heat radiating through her.

She felt his hand on her ass, pushing down hard and forcing himself deeper into her. At the same time, he continued manipulating the nipple clamps, the pain growing sharper each time.

"Ow!" she cried after one particularly painful pinch. She struggled but the hands just gripped her more tightly.

"Submit," the voice ordered calmly. "Feel all the sensations. Pain and pleasure. Familiar and strange. Known and unknown. As the rainbow is made of many colors, so too is wisdom made of many experiences."

Water splashed around them as their bodies moved harder and faster.

She felt his body begin to shudder under her as he held her as tightly as he could, moaning, his hand clenched into a claw, scratching and digging into her ass.

Daria screamed—part ecstasy, part anguish—as she and the man came together. For a moment, everything else disappeared, swept away in the tidal wave of their shared passion.

For a few moments, they lay together, sated and exhausted. After the physical and emotional workout, Daria felt completely drained and ready for the inviting softness of the big bed.

Beneath her, the man stirred, reached up and raised her enough to disengage. He slid out from under and she felt herself being dragged, literally, from the pool. Bone weary, she could barely walk, leaning heavily on her guard. Even the cool air on her bare skin did little to revive her.

A door swung heavily open in front of her and she felt cold, uneven stones under her bare feet. A few more steps and her guard pushed her down. But instead of the expected warm, pillowy bed, she fell to her knees onto something so thin she could feel the rocks underneath.

Her guard bent down and removed her manacles and blindfold. Blinking, she found herself in a small windowless cell, lit by only a single wall sconce of three candles. She lay on a dirty mattress and a coarse, dark brown blanket that smelled like it had just come off a horse.

Above her, the guard stood watching her, naked except for his mask, his cock now returned to resting, still impressive, glistening with water droplets in the candle light. With that knowing smirk at the corners of his mouth, he looked like a hunter with a prize trophy.

Without a word, he grabbed her ankle and pulled it to the wall where he slipped it into a metal, unpadded manacle chained to the wall, tightening it securely. He gently removed the clamps from her nipples. Satisfied that she wasn't going anywhere, he crossed the room and silently disappeared, the door clanging shut behind him. A moment later, a loud *click* echoed in the cold darkness.

Shivering both with cold and anxiety, Daria wrapped the thin blanket around her and settled herself as comfortably as she could. Closing her eyes, the last words of the voice came back to her with ominous clarity:

"Take her."

* * * * *

Daria woke up stiff and cold, her body sore and the weight of the heavy manacle and chain beginning to chafe a red ring.

Adjusting the blanket, she sat up, yawned and stretched as best she could, being careful of her complaining muscles.

Looking around, a metal pie plate with some kind of dark bread and fruit in it caught her eye. And beside that, a tall glass of some kind of liquid. It had no flavor, but the wetness quenched her thirst and refreshed her. The bread tasted a little like rye and with the apple-like fruit, satisfied her hunger.

With nothing to do now but wait for whatever was going to happen next, Daria curled up, pulled the blanket as tightly as she could around her and stared out into the room. Candles flickered on the opposite wall and her eyes moved to their almost hypnotic light.

In the absolute silence and the blackness broken only by the dim light, Daria found herself reliving her time in The Academy, everything re-enacted in vivid detail. The terror, the ecstasy, the anger, the exhilaration. All came back but with a sense of clarity she hadn't had before. And above all, the voice coming out of the blackness like Zeus or Jupiter or Jehovah. A god overseeing bondage, sex, submission and domination. Ludicrous, and yet…somehow…

A loud squeal announced the opening of the door and the noise snapped Daria back to reality. By the time she'd turned her head, her guard had already crossed the cell. She noted that he again had on only his short leather apron and mask.

Silently, he opened her manacle and helped her to her feet. Limping slightly, she followed him down another corridor in this seemingly endless warren. Finally, he opened another door and pushed her through.

Daria almost laughed out loud with glee. A bathroom!

"You have three minutes," the voice boomed out of the walls.

"Thank you, sir," she replied, almost giddy with relief, physical and emotional.

The door swung shut and she hurried to do what she needed to, acutely aware of the clock ticking loudly in her head.

When the door opened again, Daria smiled and started to step through but the guard pushed her back as he came in.

Grabbing her arm, he pulled her through another doorway Daria hadn't even seen.

On the other side, she found a large, brightly-lit room, taken up almost entirely by a beautiful waterfall, tumbling perhaps twenty feet in a frothy curtain over a jumble of boulders and into a shallow pool.

Leading her to the edge, he picked up a tube she recognized as bathing gel and a body ball from a flat rock. With a nod toward the waterfall, he handed the gel and ball to her.

"A shower," she squealed as the light of understanding dawned. "You're letting me have a shower! Oh, thank you, sir. I'm very grateful."

The voice did not acknowledge her.

Clutching her bath things, Daria waded quickly through the pool and under the waterfall, pleasantly surprised to find that instead of a cold, mountain stream, warm water splashed over her. Closing her eyes, she gave herself over to the total enjoyment of it. Never had she been so aware of or so glad for something as simple as a shower.

Pouring a large dollop of gel onto the ball, she placed the tube on a handy rock outcropping and began working the ball over her wet body. Immediately, the slightly coarse material erupted into cascades of lovely, soft, fragrant lather.

She took a deep breath, letting the light floral scent flow into her, cleansing and refreshing her inside as the bubbles did for her outside.

Out of the corner of her eye, she caught sight of her guard watching her intently as her hands moved leisurely over her body. Turning her back on him, she closed her eyes again and reveled in the sheer joy of warm water and soothing bubbles.

And then she felt him behind her, his body pressed tightly against her back, his arms encircling her. She could feel his shaft rubbing against her ass but he didn't seem particularly aroused.

Gently, he took the ball from her hand and began running it slowly but firmly over her skin. Small ripples of warm excitement flickered up from between her legs and spread through her. Ripples that hadn't been there when she'd been washing herself.

Under her jaw and down both sides of her neck. Across her shoulders and chest, paying special attention to her breasts and nipples, rubbing across them, feeling them become firm, erect and full. Along her arms, to her wrists, palms and fingertips. Lazy circles over the slight roundness of her stomach, filling her belly button like a mini bubble bath. At last, between her legs, moving the rough ball over her soft, wet pussy.

The ripples became a tingle and then a shudder. Their bodies moved together as he bent down, running the ball lightly over her inner and outer thighs and legs. As it played gently in the sensitive area behind her knees, she felt a small hot wave erupt and course through her. A delicious sensation that, like many others she'd experienced since she'd come to this place, rushed at her totally alien, totally unexpected.

When he'd finished his journey to her toes, he straightened up again and resumed his position behind her. Nudging with his body, they moved together back under the full force of the falling water, feeling it wrap around them like a liquid cloak, at once warm and soothing and sparkling and invigorating.

Closing her eyes against the rushing water, Daria felt oddly safe and secure in this man's embrace. Again, he nudged her out of the main stream and she felt something ooze onto her scalp at the very top of her head. Seconds later, the man's fingers entwined in her hair, gently massaging her scalp as he began washing her hair. Her hair being short, the man's fingers grabbed large chunks of it, scrubbing his fingertips briskly on the sensitive skin of her scalp.

The heavenly ministrations spread relaxing calm from his fingertips to her toes. No one had washed her hair since the nuns had done it as a child and that had never been as...as sensual as this. Even when she had her hair cut, she washed it at home before she went to the salon. After all, she reasoned logically, why pay for something she could do just as well for herself.

Slowly, he worked his hands around and down her head until she felt the balls of his thumbs come together at the base of her skull. Skillfully, he applied just the right amount of pressure in tiny circles.

Daria thought she would melt in his arms, literally. Her knees got weak, only his body supporting her kept her upright.

Waves of soothing pleasure rushed through her and collided with the heat and excitement radiating from between her legs. The combination was almost more than she could stand.

He pulled her gently back under the water and she felt the lather running down her face and neck. They stood together under the flowing water long after all the soap had disappeared. Once again he embraced her tightly, their wet bodies moving together in a tender, slow motion.

With her eyes closed, her awareness of him heightened even more. The feel of his hard cock pressed against her ass. The ragged sound of his quickened breathing. The feel of his heart thudding in her back.

A hand slid across her breasts, pinning her to him as the other hand slid between her legs. A second more and he began to massage her clit as he'd done her scalp...softly, slowly, expertly.

Daria gasped and trembled at the sheer delight of his touch. When his finger slid effortlessly back and inside, again the sensation overwhelmed her and she felt that without him, she would simply melt into the pool.

As she began to build toward climax, she felt him withdraw and release her. Regretfully, she opened her eyes and sighed softly to herself.

Submission.

Here, she had no control over anything, not even her own body.

Stepping out of the pool, the guard held out a huge towel, a blanket almost. Daria reached out to grab it, but the guard pulled it back and motioned for her to turn around. When she'd done so, he threw it over her loosely and began to pat her dry. The thick, pale blue material felt soft as velvet but incredibly thirsty, soaking up the water like a sponge.

Very thoroughly, but very gently, he took his time drying under her arms and between her thighs, bending down to catch the last trace of wetness.

Gently, carefully, he pulled the lips of her pussy apart, pulling a small piece of the towel across her. Daria shivered.

Emboldened, he let go of the towel and grabbing her firmly by the ass, raised himself just enough to lick her like an ice cream cone — short, quick strokes of his tongue that made her tremble and moan with pleasure. The ice cream strokes gave way to long, flat sweeps, sucking on her as his tongue moved back and forth like a well-trained snake.

Daria gripped the towel, clenching the soft material in both hands as she squirmed with the building excitement. But her guard held on tightly, digging his fingers into her cheeks as she wiggled.

More gasps, sighs and moans escaped her as she dropped into yet another unexpected, unthought-of experience in this place that seemed part pleasure palace, part torture chamber.

Shuddering with the first tremors of release, Daria clutched the towel, eyes closed in the joy and physical wonder of him, knowing that all that kept her from floating free was this incredible man anchoring her to the ground.

In a moment of amazement, she thought this must be how being struck by lightning felt. One monumental burst of pure, unadulterated physical sensation jolted through her, igniting a firestorm in every nerve, every muscle, every cell of her being. For a moment, everything stopped, the blue-white fire inside, outside and all around her.

After all the sensations she'd experienced, she wouldn't have believed she had the capability for such intensity, such depth of feeling. Yet in that moment, she seemed to become a spark of some cosmic fire, part of something bigger than herself. Something she hadn't even realized existed.

Little by little, the fire faded and Daria felt her body again. Sagging, she literally fell into his arms as he cradled her and lowered her tenderly to the floor.

Completely at peace, sated in spirit as well as body, she watched him through dreamy, half-closed eyes.

Propped on one elbow beside her, he wore a contented smile, taking in the curves of her body where the towel had fallen away. Lightly as the silken scarf before, he moved his fingertips over her skin, feeling the goosebumps rise where he touched.

Perhaps she dozed. She was never quite sure. When she opened her eyes again and yawned, her guard stood over her, manacles and blindfold in hand. She didn't struggle as he put them on her again.

After a short walk, they stopped and Daria felt something soft but firm against her shins. A moment later, the manacles fell away and with a gentle shove in the back from her guard, she fell forward, instinctively putting out her hands to break her fall.

She landed with a "*whoosh*" on what felt like a mattress…a harder inner surface covered by a thick, velvety material. Like the first bed and yet different.

"You are rested and well, submissive?" The voice boomed from the walls again and though slightly startled, she didn't move except to raise her head a little.

"Yes, sir," she replied meekly, "and thank you very much for the shower. I deeply appreciated the unexpected and thoughtful gift."

"It was necessary," the voice replied clinically. "You are prepared to continue?"

"Yes, sir."

A moment's pause and she felt the mattress give a bit under weight of another body. Spreading her legs apart, the guard settled himself between them. Expectant yet not fearful, Daria closed her eyes.

First, she felt his breath on her skin, just at the dip of her spine where it began the rise to her ass. Its warmth made her tingle. Next came his lips, barely brushing her flesh, not stopping to actually plant themselves but just enough for her to mark his passing. The tingle intensified. And then she felt the tip of his tongue, moving slowly, delicately, sideways between the dimples just at the top of her ass and then leisurely down the crack between her cheeks.

The sensation flowed like fine electric current, turning the tingle to a vibration that coursed through her, causing her to tremble and his tongue to zigzag but not lose contact. As he traveled downward, his hands pressed on her ass, exposing more of her to him.

Reaching his goal at last, his pace quickened, becoming small, tight circles around her anus, sucking just a little as he moved.

Daria gasped, her body and mind amazed by the powerful surge of feeling that bolted through her. There seemed to be no end to the surprises here.

Overwhelmed by the playful stimulation, Daria couldn't control her body as it wriggled under his attentions. But he simply clutched her tighter and kept going.

As he worked, his hands slid from her ass, under her undulating hips and gently raised her to her knees. Daria, only dimly aware of anything but the feel of him, obediently complied. His tongue left her for a few moments but the sensation remained.

She felt something warm and thick on her tailbone, oozing down between her cheeks, covering her anus and seeming to heat up even more as it flowed across her skin.

His lips returned to her cheeks, small soft kisses scattered like rose petals. A pressure on her asshole, so slight she almost lost it in the wealth of pleasures. A moment longer and the pressure increased. She became aware that something small, smooth and slippery had penetrated her.

Immediately, she froze, her whole being suddenly focused on her ass. Whatever had penetrated her stopped too, although she could still feel it inside her.

"Yellow!" she screamed, panic-stricken, trying to look over her shoulder but seeing only the masked bulk of her guard hovering over her.

"What is it now, submissive?" The voice had that mildly annoyed sound it always seemed to have when she objected to something.

"What...what's going on?" she demanded. "What's happening?"

"You are being introduced to new sensations," the voice replied calmly. "New experiences. You are learning to open your body as well as your mind. Is that not the reason you came to The Academy to begin with?"

"Yes," she stammered, "but not this. I don't want this. It's...it's..."

"It's what, submissive?" the voice responded. "Unfamiliar? Unknown?"

"Yes," Daria whimpered, almost in tears. "And it hurts."

"A few moments ago you writhed and sighed with pleasure."

"Yes, but..."

"You have done this before?"

"No, of course not," she told the voice, frightened now as well as angry and a little defensive.

"Then how can you know what something is or is not, unless you, yourself, have experienced it?"

"But I've heard...read..."

"Those are of no value," the voice retorted sharply, annoyance creeping now toward anger. "They are not knowing.

And if there is pain, it can be combined with the pleasure and overcome."

"I can't," she mumbled, tears beginning to come. "I just can't."

"Then say the safe-word and we are finished," the voice said simply. "It is for you to decide."

Fear and a lifetime of taboo reared up in her mind. "It's dirty! Unnatural! Perverted! Only whores and sluts…"

She felt his tongue on her again, brushing lightly over her crack, one hand gently caressing her left cheek. His touch calmed, reassured her even as his mouth aroused her. "What is your choice? Submission or end?"

Inside her, she felt him (for she knew in her soul it was part of him) unmoving, waiting. The voice had been right…the feeling, though unfamiliar, had not been truly painful. And the touch of him felt soothing and tender. His caress, his kisses so gentle, so caring…

"Submission," she answered uncertainly, throwing a last pleading glance over her shoulder then lowering her head to the pillow and closing her eyes once more.

"You must submit entirely," the voice told her, the annoyance now replaced with the tone of a patient teacher. "Your body has two barriers here. The outer is under your control. You can will it to relax and open. Tell your body now to relax and experience everything."

Daria took a deep breath and slowly exhaled, feeling the tenseness escape with the air.

The small thing inside her moved forward a tiny bit and she felt it wiggle slightly. His finger, she realized suddenly. She concentrated on keeping her breathing even, her muscles relaxed.

"You are doing well, submissive." As the first positive thing the voice had said, it made Daria feel brighter, wanting to try even harder.

Inside, she felt another finger join the first, moving slowly, carefully, further inside her.

"The inner barrier," the voice continued, "is not under your mind's control. It exists beyond you. The body must know, of itself, that it is safe, unharmed. You must let the body drift free now. Experience what it means to be open and receive."

"Lie quietly. Absolutely still. No harm has or will come to you. Feel the pleasure and the pain and know they are the same."

Physical resistance came to her as Daria felt the fingertips meet the inner barrier. Pressure as he felt for the entrance. Trying desperately to remain calm, Daria could still feel the anxiety, the fear as the inner barrier tightened in a reflex of self-protection. Outside, the hands and lips and tongue continued to reassure her silently that all was well. That nothing would be allowed to happen to her.

The fingertips stopped and nothing but the unfamiliar feeling of him inside her remained. Several moments went by as he soothed and massaged and aroused her. His touch told her, without words, all she needed to know.

Suddenly, she felt the pressure inside her again...one swift forward movement. A sting of pain that made her jump and yelp but which ended almost before she realized it and again the pleasure of his kisses and caresses wrapped itself around her. Once through the inner barrier, his fingers stopped, allowing the ring of muscles to tighten around them again.

They stopped, motionless, as his kisses continued lightly, his hand moving gently, tenderly, over her skin. In its own silent, eloquent language, his body seemed to be communicating caring, patience and reassurance to hers. Despite her fear and discomfort, his touch reached out to her, calming not only her flesh but her spirit as well.

Several long moments went by as her terrified body struggled desperately to figure out what to do with this motionless intruder. Clutching him in a stranglehold, its first reaction had been to try and expel the strange object. But as his fingers remained motionless, making no harmful gesture, her body seemed to sense the non-threatening nature of the visitors and millimeter by millimeter began to loosen its grip.

When the inner barrier at last relaxed, she felt his fingers retreating as slowly and carefully as they'd entered. As they glided out, she felt a sensual tingle and physical relief.

Opening her eyes and turning her head slightly, Daria saw her guard slipping a thin, pale yellow glove off his hand, the faint snap of some kind of plastic as he turned it inside out and dropped it over the side of the bed. Reaching down in front of him, he picked up a small, flat, foil condom package.

Fear flickered again and she felt her body tense once more in anticipation. Even as she tried to bring it back under her control, the voices in her mind renewed their horrified tirade. *"Filthy! Disgusting! The ultimate violation!"*

Yet it hadn't been truly awful. Well, not as awful as she'd believed or imagined. The sensations had been unfamiliar, certainly, and uncomfortable, but no more so than when she'd lost her virginity to another careful, patient, experienced lover long ago.

Another patient, experienced lover.

The realization jolted her as the other unexpected sensations had. Her eyes blinked wide open, astonishment streaming over her like the waterfall, energizing and flinging her headlong to a different place.

She felt as if she'd been stumbling around in a pitch-dark room, painfully bumping into things, falling down and groping blindly. Then, suddenly, the light had come on and she saw everything clearly, simply.

Pain and fear had accompanied the joy and ecstasy as she'd surrendered her girlish innocence for entrance into a more adult knowledge; a knowledge she hadn't, in her naiveté, even suspected existed. So too here, in this place of learning, she was being initiated into a deeper knowledge, of which she'd been equally ignorant.

More warm, thick lubricant poured onto her like rich syrup and his tongue began a new journey down between her cheeks, his fingers massaging the soft flesh of her ass. That same reassuring, calming connection instantly re-established itself and the serenity caused her to smile slightly and close her eyes again, sinking into a peaceful blankness. Even the voices faded away and she floated more freely than she could ever remember.

His tongue wandered leisurely, arriving after several delightful moments at her anus again. Licking, sucking and dancing in light circles around it, waves of unknown pleasure thrilling through her.

"Feel it, submissive," the voice coaxed. "There are many nerves there that have never been stimulated. Experience the sensations."

She felt one of his fingers slide forward to her clit and even in her excited state, she could feel his skin against hers. The combination of feelings intensified and Daria began her rise toward release.

Again Daria felt a slight pressure on her anus and she knew that he wanted to enter her. But instead of thrusting forward, he gripped her firmly but gently around her waist and eased her back towards him. Silently, he communicated to her that she now controlled whether or not he would proceed. No longer forcing her to submit, he asked as tenderly and lovingly as he could for her to open herself because she wanted him.

Blowing away her final shred of uncertainty like a wisp of cobweb, Daria eased herself backward a fraction, feeling his hard, full cock against her sensitized, excited anus. As she moved, bit by bit towards him, she concentrated on relaxing, on accepting him. One of his hands slid over her slick ass, the fingers of the other playing a tantalizing game of Tag with her pussy.

The tip of his cock entered her gently, stopping to let her adjust, his tender kisses on her ass and playful attentions to her clit never pausing. Daria continued her timid backward journey, feeling more and more of him as she took him up, his caring and concern for her communicated to her by the very feel of him inside and out.

In super slow motion, they continued their joining. He allowed her to guide their progress, wordlessly coaxing and supporting her but never asking for more than she could give.

By the time they reached the inner barrier, Daria's body had been inundated by all the sensations, tactile and emotional, pleasant and not so pleasant. She was literally flying on the pleasure and the pain. Her body, caught up in the whirlpool, accepted his advance with a momentary spasm.

He felt her flinch and instantly stopped, hardly breathing until he knew she'd opened the way for him once more.

Daria rested another long moment as she gathered herself and then, having cleared the last obstacle, she gave herself over to the funhouse experience spinning crazily around her.

Her guard combined his cock, tongue, fingers and hands, creating for her a symphony of sensuality. Even the feel of his stomach rubbing lightly against her ass as he moved smoothly to and fro in her was like nothing she'd ever felt before. Her whole body seemed more sensitive, more receptive, more alive than ever before.

A hot wind seemed to be blowing over her as she careened out of control through this sexual thrill ride. Blood pounded in her ears; her heart thudded, body trembled, her breath came in short, ragged gasps, like a marathon runner at the limit of endurance.

Somewhere, a sliver of her mind became vaguely aware that his movements had quickened and that the grinding pressure of him had become harder. But Daria no longer cared. The pleasure and the pain had melded and only one thing mattered to her now.

"Oh," she moaned, feeling the first waves of climax overtake her. "Dear God...oh, oh..." she mumbled as the words dissolved into shrieks and cries of joy as she catapulted into a fiery nebula of ecstasy.

Coming down, Daria became aware of her guard sagging against her, his cheek laid softly on her back, his hands resting on her ass. She'd been so engrossed in her own body, she hadn't even realized that he, too, had climaxed.

They parted as tenderly as they'd joined, Daria slowly, regretfully, inching forward, her guard motionless until she freed him and collapsed wearily back to the bed, her eyes falling closed again, heavy with sated exhaustion.

More languid moments passed as she dawdled in the twilight between peaceful dozing and blissful sleep. She felt the bed move as her guard shifted his position. She felt something warm, soft and damp, traveling over her ass and down between her cheeks. As it moved, she felt his breath raise goosebumps on her skin. It took a moment more for her to understand that her guard was gently washing off the lubricant. This last thoughtful gesture completed the experience. She sighed contentedly and surrendered both to this small pleasure and sleep.

Chapter Five

Even before she opened her eyes, the aroma came to her. A delicate scent, floral perhaps, swaddling her in its delicious embrace. And the feel of something silky against her cheek.

Reluctantly, Daria let go of the last remaining shreds of sleep and opened her eyes. Curious but not really surprised after everything that had happened to her, Daria found herself in a different bed than she'd fallen asleep in.

Sitting up and looking around, she saw a large, luxuriously furnished bedroom, much like the one she occupied in the palace. She lay in a huge bed between pale lilac sheets, dressed in a matching nightgown. A soft light that seemed to come from the ceiling, bathed the room in a pale glow.

As she yawned, the light grew brighter and the right wall near her bed suddenly parted, revealing a small being.

"Mistress Daria," it chirped in a tiny, childlike voice as it approached her, "you are sufficiently rested?"

He reminded her of one of those sorcerers from her childhood picture books...no more than four and half feet tall, a shiny, pale, perfect marble-round head, round black eyes, button nose, toothy grin, dressed in a flowing, dark green floor-length caftan with full sleeves he held in front of him. As he glided toward her, he almost seemed to shimmer.

"Yes, thank you."

The pleased grin expanded. "Excellent, excellent." He dipped his little cue ball head in her direction. "I am Tovah," he told her. "The Headmaster has given me the most pleasant task of attending you. Whatever you desire, you have only to make known."

"Headmaster?" she repeated still confused.

"Yes, Mistress."

"Then...then I'm still in The Academy?"

"Of course, Mistress," Tovah replied, trying to hide his surprise at her question. "Having finished your submission lessons, it is now time to begin your domination lessons."

"Oh," she replied, still somewhat dazed.

"Well then," the little man continued brightly, "are you ready to refresh yourself by bathing?"

"Yes, that sounds very nice."

"Excellent. Excellent," he beamed, removing a bony little hand from the huge sleeves and touching his skinny child-sized fingers lightly on her arm. "If you'll come with me, I'll show you the bathing pool."

They moved across the room, the wall sliding open just as they reached it and Daria gasped at the splendor beyond.

To call it a mere 'bathroom' would have been like calling the Grand Canyon a little ditch. Huge like the bedroom, it seemed both bright and at the same time warm and restful. The walls were covered with paintings of placid emerald lakes, green sky, and forests filled with strange looking trees in hues of orange and gold and brown. Even stranger animals contentedly grazing in fields of yellow grass, keeping a wary eye on their young as larger, more ferocious-looking creatures lurked in the background.

A pool dominated the room, a square perhaps twenty by twenty feet, filled with sparkling water. Smooth, black stone benches and chaise lounges, padded with a thick, velvety crimson fabric ringed the pool, and matching smooth black steps led down into the water.

"It's beautiful," she breathed, swiveling her head in awe. "Just beautiful."

"Indeed it is," Tovah agreed, a wistful note creeping into his voice as his eyes traveled along the walls. "It's called *Gettaluan*. What you would call in your language, 'Paradise.' In the Time Before, almost all of Utan appeared as these blissful pictures portray. Of course, here, in these pictures, the artist has brought together all of the trees and animals in one place which actually spread over the whole planet, but this is truly how our home looked."

Looking around the room and at the little man at her side, Daria felt an unexpected pang. For her, Paradise existed only in the Sunday school of her childhood, lost long ago…relegated to a forgotten antiquity along with Hercules and Hera.

But for the Utanians, Paradise remained with them always, far over their heads and coated almost entirely with a sheet of ice two miles thick, but as real and present as the holograms in every home and the paintings on these walls.

"I'm very sorry," she murmured. "It's a great loss and the Utanian people are both wise and strong to have overcome it."

"Your kind words are deeply felt, Mistress Daria. But alas, all that really sustains us is the knowledge that one day this icy evil will end and we will return to our true home on the surface."

Silently, his eyes swept around the room one last time. Straightening his shoulders, he turned back to her, the smile again firmly in place. "I trust you will find all that you require. I have personally selected and laid out an assortment of bath supplies. Also, a tray of small edibles and drink. I hope everything is to your satisfaction, but if not, you have only to make your wishes known."

"I'm sure everything is wonderful," she told him. "But there is one thing."

Concern clouded the little face. "Anything, Mistress."

"Could you tell me what time it is? For that matter, what day is it? I've lost track of time and don't even know how long I've been here."

"In The Academy," he replied solemnly, "time has no meaning. We are apart from the outside world. Here, only learning and knowledge exist."

"But how will I know how long I've been here?" she persisted, caught between anger and anxiety. "Or how long I'll have to stay? I have people..." The words died in her throat, killed by Trout Erdman's image, his words.

"You have been here as long as it has taken for you to complete your submission lessons," he told her in a patient squeak. "You will remain until you complete your domination lessons." He paused a heartbeat and studied her eyes. "Unless, of course, you choose to leave. That is your decision entirely and you are free to go at any time. As for the people who may be concerned about your absence, it has already been explained that you are away in the outer areas on a fact-finding trip. It is...almost the truth."

It was no use, she knew. With a sigh, she smiled weakly. "All right then," she conceded, "I won't worry about it."

The smile returned to the little face, brighter than ever. "A very wise decision, Mistress. Now I will leave you to your bath. Should you require anything further, you have only to call out." He turned to leave.

"Excuse me. I need to use the..."

"Ah, yes," he grinned. "Through there." He pointed to an archway to their left. "Forgive me for not pointing it out sooner. I hope the delay has not caused you undue inconvenience."

"No, thank you."

"When you have finished with your bath, please call."

"I will. And thank you again."

When she finished, Daria stripped off her nightgown, draped it over a bench and padded carefully down the steps into the pool, bathwater warm and about five feet deep at its deepest point. Lazily, she swam a couple of complete circuits before returning to the steps. To one side stood six small bottles, a rainbow of colors, each exuding its own fragrance, situated nearby so she reach them while reclining comfortably. Beside the bottles sat several items; a fat, pale yellow bath ball, a long handled soft-bristled brush, and a beautiful gold tray holding fruit, bread, cheese and a bottle of Utanian water.

Picking up a handful of small, red berry-like fruit, she leaned back, popped them into her mouth and closed her eyes.

She remembered one of her favorite childhood movies of ancient Rome or Egypt where the queen bathes in unimaginable splendor, surrounded by attentive slaves and pampered with every luxury.

Whatever else, she had to admit to herself, domination certainly had better bathroom facilities than submission.

And the fact that time here had no meaning had definite advantages. For one thing, one could indulge in the unhurried pleasure of a long, relaxing bath.

By the time she'd finished the fruit, Daria's skin had begun to prune, and reluctantly she went back up the steps. A beautiful peach-colored bath sheet, like the one her guard had swaddled her in after their sensual shower under the waterfall, lay neatly folded just beyond the pool's rim.

Dry, she wrapped it around herself and tucked in the top, making a sarong that reached the floor.

"Tovah," she called timidly. "Tovah."

Again, the wall separated and the little man appeared, tottering toward her on his impossibly tiny feet.

"You are refreshed, Mistress Daria?" he asked, bowing his little head toward her.

"Yes, thank you. I feel much better."

"Do you require more food or drink?"

"No, thank you. I'm fine. I, uh, could use something to wear though."

"Of course."

He pulled his hands from the voluminous sleeves, producing a small black box about the size of an old-fashioned PDA. It had a keypad of about ten keys on its face, covered with white symbols she didn't recognize.

For a few moments, he studied her critically, scanning her from head to toe and muttering to himself.

"You will turn around please?" he asked, making a circle in the air with a downward pointed finger.

Obediently, Daria did a slow circle, coming back to face Tovah, confused but knowing there was no point in asking questions. She would get her answers when he wanted her to know.

"Ah, yes," he muttered, again, more to himself than Daria. "Excellent, excellent."

Quickly, he tapped the keypad, his little fingers flying so fast her eyes couldn't keep up. With a little flourish, he pointed the black box at the bench beside them and punched a large button with his thumb.

A beam of bright light sprayed on the bench and Daria heard a sort of low-pitched whirring sound. An instant later, a pile of midnight-colored clothing appeared. Aiming the box at the floor under the bench and firing again, produced a pair of short black boots.

"For your approval, Mistress Daria," he announced, a slight note of pride in his voice. "These are your domination clothes."

Daria leaned down and ran wary fingertips over the material. It felt like some kind of leather, but softer than any suede she'd ever known and creamy smooth as butter. Picking it up, she held it out, amazed to see a one-piece jumpsuit, with long sleeves and a high neckline.

"It's beautiful," she said, bringing the garment to her body.

"If you will try it on, I think you will find the fit to your satisfaction." The little face looked up at her like an eager, expectant child. Obviously, he expected her to drop her towel and change in front of him.

"Excuse me," she ventured cautiously, "but what about...undergarments?"

"Undergarments?" he repeated slowly, the look on his face telling her he didn't have a clue what she meant.

"Yes," she tried to explain. "A bra." She made a quick swipe of her hand across her breasts. "And panties." Another nervous motion toward her crotch. "Human women wear them for support and comfort under their clothes."

Still no flicker of comprehension.

"I think," he answered finally, "that you will find the garment most comfortable. If not, I can make whatever alterations you deem necessary."

With a sigh, she realized there was no use in pursuing the matter.

"How do I put this on?" she asked, resignation edging her voice.

"There is a slide in the back which opens and closes. You will find that the garment is designed to be worn snugly."

Wriggling into the jumpsuit, Daria quickly discovered that 'snugly' in Utanian must be measured differently than on Earth. As she stepped into it and began pulling it up, the material seemed to meld itself to her skin. Almost like slipping into the animal itself.

"If you will allow me?" Tovah said, stepping up on the bench and pulling the slide closed. Stepping down again, he eyed her, the look on his face indicating his satisfaction.

"The garment looks well on you, Mistress Daria," he told her. "I hope the fit is to your liking."

Amazingly, even though the material hugged her like paint, it wasn't the slightest bit tight or constricting. In fact, it felt very comfortable, as if it had been tailored for her especially. She could even wiggle her toes in the boots.

"Yes, thank you. It's wonderful. So soft and comfortable. Is it leather? Animal skin, I mean?"

"Yes, Mistress."

"I thought you didn't have any animals down here?"

"Unfortunately, you are correct, Mistress. You are wearing the skin of a Balmeer, replicated exactly from the original, down to the very cells."

He pointed to one of the wall paintings. A herd of some kind of animal grazed peacefully except for one standing on a rock, watching…listening intently. In the corner, a huge, wolf-like creature crouched in some bushes, seeming to be biding his time for an attack.

"In the Time Before," Tovah continued quietly, "the Balmeer was the most ferocious, feared animal on Utan. They ranged over the whole planet in small blood groups, led always by the fiercest female. They did not kill for food or in self-defense as other, ordinary predators. Balmeers killed without conscience, without mercy. The clans believed that sometimes they killed merely for the sport of it. Balmeers would attack and cripple a mother animal and then leave her to watch helplessly as they ripped apart and devoured her young."

"That's awful," Daria replied with a shiver. "How could something so terrible have such a beautiful skin?"

The little man smiled knowingly. "Sadly, Mistress Daria, in this universe you will find that very often the foulest, most bloodthirsty beasts prowl among us in the most beautiful, most inviting skins."

A picture of Trout flashed suddenly in her mind, smiling sweetly, lovingly at her.

"Yes," she agreed quietly, "I know what you mean."

"Those in the Time Before believed that by putting on an animal's skin, you took on a portion of the animal's soul. In effect, became one with the animal."

"Why then would you pick such a horrible animal? I mean, there must have been other animals with skins you could have used."

"Perhaps, Mistress Daria, but as I said, females dominated the Balmeer. It has always been believed fitting that females learning domination might take something from the most dominant females in our history."

"I see," she told him, suddenly keenly aware of the skin covering her own. Feeling it against her, joined almost. But Daria had another, more practical thought. "Excuse me, but…but what should I do if I…if I should need to…you know…refresh myself Especially in…in an emergency?"

"Ah, yes," he smiled broadly, "that could be a problem. However, if you look closely, you will see there are slides in several strategic places in the garment. These provide…ready access to any part of your body you may deem necessary without having to remove the garment itself."

Daria ran her fingers over the smooth, soft material and discovered thin lines at her bosom and crotch. She had no difficulty imagining others elsewhere on the garment.

"Now," he continued cheerfully, "you must have a *gorlach*. I may see your hand, please." He held out his little hand to her.

"A *gorlach*?" she repeated, putting her hand in his.

"Yes, Mistress. The symbol of your authority, your dominance." He took her hand, turning it over and examining it carefully. "Excellent, excellent," he muttered. "You have a most beautiful hand. Small and delicate yet strong and capable. Very much the hand of a dominant female. You will do very well."

Carefully he let go of her and retrieved the black box from his sleeve. Still muttering, he aimed it away from them and punched the buttons. Immediately, a small table appeared about six feet away. Horrified, Daria saw it was covered with whips of all sizes and descriptions.

"For your consideration and approval, Mistress."

"I…I don't want a whip," she answered, almost too upset to speak. "That's…that's barbaric."

The little man looked up like she'd slapped him.

"I do not understand," he told her sincerely. "The *gorlach* is part of your outfit…as your boots or garment. You must look and feel a dominant female."

"I would never *consider* using a whip on anyone. On anything."

"It is not necessary that you use the *gorlach*," he assured her, "only that you carry it. You may use it if you wish, but mostly it is for you to more fully assimilate to your role." Those big, dark, pleading eyes melted her.

"All right," she conceded, "I'll carry it, but that's all."

"Yes," he breathed a sigh of relief, "that is all that is required. Please, if you will come, we can select your *gorlach*." He gestured for her to precede him.

"Now," he announced, turning a critical eye to the tabletop, "we must have something that suits both your taste and your hand. Do you have any preference?" He gazed at her earnestly.

"No," she mumbled, "just pick something."

"Ah, then," he replied turning back to the table, "I would suggest the *Otkan*." He picked up one of the whips and held it out to her.

She saw a slender black leather wand, perhaps ten inches long and an inch around with a small knot at the end, like a baseball bat, tapering out to a bouquet of perhaps ten thin black lashes about six inches long. Feeling slightly queasy, Daria reached out and wrapped her hand around the shaft.

Tovah surveyed her, his eyes narrowed in sharp concentration, his little fingers adjusting her grip. "The *gorlach* must fit your hand as naturally as your fingers," he commented. "The grip must not be too big or too small and the lashes must not be too long or too short." He glanced up at her. "It meets with your approval, Mistress?"

"Yes, I guess so," Daria replied, feeling as though she'd picked up a snake and couldn't find anywhere to drop it gracefully.

"I have been fitting females for their domination training for a great while. I've developed a good eye but nothing can replace the actual feel. You must be honest with me. If this is unsatisfactory for any reason, I have many more."

"No," she said quickly, "this is fine. Really."

"Very well. Now we will test it to make sure it handles smoothly."

"I don't want to test it," Daria almost screamed. "I mean, you said I just had to carry it as a symbol."

"Quite right," he answered, a little taken aback by her reaction. "But should you decide to display it, it must respond to you as a part of your own body. Let me show you."

A few more quick taps on the keyboard and he aimed it away from them again. In an instant, a metal frame, some six feet square appeared, a fat pillow, at least two feet square hung suspended in the center. As they walked to it, Daria noticed the pale beige pillow had a slight nap.

"You will stand just there," Tovah instructed, moving her to within an arm's length of the pillow and slightly to the side. "The secret to wielding the *gorlach* properly is in the wrist." Taking her hand in both of his tiny ones, he flipped her wrist loosely twice. "Always keep it flexible. Now, bring your hand to your waist and back slightly. Yes, that's right. Now, bring it forward quickly, snapping your wrist in front of you and keeping the lashes together until they connect with your intended target."

Daria hesitated but Tovah urged her on. "Try it, Mistress. Do not worry about getting the technique correct on your first attempt. We are merely trying to determine if the *gorlach* is suitable for your hand. Please." He waved in the direction of the pillow.

Reluctantly, Daria did as the little man had instructed her. She heard a hard 'smacking' sound as the leather connected with the pillow, sending it twisting slightly on its long, thin ties.

"Ah," Tovah chirped approvingly, "for a first time, a most satisfactory strike."

Craning forward slightly, Daria could plainly see the track of the lashes where they'd landed in the nap of the soft pillow. With a couple of stragglers on either side, most of the tracks ran together just right of center.

"If I might suggest," he told her, gently taking her hand and readjusting her grip a bit, "you might move just a fraction to your left and bring your hand up so much." He raised it about two inches. "Now, if you would care to try once more."

Again, Daria reached out, striking the pillow almost dead center, the small stripes almost showing as one. Looking at the closely laid marks, she felt a sudden and completely unexpected surge of something she could only describe as pride. Shocked at her reaction, she immediately tried to force it down. After all, a civilized person couldn't enjoy something this primitive, this barbaric. She must face it as just another trial to be borne.

"Oh, excellent, excellent, Mistress Daria," Tovah gushed. "You have done this before?"

"Certainly not," she countered, trying to feel righteous indignation at the suggestion but missing by a beat.

"Then you are most certainly a natural talent. Please, continue until you feel perfectly comfortable with the implement."

"No, really…"

"Nonsense. You must wield the *gorlach* as an extension of your hand." He stood back and waited.

Uneasily, Daria tightened the fingers of her right hand around the hard leather shaft and pulled the thin leather tails through the fingers of her left hand. Something about the feel of this whip in her hands both frightened and excited her.

Bringing it back, Daria hesitated another moment and then started let it go, feeling the roughness on tender palm as she pulled her hand away. Stopping only long enough to gather the tails between the fingers of her left hand, she struck the pillow again and again, each blow delivered with a fraction more power, more accuracy, landing with a sharp *thwack* and leaving their marks just where she'd intended.

Beneath the Balmeer skin, she felt a hot, excited rush envelop her. More than the physical exertion, it welled up from deep inside her, igniting both her body and her mind with something...the thought both intrigued and repulsed her...something almost sensual.

Tovah grinned like a delighted four-year old. "Excellent, excellent," he crowed again, running his tiny fingers over the whip's tracks. "I knew you would do well, Mistress Daria. When you have honed your natural talent, you will most certainly be a formidable dominatrix."

Daria realized he'd paid her a great compliment, but combined with her unexpected and totally inappropriate reaction to the flogging, even of the pillow, it revolted her.

"Thank you," she choked out. "But I have absolutely no interest in this, whatsoever. I'm merely fulfilling my commitment to The Sildor."

"Perhaps," he replied cryptically. "Perhaps not."

She opened her mouth to ask what he meant, but before she could, he waved his hand and continued. "At any rate, I believe you are almost ready to begin."

From his sleeve, he produced another small, black box, which he held up for her to see. It had only a small blank screen, a triangular green button and a square white one.

"You will, under no circumstances," he told her earnestly, "address your submissive directly. The only time he will speak is to utter his safe-word, *kaytack,* or 'red' in your language. You will convey your wishes to your instructor who will convey them to your submissive. Your instructor will also see to it that you have the appropriate setting and equipment for whatever scene you wish to play out."

"What do you mean, 'scene'?"

He shrugged his thin little shoulders. "Whatever you desire, Mistress Daria. Here, whatever your fantasy, it can become reality. The Academy and all within its walls are at your command."

That same hot, excited tingle rippled through her, a mixture of excited anticipation, tinged with a trace of fear.

"Simply press this," he pointed at the triangle, "and various scenes will appear on the screen. When you see something that interests you, press this one." He pointed to the white one. "When you have selected a scene, the instructor will direct the submissive and appropriate items will appear on the screen. You may choose whatever you wish by pressing the button again. If, for any reason you should need to speak to your instructor, touch the bar here." His little finger indicated a slight indentation at the bottom of the box.

After a few moments of staring dumbly, the small man gestured to the box again. "Please, Mistress Daria, try it," he coaxed. "It is very simple. Really."

Cautiously, Daria tapped her thumb on the green button. Instantly, the small screen came alive, what she saw amazing her. Not exactly a video screen or even a hologram, it seemed more like looking through a window.

The first scene showed a man, naked — and well endowed she noted almost in spite of herself — chained spread-eagle to what looked like a dungeon wall. The view focused in more closely on him and in the flickering light of several torches, she could see he had something wrapped around his balls, separating them, and cinched securely around the base of his erect cock, making it stand up almost straight.

Another scene. A woman, much bigger than Daria but dressed almost identically, except for a close-fitting, black half-mask, was standing just behind and to the side of another naked man, this one bent over at the waist, wrists handcuffed to his sides, legs spread wide apart, ankles secured. The *thud* of a large, multi-tailed leather whip landing on bare flesh and an obviously pained, 'uh' the only sounds.

Still another. A naked woman atop a naked man, riding furiously toward climax as he writhed and squirmed beneath her in his own building ecstasy.

"I'm sorry," she snapped, practically pounding the triangular key again to make the screen go blank once more, "but I really can't do this. It's...it's just..."

"I'm sorry, Mistress Daria," Tovah murmured, his face a pathetic mixture of confusion and dismay, "but I do not understand. Please, tell me what the problem is."

"I can't whip someone for no reason. I can't chain them up and torture them. It's not right. It's certainly not me."

"But these are only some of the scenes," he insisted. "You may do whatever you wish. The submissives are never compelled to do anything that they do not wish to. Submission is not the same as slavery."

"How…why, would a man…anyone for that matter, choose to undergo such things? I certainly didn't choose to undergo what I went through as a submissive."

"No, you did not," he agreed quietly, "but you did agree to come here. And once here, you agreed to submit to whatever happened, even though you always had the choice to stop."

"What choice?" she replied bitterly. "If I don't go through with this, The Sildor won't sign the contract and that will hurt both our worlds."

"Ah," he nodded knowingly, "I see. You did not come here to gain knowledge. You came here to gain advantage. You hoped not only to curry favor with The Sildor, but to maneuver her into a position wherein she would feel, if nothing else, obligation to sign your contract." He shook his little head and made a sort of 'tsk, tsk,' noise in the back of his throat. "No wonder your progress has been so slow and your ability to learn so limited."

Words of denial and defense leapt to Daria's mouth but died before they could be uttered, stopped cold by the look in those big black eyes. They held no reproof, no anger. Only bottomless wells of pity for such a hapless creature as he certainly thought she was. So they stood there, gazing at each other for several silent, uneasy moments. Finally, the little man shook his head a fraction and continued.

"Whatever the reason," he told her, "you are here and the lessons must proceed. You will come with me." Turning, he led her through an archway off to their right and down a long hallway.

"How will I ever be able to find my way through this maze of halls?" she asked tentatively.

"When you decide upon a scene, you will be directed where to go," he replied simply.

They stopped in front of what looked like a blank wall to Daria, but Tovah reached out and pressed the smooth surface with his palm. Instantly, the wall melted away and was replaced by a window facing into a small, spare room. Seated on a plain wooden stool was a man that she immediately recognized as her guard. His short leather apron barely covered his cock and he was still wearing his leather mask. Now though, he also had on a black leather collar, stretching between his chin and shoulders. It was so wide, in fact, that she could see he had to tip his head up slightly to accommodate it. From the back of the collar, a chain ran down his back to his wrists, bound with metal handcuffs.

"Do not worry, Mistress Daria," he explained. "The submissive can not see you as yet. To him, this viewing panel remains a solid wall."

Daria stood transfixed, again, not comprehending why this sight both excited and repelled her. And she felt a shiver of warm anticipation flow through her.

"This is your submissive," Tovah told her. "Male submissives always begin in this manner. Not only does it immediately establish the dominance of the female by making the male physically submissive but also prevents even the possibility of disobedience."

"I don't understand."

"From this point until your domination instruction is complete, only you will be able to release him. Not just from his physical captivity, such as the chains he is wearing now, but from The Academy itself. Should you will it or should something happen to you, he would remain here in submission until his death."

"But…but why did you pick him?" She gestured toward the window.

Surprise flashed across Tovah's little face. "Pick him?" he repeated in astonishment. "We did not pick him. That is not the way of The Academy. He made the choice, both to participate in your submission lessons and now, to undergo your domination."

"I don't understand." Daria answered, utterly at a loss.

"Regrettably," he sighed, "I agree. You understand almost nothing, even after your submission training." He stood silent for several moments, looking up at her as if trying to figure out how to explain quantum physics to a four-year old.

"There are many such places as this," he began, "all over Utan. They have existed almost as long as we have existed as a people. They are places where knowledge is obtained and wisdom earned. For us, they are what you would call in your language, sacred. This place, because it trains the best the planet has to offer, is the most important of all of us. Many come, few are accepted. To be selected and go through the training is very special. At least to us. For him," he nodded again toward the window, "this is a great honor and he strives to experience and know all that happens that he may learn as much as he can. He looks on this, not as torture or humiliation, but as an opportunity to step outside himself. To acquire that which can not be known in the mind but which can only be grasped with the soul."

The little man paused, realizing that his words were not sinking in. He knew she had no way of understanding and he pitied her deeply.

"At any rate, the lessons have begun and must now either be completed or ended with your safe-word. Do you wish to continue?"

She looked back at the helpless man before her and examined her options. She'd certainly passed the worst. Having survived the submission, she now had control. Things would go as *she* wanted. There didn't need to be any violence, any brutality. In fact, she could take this opportunity to show them all how much more civilized, more humane she could be, even amidst these barbaric practices. And even though this man had whipped her, tried to drown her, and violated her in a way she didn't even want to think about, she'd show him mercy. And The Sildor would be so impressed, she wouldn't have any other choice but to sign the contract.

"Of course I'll continue," she replied, turning back to Tovah and smiling just a bit. "After all, now I understand the importance of these...these rituals."

Tovah merely shrugged. "As you wish. There is one more thing, though. You will put out your hand, please."

As Daria did what the little man asked, he produced his box again, tapped the keypad and aimed it at her hand. A black object appeared and Daria held it up. It was a black mask, small, that would cover only the upper half of her face.

"You will wear this at all times. And the submissive will wear his. We have found that with the females, it is better that both of you remain anonymous as you seem to have an unfortunate tendency to form attachments, especially to male submissives, if you can see the face, eyes, expression and therefore fail to exercise your dominance fully."

After all she had been through, it seemed silly, but she slipped it on knowing the futility of arguing. The soft leather molded itself to her face and the flexible band settled comfortably around her head.

"Now, what scene would you like to begin with?"

"I really have no idea," she replied slowly. "Perhaps...perhaps you could suggest a sort of beginner's scene. To help me get started."

"Very well," he answered crisply. "Perhaps the best way would be for you to simply go in and make your presence known to the submissive. Feel each other out."

"Yes," she breathed, smiling and relieved. Even though she knew they were being watched, perhaps she could convey to him her non-threatening intentions.

Tovah pressed the wall again and part of it slid open, creating a doorway for them. As they approached the stool, the man's head came up and turned in their direction and Daria realized that the eye slits were closed, blinding him as she'd been. Pity, anger and that unexplained little ripple of excitement, coursed through her again.

"On your knees, submissive," came the same deep voice that had commanded her when their positions had been reversed, "your Mistress has arrived."

Quickly, unsteadily, the man raised his large body and managed to bring it to the hard stone floor, the collar forcing his face to turn up.

Tovah nudged her slightly and jerked his head in the direction of the submissive. "Go on," he mouthed, "go on."

Tentatively, she moved across the room until she stood over him. Uncertainly, she turned back to Tovah.

"Touch him," the small mouth formed insistently. "Run the tails of your whip over his body." He made a slow dragging motion in the air in front of him.

She settled her palm firmly against the knob at the end and wrapped her fingers tightly around the leather shaft. Carefully, she raised the whip until the tails dangled in front of her, slowly moving them across the submissivie's shoulders and chest, twining them around his neck. As she did so, his body trembled, from fear or anticipation, she couldn't be sure, but she felt herself relaxing a bit.

Still moving the whiptails over his body with one hand, Daria suddenly seized a handful of his dark hair in her other gloved hand and yanked his head back fully. She could see only the lower half of his face, his eyes hidden behind the closed slides, but she sensed something pass between them...a knowingness about their roles. As he gave himself over to her completely, that knowledge excited her in ways physical and emotional she wouldn't have guessed at before her time in this place.

For a moment, she looked into that helpless, blank face. Abruptly, she leaned down and pushed her lips to his, crushing them with her ferocity. The force would have knocked him backwards if she hadn't been clutching his hair so firmly. Recovering from his surprise, he steadied himself and opened his mouth to her, allowing her tongue to roam at will as she explored every part.

Satisfied, she freed him, releasing his hair with a small, almost dismissive shove. He tottered but didn't fall.

"Tovah," she began, turning slightly back to where the little man had been standing. Surprised, she found him gone, the door now closed, the wall seamless once more.

Anxiously, she consulted her black box, pressing her thumb into the green key. As before, the screen instantly lit up, various scenes of sex and bondage flickering before her. Something with a bed and lots of pillows appeared and she punched the other button.

The door slid open and the familiar voice boomed out. "Rise, submissive," it ordered simply.

Awkwardly, he began trying to get to his feet. Instinctively, Daria reached out to help him but something froze her in place, almost as if one part of her actually wanted to see him struggle even as the other part felt appalled by it. But the feeling disappeared as he stood up, dwarfing her as he did so.

A bright light flashed on the stool and a short, thick, black leather cord appeared, coiled neatly. At one end, she could plainly see some kind of silver metal ring, and at the other, a small loop, about the size of her fist.

"Turn around, submissive."

As he turned, Daria saw a metal loop on the back of the collar, just above where the metal chain attached. It took only a few seconds for her to realize the cord was really a leash.

She had a fleeting thought that this was too much. That she couldn't possibly treat this poor man like an animal. After all, she wanted to prove to these people... But the thought disappeared, swallowed up by another, darker one. They were just playing a game, she reasoned, a 'scene' Tovah had called it. And the submissive had agreed to participate willingly. And she'd never actually had physical control over another person...especially a large, attractive man who'd very recently had control over her.

A memory of being chained by the ankle in that cold, dark cell came to her. He certainly hadn't had any compunction about exercising his power over her. Hadn't he used his whip on her? Stood by while she practically drowned?

Daria felt a distinct sense of satisfaction as the metal ring of the leash snapped into place on his collar and she adjusted the loop in her hand.

Silently, they crossed the room and out into the hall. A row of red lights now blinked in the floor, leading off to her left. Obviously a trail had been laid down for her to follow to the place where they would play out their scene. Funny, she thought idly as the moved along the dark corridor, but she hadn't noticed any lights when she'd been the submissive.

They walked down the maze of halls, the red trail blazing in the shadowy half-light of the candles in their sconces, high up on the walls.

At last, the lights ended at a wall that slid open as they reached it. Inside it looked much like some of the other rooms she'd been in except for its bright lights and walls and ceiling covered in huge mirrors. It reminded her of pictures she'd seen of twentieth century Earth amusement park attractions called, funhouses. And like the other rooms, a large bed with pillows of all sizes strewn across it took up a major portion.

As they neared the bed, she saw a large key lying on a low table beside the bed. She knew it must be for the handcuffs and collar. Metal manacles on short chains lay open and ready at each corner of the bed. Grabbing the key, Daria quickly released him, untying his apron and dropping it on the floor. Next, she pushed him gently down on to the bed, indicating for him to lie on his back and raise his arms.

After slipping off her gloves and boots, Daria unfastened the slide at her crotch, exposing her entire bottom, from pubic hair to ass and the one across her breasts, spilling them out, pale and pink against the dark leather. Ready, she slowly climbed on to the bed and straddled him. She felt him tremble again as she settled herself on his naked body.

Leisurely, she stretched her body over his as she reached up and secured the metal cuffs, first around his wrists, making sure not to close them too tightly and then his ankles, rubbing herself casually against him. Even through her leather 'skin,' she could feel his cock growing aroused. And she felt her own growing excitement.

Sitting up, she took in every inch of him, arm and leg muscles defined by his spread eagle position, his fully extended shaft rising out of a nest of curly black pubic hair and resting impatiently for her against his flat stomach. He belonged to her, totally and completely. Helpless. Powerless.

She leaned down once more, laying herself out over him again. As she moved up a bit to his lips, she felt her wet pussy glide over his cock and her tender nipples dragged over his chest. The Balmeer skin seemed to tingle with an electricity of its own, heightening the sensations for her.

Daria put her lips on his, brushing them lightly as she moved across his cheek and down to the junction of his neck and shoulder. Because of the tension of the manacles, his shoulder muscles had tightened, making a firm bulge, but his neck, rested on a pillow, relaxed and supported. Slowly, carefully, she began nibbling on the soft, inviting flesh, nipping gently, feeling it against her tongue and lips.

Under her, the submissive wriggled a little and a small moan escaped him. She took a larger piece in her mouth, pulling it over her teeth and pressing down harder. The moan deepened and changed pitch a little. Releasing him, she ran her tongue down the side and into the hollow of his throat. His damp skin had a slightly salty tang to it.

A very nice throat, she thought, raising her head and examining it closely, the depression in the front of his thick, masculine neck, just big enough for a playful tongue. On either side, she could see the big veins, distended slightly, filled with life sustaining blood, framing that beautiful, vulnerable throat.

For a moment, Daria imagined her teeth, sharp and deadly as the fangs of an animal, sunk into that soft, exposed flesh...skin tearing, blood gushing, agonized screams filling her head.

Snapping back, Daria found herself hot and anxious to have this stranger. In fact, her need for release seemed to be more than just a physical ache...almost as if something inside her demanded she have him.

Sliding the eye holes open, she watched as he blinked, turning his head as much as he could to see his surroundings and then back at her. She smiled a little and leaned forward so that her breasts hung just over his mouth like sweet, tantalizing fruit. Obediently, he opened his mouth and the tip of his tongue ran along the bottom swell. The feel of his touch made her shiver and she lowered her nipple, hard and erect as his shaft, into his mouth.

"Oh..." she moaned, closing her eyes and giving herself over to the pleasure. The broad, flat part of his tongue swept over her nipple, alternating with quick little circles around the tip.

Trembling, Daria eased herself away from his mouth, settling herself over his rigid cock. Immediately, she felt his heat filling her.

Through half-closed eyes she watched him struggle like a captured animal, his metal restraints squeaking and scraping as they strained against his writhing body. Soft moans escaped him, each one fanning her own internal fire.

The thought came again; completely helpless...completely hers. Passion. Pain. Ecstasy. Torture. Perhaps even life and death. She had only to make her desires known.

That sense of something forbidden rushed through her again, a hot, pulsing, powerful wave pushing her toward climax.

A shudder rumbled through him, moans becoming excited cries as he peaked, pulling her into their shared fulfillment. Ecstasy, excitement, pleasure ripped through her, so intense the mixture blotted out everything in a sunburst of physical sensation she could feel from head to toes. For an instant, she felt as if she was larger, more than herself. As if she'd melded with some cosmic force.

Sprawled on him, Daria gasped for breath, feeling like an exhausted marathoner and yet strangely exhilarated. Perhaps, she mused idly, like a wild animal, ravenous from days on the hunt, finally bringing down its prey. Eating its fill and then dozing peacefully, sated and victorious. Yes, she thought contentedly, that was exactly how she felt.

"Mistress Daria?" a little voice whispered in her ear.

"Mmmm...?" she sighed.

"It is Tovah," he said softly. "I've come to attend you."

She opened a sleepy eye and focused on the little head inches from her own. "Go away," she hissed. "I need to rest."

"Certainly, Mistress Daria," he agreed, "but not here."

"I'm perfectly comfortable, thank you."

"But you must have proper resting accommodations," he insisted plaintively. "A place to refresh yourself and consider your next scene. The submissive must be seen to also."

Looking down at his limp form, she realized with a start that she hadn't even thought about him.

"Yes, of course. See that he's taken care of."

"As you desire, Mistress. If you will allow me?" He put out a child-sized hand and smiled.

"All right," she conceded reluctantly. "If you insist." Slowly, she raised herself to a sitting position and with Tovah's help, made it to her feet. Turning his head discreetly, he waited while Daria readjusted her garment and closed the slides. Picking up her boots and gloves, she nodded and they left the room. In the hall, she stripped off her mask and shook her head.

"I trust everything was to your satisfaction," he said as they started back through the long, meandering passageways.

"Yes," she giggled, "everything was very…nice."

"Excellent, excellent." He glanced up and smiled a little. "I believe that once you become comfortable in the role, you will find domination very much to your taste."

Inexplicably, the cryptic remark made her feel very uneasy.

"I have no intention of becoming 'comfortable' in the role, as you put it," she responded, trying to sound more confident than she felt.

"Perhaps," the little man answered quietly, but not looking up again, "perhaps not. We cannot see the future and sometimes it's very different than we imagine."

She opened her mouth but they arrived back at her room.

"Yes," she agreed wearily, "but for the present moment, I don't want anything but to get out of these sweaty clothes and into bed for a good nap."

"Most understandable," Tovah nodded. "I shall leave you to your rest. If you have need of me, you have but to call."

Alone, Daria quickly slipped off her jumpsuit, stepping out of the discarded pile and stretching, feeling as though she'd shed an old skin.

Turning to the bed, she caught sight of herself in the huge wall mirror. Something seemed different about the familiar face and body. Something too subtle for her conscious mind to snag, but there nonetheless.

She stepped to the glass, almost touching it. Anxiously, she searched every inch of her face and body, trying to put her finger on it. Her skin, flushed a healthy pink, no doubt from the tight clothes and exertion, and a thin sheen of sweat made her seem shiny, the remnants of her own wet climax still lingered between her thighs. But try as she might, nothing remained except a sort of shadow and a vague sense of unease.

Curling up in her big bed, Daria tried to convince herself it was this place and nothing more. Here, she'd fallen down the rabbit hole or wandered behind the looking glass. Everything got turned around and inside out. And everything would be restored to normal as soon as she finished up this ridiculous exercise and got out of here.

"Normal," she muttered like a sleepy child, "normal."

* * * * *

Daria awoke feeling rested in body, but not in spirit. There seemed to be an anxiety…no, anticipation…hanging around her mind like a wisp of fog.

Her soiled, sweaty jumpsuit had disappeared, replaced by a fresh one, laid out at the foot of her bed. Across the room, a table had been set with bread, fruit, cheese and a pitcher and goblet. Beside them lay the little black control box and her *gorlach*, the tails hanging down like limp black streamers.

For a moment, she felt the weight of it in her hand, her fingers wrapped securely around the hilt, her wrist poised. In her mind, she heard the sharp *smack* of thin leather striking naked skin and the answering rush of excitement in her body.

Almost in spite of herself, Daria got out of bed and padded to the whip. She felt as if she were standing outside herself, off to the side, watching.

Picking it up, it seemed to settle into her hand naturally, filling it with a welcome hardness, the roughness rubbing on her sensitive palm. A sensuous tremor fluttered through her.

Holding it tightly, she sat down, the soft chair material cradling her butt and back as she picked up a piece of bread and began to nibble distractedly, never taking her eyes or mind off the whip.

"Whatever you desire." Tovah's words echoed in her brain. "You have only to utter the words to make them a reality."

Her thoughts turned to the submissive.

Tovah had said that her submissive had come there for her pleasure, whatever that might be.

She heard the crack of the whip again in her mind, louder, sharper, more forceful this time. And the room grew warmer.

He wasn't a slave. He'd gone there of his own free will. To gain wisdom, she thought derisively. He had agreed to whatever happened, and he had his safe-word.

Grunts of pain added their voice to the mixture and she could almost feel the impact of the whip traveling from her hand and arm through her body.

After all, a little voice cajoled, he'd struck her. Hard. Stood by and watched her almost drown. Chained her and left her naked and alone in a dungeon. Wasn't she entitled to retribution? To justice?

Yes, she thought, a cold smile curving the corners of her mouth, *justice.*

If she'd learned nothing else in this demented sexual Wonderland, she knew the rules were dictated by the powerful. Now she was dominant…had power…she intended to use it. Of course, she wouldn't sink to their level of barbarism and cruelty, but she'd show them she wouldn't be bullied.

Keeping one hand on her *gorlach*, she pulled the little black box to her. Casually, she pressed the button and watched as various sexual scenes filled the screen. Funny. When Tovah had first showed it to her, the scenes had made her uneasy in their explicit variety. Now, they seemed interesting…intriguing even.

A particular scene struck her fancy and she played it over twice, relishing the details and imagining herself in the other woman's place. Finally, she pushed the button to mark her choice. Sliding it back across the table, she leaned back contentedly and began attacking the food in earnest.

* * * * *

He stood in the middle of the room like a statue in a mirrored box, his hands manacled behind him, the eye slits in his mask closed.

Silently, she crossed the thick carpet, taking in all sides of his naked body reflected in the completely mirrored walls. At her approach, she saw his body stiffen slightly, as if he knew somehow she'd arrived.

Making a slow circle, she studied him carefully, running the tails of her whip through her fingers. The thought of them across his flat, inviting ass made her shiver with anticipation. But she wanted to move slowly, relish every moment.

Standing in front of him again, Daria slowly undid the slides covering her breasts and pussy. She'd come to enjoy the feel of the tight leather and had no desire to be naked.

Leaning toward him, she brushed her nipples lightly across his chest, feeling them harden as they passed over his warm flesh. Immediately, his body moved to meet hers. He bent his head down and forward, searching for her lips. Obligingly, she tipped up on her toes a little and allowed his mouth to find hers.

His growing arousal pressed itself against her and she smiled that her light touch, a kiss, could have such an effect on him.

As they kissed, she brought her whole body against his, pushing her wet pussy against his erect cock. He rewarded her with a groan and the feel of his body quivering.

Pulling her lips away, she moved around him, never allowing their bodies to part. At his back, she grabbed him around the waist, pressing herself tightly against him, feeling him helpless and hot. As she moved her rock hard nipples over him, tingles of sensual pleasure raced in her blood. And if she moved just so, she could feel his hands and manacles across her pussy. The combination of hard metal and soft skin increased the passion she felt increasing within her.

Reaching up, she put her hands on his shoulders and pushed down. Obediently, he got to his knees as Daria finished her lazy circle and returned to his front. His cock seemed to be pulsing with a life of its own, straining and searching for her.

Keeping her hands tight on his shoulders, she spread her legs on either side of him and pressed herself against him, her wet, anxious pussy bringing itself to his lips.

Even with his eyes covered, his mouth found its target and began to devour her hungrily, his tongue moving across her clitoris, alternating its hungry dance with nibbling and suckling at her pink, swollen flesh.

Fire flooded through her, raging in her blood and dizzying her like a small car suddenly hitting air turbulence and making its first sudden drop. Air seemed to rush out of her lungs, her breath coming in ragged, excited pants.

She squirmed as the pressure built inside, digging her fingers into his hard, muscled shoulders and back. Soft, kitten mewling noises became moans as his mouth played a rhapsody on her pussy, his tongue seeking out her every secret place and drawing her to him.

The shaft of the *gorlach* pressed into her palm, rolling slightly as he leaned further, moved faster, the fringe brushing the hot flesh of his back.

A sudden burst of white hot energy shot from between her legs, the power of it sending sparks to every atom of her body, bringing her rigid with pleasure and the next instant causing her to sag bonelessly against him. Her only awareness, only thought, the feel of him lapping and sucking her juices.

Even as she got to her wobbly feet and tried to pull away, his tongue tried to follow. Gently, she put out her hand to keep him in his place, pleased and still aroused as his tongue whipped around his lips in search of the last drops of her.

But the fire smoldering inside told her that the party had only just begun.

With a gesture of her *gorlach,* she signaled to the unseen voice that she wanted to proceed.

"Arise, submissive," it ordered and obediently, he got to his feet.

Playfully, she flicked the tails of her whip over his thick, pounding erection, dragging them over the bulging tip and down the solid sides. *He's beautiful*, she thought. Aroused by the mere taste, smell of her, his whole body cried out for the one thing that only she could give him.

He belonged to her; to command, to do with as she pleased. No longer just a submissive playing a game with her, he wanted desperately to be freed from this exquisite agony for which she was responsible. She knew in her soul that even free of his blindfold and manacles, he would do anything she asked, endure anything, for his release in her body.

Carefully, she took his cock in her hand, feeling him immediately, hot and ready, alert and hopeful. He twitched and she closed her fingers more tightly. Tugging on him, she made sure he knew she wanted him to follow her but not that she would relieve him just yet.

In a few steps, she'd guided him to the corner of the room and a large metal frame with manacles attached to stout leather strips hanging down from the top corners and laying on the floor from the bottom corners. Positioning him in the frame, she quickly bent down and secured his ankles. Unlocking his hands from behind his back, she immediately re-manacled him to the frame. When she'd finished, she stepped back to admire her handiwork.

Daria stretched him tightly, his long legs and strong arms pulled as far apart as she could manage, making the muscles beneath that smooth tanned skin stand out. His ass flat, his cock straining against that perfect belly, he was all hers.

Gazing at him, she felt a moment of indecision. The heat of her desire momentarily edged with the ice of doubt. It was…was what? Wrong? Bad? Dangerous? Those words didn't exist here. All that existed here was control. Sex. Power.

The word rang through her like waves through a tuning fork, pitching her to something bigger, stronger than herself. And the heat of the Balmeer's skin seemed to have welded its flesh to her. It sent the hunger of its primal need coursing through her blood.

She wanted this and would not be denied.

The *gorlach* settled easily into her hand, seeming to understand her wants and conform itself to her readiness. Picking her spot and planting her feet, Daria raised the whip and let the tails fly as she'd done on the practice pillow.

All the sensations ran together. A smacking sort of sound, different than the dull thud of leather hitting a padded pillow. A sharper, more distinct sound followed by a sharp breath and an *umph* of surprise and something else. Tingling ran up her right arm and blossomed in her chest to a shiver of pleasure. Bands of thin red appeared magically on tender, pale flesh. She realized with a start of satisfaction that the groupings stayed tightly together, as they'd been on the pillow.

"You are a natural talent," Tovah had told her.

The *gorlach* twitched impatiently in her hand.

Smack! Smack! Smack!

More red bands, covering that ass like thick marking pens on white paper. And every time the *gorlach's* tails connected with the submissive's body, it jerked and flinched like small jolts of electricity had touched it.

More! More!

Something snarled ferociously in Daria's brain even as waves of aroused fire broke over her, making it hard to breathe or think of anything but the growing red marks and the hot, erotic, overwhelming rush enveloping her.

She leaned closer, raising her arm higher and higher, bringing it down with greater force and frequency. The *umphs* had become grunts and the electricity no longer seemed to energize his body. Instead, it seemed to be slumping forward, held up only by the leather and steel at his wrists. And still the red bands grew, the electricity now seeming to course through her body as if taking it from his.

Power, came the growl in her brain. Trout Erdman. Unitech. The Sildor. This was how it felt to have power. To be them. Security. Wealth. Position. Politics. Even life itself. This was how it felt to be them. To dominate without fear. To be truly powerful.

The electricity surged through her like an erotic high, pushing her further and further but refusing to release her to that blissful peace of orgasm. Instead, it taunted and tortured and tantalized but never achieved its promise.

You've been powerless all your life, the voice cajoled. *At the mercy of everyone who made you feel small and helpless and worthless. All the people who treated you like dirt. The petty tyrants and the fools. Well now you have the power. Use it. Feel it. Enjoy it. Luxuriate in it. Exercise it. Experience the god-like sensation of life and death. The ultimate act of power. It will be as nothing you've ever known.*

A long moment of swirling dizziness engulfed Daria, as if the room itself had begun to spin. Nausea welled up, mixing with the acute awareness of damp leather in her hand, a sheen of sweat on her face, the sound of her thudding heart in her ears. And those awful, ugly, swollen red bands.

Lowering her arm, she felt as if all the life had drained out of her suddenly. Her stomach did a slow roll and for a second she feared she would be physically as well as emotionally sick.

Finally, she managed to rouse herself enough to look up. "Red," she murmured hoarsely. "Red."

Chapter Six

Voh bowed slightly and waited another moment until the barred door swung open a little and she stepped into the hall.

"It is good to see you again, Miss Evans," he said in that same, quiet gentle voice that he'd used when she'd entered. "The Sildor sent me to escort you back to your rooms."

Walking back down these deserted halls, Daria experienced a feeling of unreality. After she'd uttered the safe-word, Tovah had arrived almost instantly and taken her back to her room.

"You must sleep now," he'd told her softly as he'd helped her out of her jumpsuit and into the large bed.

"The submissive…"

"Shhh," he'd answered, putting one of those tiny fingers to her lips. "We will talk afterwards. When you are refreshed."

But when she'd awakened, Tovah hadn't been there, even when she'd called. The bath had been prepared for her and when she'd finished, she'd found her clothes, including underwear, neatly laid out on the bed. Just as she finished dressing, a hooded figure, like the one who had brought her into this place, appeared. Silently, he'd pointed and begun to walk away. Daria followed, and she'd found herself walking back along the corridor where, at the end, Voh waited, much to her relief.

Voh opened the doors of her room and stepped aside. "There is food and drink for you. We had no way of knowing exactly when you would return from The Academy, so your attendant is not waiting. I will remain out here until he arrives. If you have need of anything before he returns, you have only to make your desires known."

"Thank you, Voh," she smiled weakly, "but I'm fine, really."

Closing the doors behind her, Daria looked around. Everything was just as she'd left it, even to the bowl of fruit and decanter of *Fal-Trank* on the table. She couldn't, however, remember a time in her life when she'd felt less like eating.

Going to her briefcase, she took out her clock to check the date and time. It surprised her that so much time had gone by so quickly. And yet, now, time did not seem as important as it had before she'd gone away.

Plopping down beside the communication device, she punched the recall button and scanned the list of calls. Three from Trout when she'd first gone into The Academy and one from Analet, no doubt after she'd received Daria's letter. With a resigned sigh, she hit the 'erase all' button and the blinking red light went dark. There would be time enough to talk to Analet when she'd sorted through The Academy more clearly in her mind. And she had nothing to say to Trout.

Absently, Daria wondered where Ston was. She'd expected to find him waiting for her and the fact that he wasn't made her feel even more lonely. But she needed to be alone, anyway. She needed time to think and reflect and plan.

Picking up the fruit, the decanter and the goblet, Daria moved to a pile of comfy cushions on the floor and settled in. Some quiet time and some *Fal-Trank* sounded like just what she needed now.

* * * * *

"I'm sorry I was not here when you returned from The Academy," Ston told her quietly. "We did not know how long you would be away and I had other duties."

"That's perfectly all right, Ston," she smiled. "I understand completely."

"It is good to see you again," he continued shyly. "You look well."

"Thank you. Although I think you're looking a little peaked." She cocked her head and studied him. He seemed to be moving a little slower, his face a little paler than she remembered.

"Peaked?"

"A little tired. Not your usual self."

"Ah. Well, I have been busy since you left. But there is nothing wrong, I assure you."

"Aren't you going to ask me about The Academy?" The complete lack of interest both of Voh and Ston surprised her.

He shook that mop of black hair slightly. "It is forbidden to talk of such things," he said earnestly. "The Academy is very personal."

Pictures of what had happened to her flickered in Daria's mind and she chuckled. "Yes," she agreed, "I would say that The Academy is *very* personal."

"I hope that your experience there was enlightening."

Daria sighed and looked away for a moment. "Yes, Ston. You might even say, painfully so."

A furious knocking started at the door and Ston went to answer it. A moment later, Analet raced through the room like a pale blue whirlwind over to where Daria sat.

"Daria!" she shrieked, throwing herself down in the midst of the cushions and wrapping her friend in her huge arms. "I am so glad to see you! Are you all right?"

"Yes, Analet," Daria reassured her, trying to untangle herself gracefully from Analet's embrace. "But what are you doing here?"

"The Sildor sent me a message as soon as she knew you were coming out. I would have been at the door to meet you except that I could not escape the long, boring meeting in which I was trapped and only learned of your arrival back here a short while ago. I came as quickly as I could."

"Do you require food or drink?" Ston asked quietly.

"Analet?"

"Nothing for me, thank you."

"We're fine, Ston. I'd like to speak to the Ambassador alone for a while. Perhaps you'd like to go and rest?"

"I'm fine..." he started to insist but Daria held up her hand.

"I'm sure you are, Ston," she told him firmly but gently, "but the Ambassador and I wish to be alone and since you look tired and I have no need of you at this moment, I think you should rest. Please. It's what I want."

"As you wish," he replied glumly and with a slight bow to each of the women, he backed slowly, and Daria thought again, almost painfully out of the room.

"I have to tell you, little friend," Analet began slowly, "the letter Ston brought both alarmed and confused me more than a little. I honestly did not know what to do when you wrote of being forced into some kind of slavery at this 'sex university' and that I should go immediately and tell The Sildor that I knew of your plight and that I would go to the galactic authorities if you did not return safely."

Surprisingly, Daria laughed. "I did write quite an epistle, didn't I? You'd probably be horrified at some of the things I imagined."

"I could not imagine how you managed to get The Sildor to invite you to attend The Academy, even for a short time. Especially not without explaining in great detail what you could expect to find there." She shook her head. "Most perplexing. And unnecessary."

"I know that now," Daria agreed, "but I didn't then."

"That is not what I mean," Analet continued. "You are my friend. Do you think that if you suddenly disappeared, even in the palace of The Sildor, I would not notice? That I would not seek to find you? No, Daria. Even The Sildor could not hide you. I know many powerful people...more powerful even than the ruler of Utan. I would have broken down the walls of The Academy with my bare hands if it had been required to find

174

you. And I would not be put off either. I am…" she sought for the right word. "I am tenacious. Like the bullfrog of Earth."

Daria reached out and put her hand on her friend's. "I know that, Analet. You've always been a dear friend and I should have had more faith that you wouldn't let me just vanish without at least trying to find out what happened. You make me very proud to call you my friend."

"That is a kind thing to say, little friend," Analet murmured, her voice harsh with emotion. "I have always treasured our friendship even if sometimes…" She stopped and stared deeply into Daria's face, a questioning look in her deep amber eyes.

"Even if sometimes what?"

Analet continued to stare intently for a few more seconds. "Even," she finished quietly, "if sometimes your habit of correcting my speech is annoying. Such as just now when I said, 'bullfrog,' I expected you to say, it should have been something else."

"I know, Analet," Daria replied apologetically, "I've been pretty awful about that down through the years, and I want to tell you how sorry I am. I should have paid more attention to what you told me rather than the words you used. I promise to try and not be so picky in the future."

"Then bullfrog is correct?"

"Uhm…not really," she said sheepishly. "It's actually bulldog. Bullfrog is another animal entirely. But I knew what you meant and that's all that matters."

"What has come over you, Daria?" Analet asked warily.

"You mean about the language? I told you…"

"No," she replied emphatically, narrowing her eyes and searching her friend's face. "It is more than that. There is a different look about you…a different sound not just to your words but to your voice as well. Something that was not there before…"

"So after you received my letter, did you go immediately to The Sildor and demand my release?" Daria asked, hurriedly changing the subject.

"I called the palace and begged audience with The Sildor on an urgent matter."

"Very wise of you. She probably wouldn't have seen you if she'd known you wanted to talk about me. What did she say when she found out that you knew about me...going into...into The Academy?"

Analet shrugged slightly. "I told her that you had communicated to me your fears about entering The Academy. She told me that you had agreed to go as part of the contract for the mining rights. That it was important for both of you to understand the gravity and enormity of the commitment you were making and that you establish a bond of trust. She assured me that you always had control because of your safe-words but that if it would ease my mind, she would send daily reports to me, which she did."

"You mean...you mean you never worried about me? At all?" Daria could barely believe her ears.

"I had no reason to. Many have come and gone through The Academy. In fact," Analet smiled broadly, "even though she could not tell me specifically about your lessons, she seemed quite pleased with your progress."

Daria looked away for several long moments. When she turned back, Analet saw unshed tears in her eyes. "Did she...did she tell you I failed?" She could hardly get the words out around the lump in her throat.

"Failed?" her friend repeated in disbelief. "But how..."

"Let's just say I failed and let it go at that."

"You need to rest," Analet told her gently. "You have been through much in body and spirit. I should not have come so soon after. I just wanted to make sure you were well. I'll go now."

She squeezed the fingers of Analet's huge hand and smiled a little. "I'm so awfully glad you came, Analet. Really. I'm sorry I'm not better company. I feel as though...as though I've just come off a month's suspension on a liner to the other side of the universe. Let me get some rest and I'll call you. Tomorrow, maybe. And we can go to lunch. Dinner even."

"That sounds very good." She raised her large body to a standing position. "I will see myself out. You should rest. Good-bye, little friend."

"Good-bye Analet. And thank you. For everything."

When Analet left, Daria closed her eyes and sighed heavily. Tomorrow she would go and see The Sildor. Better to get it over with as quickly as possible and be done with it.

And then she would deal with Trout.

* * * * *

"The Sildor will see you now." Voh bowed slightly and closed the door of The Sildor's office. Everything remained just as it had been when she'd stood before this very same desk and received the ultimatum about The Academy. Here she'd stood when she'd entered into this devil's bargain. It seemed like such a long time ago. She supposed it was only fitting that the whole thing should end where it had begun.

A door opened and The Sildor emerged, followed by Albre. Daria waited while she seated herself behind the desk and he took his place beside her.

"Good day, Daria Evans," she said solemnly.

"Good day, Sildor Minsee," Daria replied with a small bow and an equally solemn tone.

"You are well?"

"Yes, Sildor. I hope you are the same."

"I am as always." She paused a heartbeat. "I suppose you have come about the contract."

"My purpose for this gracious audience, Sildor, is three-fold."

"You may proceed."

"First, I would like to apologize to The Sildor, to her Counselor and to all the people of Utan and to humbly beg your forgiveness."

A perfect eyebrow arched in surprise, and Minsee and Albre exchanged confused glances. Secretly, Daria chuckled, pleased that she'd caught them both off-guard.

"And for what do you apologize and beg forgiveness?" The Sildor leaned forward a little.

"For my thoughtlessness and my rude behavior. In my ignorance and ape arrogance," she flashed a small grin and threw a quick glance at Albre, knowing now his voice as the Headmaster, "I believed myself better than the Utanians. I believed you had nothing to offer but your natural resources. That we humans would be the teachers, the benefactors and that in time we could remake you in our image. My shallow, selfish thoughts did not take into consideration all that Utan could teach. I believed that because I could pronounce the name of your capital city and the index of your mineral riches, that I knew everything necessary about you. I truly lacked an understanding that simply because you are different from we humans, does not automatically make you less."

"And the second purpose?"

"To thank The Sildor for the great gift of allowing me entrance into that most exalted and sacred of Utanian places, The Academy. Being so very ignorant in so many things, I had no concept of the magnitude of my ignorance. By permitting me even these few, brief lessons, I have learned much. At least now I have an inkling of how little I know...truly know, and how much more there is left in the universe for me to understand.

"I have learned that one can not know simply in the mind. To truly know, one must feel...experience... understand with the heart as well. If you had told me before I came to this great place that I would be so changed, I would not have believed you. It is a gift for which I will be eternally grateful and for which I will never adequately be able to repay The Sildor."

Suddenly, the old woman's face broke into a smile, as warm and friendly as a summer's day. It softened the hard mask of her face to such an extent, it amazed Daria. Years faded away and her whole being seemed to uncoil and relax, transforming The Sildor into a different person.

"I am glad that you have received the gift of enlightenment which I sought for you," she said gently. "I knew when I first read the project that you possessed a truly brilliant mind and I wished to know if your spirit matched it. It disappointed me greatly to find your soul so barren. I could not turn the future of my world over to such a person or the group to which such a soul would belong. I almost sent you away.

"But part of me knew that this project could be of great value to my people if I could find a shepherd to keep them safe from the Balmeers who would most certainly follow the trail of riches and plenty it would bring. And I felt that if I could light the spark of truth in your soul as in your mind, that you would be that person. You have learned well the lessons I sent you to learn."

"Surely The Sildor must know that I did not finish the lessons." Daria looked at Albre. "Your Counselor must certainly have told you by now that I uttered the safe-word because I could not exercise even the tiny fragment of power you gave me over my submissive. I saw a side of myself that was both weak and cruel. I didn't realize enlightenment could leave such a bitter taste."

Albre smiled. "You looked into the darkest, ugliest side of power...the absolute power of life and death...and you made your choice.

"You knew that you could have beaten the submissive and as long as he chose not to utter his safe-word, you could have taken his life and no punishment would have been meted out. And you knew too, that if you uttered your safe-word and ended the lessons, you would lose your contract and all that you might have gained because of it. You chose that which was right over that which was easy.

"On Utan we have a saying: 'Only those who have known the lash should hold the whip.'"

"On Earth we say, 'power corrupts...absolute power corrupts absolutely.' I was tempted...very tempted."

"But you resisted the temptation," Minsee added, her face now almost glowing with satisfaction. "You have proved yourself not only trustworthy, but a caring and understanding soul. Just the sort of person I must have to stand against the Balmeers.

"Therefore, by decree of The Sildor, Daria Evans is hereby appointed Minister of Natural Resources for all of Utan. This appointment is for life. You will reside in the palace that you may be available to me at all times. Apartments commensurate with your office will be provided which you may decorate to your taste. Also clothes, furnishings, jewelry and whatever else you may require. A sum of money will be placed at your disposal for personal spending. And as a minister of The Sildor, you will be entitled to..." she frowned and whispered to Albre.

"Ah, yes. You will be entitled to mates up to twenty-five in your numbers. You will contact Unitech to sever your ties with them and take up your duties immediately. We have much to discuss before the contract is officially signed."

"The Sildor does me a great honor," Daria replied, almost overwhelmed by the generosity of the offer, "and I truly wish I were the person about whom you both speak. But I have failed...The Sildor, Unitech and most importantly, myself. It would be dishonest of me to take advantage of your mistaken impression and I do not wish to add that to my transgressions.

"As I said, my purpose in seeking this audience was three-fold. The last purpose is to tell The Sildor and her Counselor that I will be leaving Utan and returning to my own planet on the next available liner. I've already made arrangements. Unitech will send someone in my place, the contract can be signed and everything will be just as it should be."

"I do not wish you to leave," Minsee told her flatly, the regal mask now firmly back in place and darker than ever. "You will remain and be my Minister. It is the will of The Sildor."

"I'm sorry, Sildor," Daria apologized, "but that is not possible. I must return to Earth. I will always remember the kindness and the greatness of The Sildor and when I return to my people, I will tell them of the wise and gracious ruler of Utan and how much I owe her. And now, Sildor, with your gracious permission, I will take my leave."

She bowed and departed.

"She can not do this!" Minsee bellowed suddenly. "I am The Sildor, absolute ruler of Utan! She must stay if it is my will! Do something!"

"What would you have me do, Minsee?" Albre teased. "She is human, not Utanian. You have no power over her to make her stay if she does not wish to."

"She will stay if she's shackled to the wall in my dungeon!" the old woman fumed. "She will stay if I strip her naked and turn her out."

"And with her dying breath she would probably spit in your face."

"I will not tolerate such defiance!"

"I thought this is what you wanted," he continued good-naturedly. "Not a timid, uncertain little *Regin* but a self-assured, confident Balmeer, although even you, Minsee, must know that even The Sildor can not make a Balmeer into a tame house pet."

Minsee suddenly slumped back in her chair and began to nibble nervously at the ends of her fingers. Albre knew something was truly wrong. Gently, he reached over and pulled her to him, resting her head on his chest.

"What is it, my love?" he asked tenderly, stroking her hair and brushing his lips along her hairline.

"This is too much for me," she confided sadly, sounding, he thought, like a frightened, exhausted child. "I have read this project, of the minerals and their values and the great quantities. But I could live a thousand years and not understand it…truly understand it. I must have someone who knows these things to advise me and help me make the right decisions for my people. Not just for the now but for all the years to come that will be affected by those decisions. I must have someone at my back whom I can trust." She looked up at him, helpless and desperate. "I must have Daria Evans."

"It is as she said. Unitech will send someone else. Someone just as good."

"But how can I be sure?" she whimpered. "How will I know that they are as smart or as good as Daria? I cannot send everyone at Unitech through The Academy. I must have an advisor, a counselor *now*. If I wait too long or choose unwisely, we will be swallowed up like ripe tomatoes."

"Perhaps you could talk to her," he suggested. "Tell her how you feel, how great the need is for her here."

"I am The Sildor," she sniffed. "I do not beg anyone for help."

"Even when you need it desperately?"

"Even then."

"Well, you are probably right. You forget, she is a solitary human female, far from her own kind, her own place. And there is the male she speaks of. The one she is promised to mate. Perhaps her blood runs hot with the thought of him."

Minsee nibbled silently on her fingers again for several moments. "No," she announced at last, "hers is not the face, the voice of a female returning joyfully to her mate. From her speech, her manner, I have never believed that her blood runs hot for this male but I know in my female heart that it runs cold as our planet's surface for him now."

"Well, she has turned down your offer to be a royal minister. If you can not appeal to her greed and her ambition, what will you do then?"

"We must find something else that will make her wish to stay."

"Such as?"

"A mate."

"What?"

She raised herself and looked at him, mischief and excitement dancing in her eyes. "We will mate her to an Utanian male. Once she is mated, she will have to remain."

"And do you have any particular male in mind," he joked, "or will you just go out and round up the first one you find on the street."

"Of course I have a particular male in mind. Ston."

"Her attendant?"

"Certainly."

"I do not know…"

"Of course you do not know," she laughed. "You are a male. But I have seen how he looks at her when he thinks no one is watching. He will make an excellent mate for her. He will be gentle and loving and attentive and will allow her the freedom to be as she is but he is also strong enough to match her willfulness and not be trampled by her." Minsee nodded once.

"Yes. It will be a good mating. Their offspring will be the best of both our people."

"Suppose, as you believe, Ston has feelings for Daria Evans. But perhaps she has no feelings for him. Have you thought of that? Without feelings, she will not take him to mate simply because it is what you want."

"Daria Evans has feelings for Ston," Minsee assured him. "She just does not realize it yet."

"But you intend to remedy that situation?"

"Yes."

"And may I ask how?"

"Better than that," she chuckled, "I will show you."

A push of a button summoned her attendant.

"Voh," she smiled, "I wish to speak to Ston, immediately. He will most likely be in the chambers of Daria Evans. Find him as quickly as possible, and tell him to cease whatever he is doing and attend me now."

"What is it that you have on your evil mind?" he continued to tease when Voh had departed.

"Do you remember as children how you went around telling me always how much you loved me and how you wished for us to mate and produce offspring?"

He nodded. "And you used to abuse me and tell me to go away and ignore my pleas for your favor."

"Yes. But there came a time when you no longer attended me. When your attention drifted to other females and soon you forgot about me entirely."

"Simply because you did not find me attractive, did not mean I repulsed all females."

"Well, I have a secret to confess. Only when I stood on the brink of my maturity did I realize I had loved you always. Being always there, always available, I paid little heed to you. When you no longer paid me court, that truth became known to me. I went to my female parent and cried for you. You may not realize it, but I had a very difficult time convincing her the offspring of her headmaster would be a suitable mate for the next ruler of Utan. But I wept and she relented."

She ran her fingertips along his cheek.

"Do you remember the first time?"

Albre took her fingers in his own and kissed them tenderly. "You had gone to The Academy to begin your lessons. My male parent had informed me that I had been selected to be your instructor. Only my lust and fear exceeded my love and joy.

When I opened the door and saw you there in the candlelight, naked, blindfolded and manacled to the bed, howling and clawing like a wounded Balmeer, your perfect tawny gold body covered with a sheen of sweat, your beautiful pale curls just barely concealing your female treasure, all that filled my mind was your beauty and my need for you."

"I knew you would be my instructor," she whispered lovingly. "I selected you myself. But I was not going to let you have your prize without a fight. I wanted you to believe that you had won it and that it had been worth the struggle."

"My cock had long been hard from the thought of you. When it beheld you finally, I thought it would burst without ever having touched you. And when I climbed onto the bed and rested between your legs, I feared I would not be able to pleasure you without coming myself, simply by being so close to you."

"I remember being afraid, then, myself," she told him softly. "Afraid that I would not be able to please you and that you would not love me when we finished."

"How could I not love you?" He kissed her gently. "Even now, I can still smell your sweet, aroused scent, the feel of your soft hair as I moved to give you your first pleasure. That first delicious taste of your flesh as my tongue moved across your beautiful pleasure point. It is as clear to me today as that first moment."

"I could not believe the power of that first surge through my body," Minsee sighed. "I had never dreamed such physical pleasure existed."

Albre chuckled. "It amazed me how quickly your howls of anger turned to moans and mewls of ecstasy. And when you released yourself to me, your wetness flowing out like the sweetest wine...well, only that which came after was greater."

"I lay there, sated, barely able to breathe with the wonder of your gift, when I felt the heat of your cock, throbbing and hungry for me."

"You looked so beautiful, so peaceful and my blood burned for you. My cock felt as if it had grown too big for my body and I knew that the only way to extinguish the flames and bring it back under control, lay inside you and our joining."

"It seemed that you took forever," she giggled. "Perhaps you did not understand that even after the pleasure you'd given me, I ached for you as you did for me."

"I knew that I must be careful, patient, even though every bit of me screamed to rush inside and quench that unbearable hunger. When the tip of my cock found your entrance, I feared I would come then, my need was so great. Only the fear that I would hurt you, cause you even a moment's discomfort, kept me in check. So I concentrated on your breasts and your mouth and the soft flesh of your throat, knowing that I must raise you to my heights. Quickly."

"I remember the feeling of growing excitement. The feel of your lips on my breasts felt like fire."

"And then I reached your barrier and I knew that I must take care or there would be pain."

"With my mind spinning and my body writhing, I did not even notice the moment's pain as you took me from childhood to maturity." Her eyes became dreamy and far away as they relived the long ago passion.

"I felt you flinch and cry out," he replied softly, "and for a moment terror gripped me that all my care and planning had been for nothing. But you continued to accept me and when I arrived in you fully, joined as one, I felt you hot and slick and tight around me, the movements of your body pulling and squeezing my cock."

"And then we stepped off into Paradise, together," she finished, looking up with love filled eyes.

"And you would have me believe that our lives together are because of your little scheme?"

"It has been a good life has it not? I mean, we have been happy all these many solar revolutions together?"

He sighed deeply. "Every day with you, Minsee, has been a trial both to my body and my spirit. You are willful, headstrong, devious and not just a little cruel when you set your heart to it." A smile touched his lips. "You are also as much a part of me as my heart or my head, and I could no more imagine my life without you than without them. Yes, my love, it has been a good life and we have been blessed with much happiness."

"Then you see why I want this for Daria and Ston. So that they may know what we have known and when they reach our time in life, they may look back on many offspring and a love that still makes their blood run hot."

"You want Daria and Ston to mate so that you can have your own way," he chided gently. "If they find happiness, so be it."

She tried to look distressed but missed. "Why must you always think the worst of me?" she pouted. "I am only doing what is best for a female I have come to feel very strongly about. She has been too long alone and it is time for her to take her rightful place in the universe."

"You are plotting and manipulating so that you get what you want. It would be well if once in a while you chose simply to be honest and straightforward. One day, your games will bring you to grief."

"Perhaps," she agreed, a wicked gleam in her eyes, "but not now. I tried being straightforward and honest and it did not work. Now I will resort to other measures. But I will get what I want."

"You always do," he answered with a resigned sigh. "You always do."

A sharp rap sounded on the door and Voh appeared.

"The attendant Ston is here."

"Good. Send him in." They moved apart quickly, Minsee to her desk chair, and Albre at her side.

Minsee sat straight up in her chair, her hands folded on the desk in front of her and by the time Ston stood before them, both she and Albre had returned to their formal selves.

"The Sildor sent for me?" Ston asked, bowing.

"Yes," she replied gravely. "I have been looking over your record since you came to the palace as an attendant. Your work is diligent, competent and thorough. All tasks assigned to you, both great and small, are attended to promptly and carefully. I am most pleased."

"I try to serve to the best of my ability," he replied, secretly overjoyed at the praise, but careful not to show any emotion in the presence of his ruler.

"Your service is being rewarded. By my decree, you are henceforth elevated to the rank of Lord Chamberlain of my household. You will be in charge of the palace and its staff. You will, of course, receive all the trappings of your new responsibilities including a bigger apartment, uniforms, symbol of authority and an allowance for personal needs."

"The Sildor does me a great honor," he breathed, barely able to believe her words but keeping his composure nonetheless. "I will strive to continue to serve you to my utmost and hope that I may continue in your service for many more solar revolutions."

"I am pleased that you accept these new responsibilities," she told him carefully, watching intently as she prepared to spring the other part of her surprise. "You will have three solar rotations to take care of any personal matters which may need your attention and to gather whatever items you wish to take with you before you leave."

"Leave?" Ston repeated cautiously.

"Yes. Oh, perhaps I did not make myself understood. You are to become Lord Chamberlain of the summer palace in the eastern region. My oldest female offspring makes her residence there and I spend some time there myself. It is important that she have someone who can run her household efficiently."

"But…but I have duties here," he told her anxiously. "The Sildor herself assigned me to attend the human female, Daria Evans. I must stay and do that."

Inwardly, Minsee gave a whoop of triumph although her outward appearance hadn't changed. She'd been right. He had feelings for Daria. Everything would work out as she'd planned.

"Ah, well that is one of the reasons I chose now to give you this new assignment," she replied carefully. "I have only just now been informed by Daria Evans that she is leaving Utan and returning to her home planet by the first available liner."

Ston's reaction was almost more than The Sildor had hoped for. His mask of calm civility fell away, stripped by the power of her words like a punch in the stomach.

"But…but what about the contract?" he sputtered helplessly. "I…I thought she was to stay and oversee the project for many solar revolutions?"

"She did not give a reason," Minsee responded, trying to pretend that she neither knew nor cared but knowing inside she must turn up the heat even more.

"As a female, though, I believe it has to do with the male to whom she is promised to mate. After The Academy, perhaps her blood runs hotter now than before. The urge to mate and produce offspring can be very strong." She paused to watch Ston's distress turn to full-fledged pain.

"Whatever it is, her reason for going is of no consequence. She is going and you are released from your duties. You will begin making arrangements to leave for the summer palace. You are dismissed."

Ston bowed, and quietly left the room.

"Did you see the look on his face when he learned of Daria's going?" Minsee exalted gleefully. "I thought he would break down and weep."

"So beyond causing Ston a great deal of misery, what do you intend to do?"

"I will do nothing. Ston, however, is faced with the loss of his female and has only a short time to prevent it. Unless I am very much mistaken, and I never am in these matters, he will go straight to her, declare his feelings and this whole matter will be concluded by nightfall."

She scooted back her chair and rose quickly.

"Now where are you going?"

"I have decided it is a good time to inspect the listening ports in the west wing of the palace," she replied regally. "It has been much too long since I saw to their working order."

"You are going to listen in on Ston and Daria Evan's conversation," corrected Albre as he rose. "You are a vile, wicked creature Minsee, and it shames me that I love such a female as much as I do. Someday, though, one of your schemes will turn on you."

"Hurry or we will miss the best part."

* * * * *

"Miss Evans?"

"Yes, Ston?"

"I may be permitted to speak with you?"

Daria, noting the anxious, almost fearful note in his voice, closed the book she'd been reading and set down her goblet.

"Of course, Ston." She pointed to a cushion beside her. "Please, sit down. Would you like a glass of *Fal-Trank*?"

"No, thank you," he said nervously, settling across from her.

"What is it you'd like to say?"

Ston swallowed and ran his tongue over his lips. "The Sildor tells me that you are leaving Utan to return to your home planet."

"That's right."

"And that you will be going very soon."

"The liner leaves in four days...I mean, solar rotations."

"Do...do you go back to complete your mating...your marriage to the male you are promised to?" He leaned forward and stared at her intently.

She sighed and reached for her goblet. "That's a very personal question, Ston," she answered wearily. "As close as we've been in the time I've been here, I don't feel it's something I can discuss with you."

He felt his heart sink. Of course she wouldn't want to discuss the male with him. "Then perhaps you are leaving because of...of what you endured in The Academy?" She thought he sounded like a frightened little boy trying to work up the courage to tell his mother of a childish misdeed.

"No, Ston," she reassured him, putting her hand on his arm and grinning weakly. "I'm not leaving because of The Academy. Well, perhaps not for the reasons you think, anyway. Let's just say that I'm leaving because it's time for me to go."

Those gorgeous, anxious, worried eyes bored into her and she had the distinct feeling he was wrestling with himself about something.

"I...I do not wish you to leave Utan," he said finally, the words flowing out as slowly as syrup. "I...I wish for you to stay so that...that I may continue to attend you."

"That's very sweet of you, Ston, and I appreciate your thoughtfulness. But it really isn't possible."

"Then I will go with you to your planet and attend you there," he told her, the anxious tone becoming almost panicky.

"On my planet, Ston, there are no attendants. We live very differently than you do here. Besides, you'd be very unhappy separated from your own people. I'm sorry but it just isn't possible."

"I would be happy wherever you are," he insisted. "I would follow you anywhere. I went even into The Academy so that I could be with you."

Too late he realized what he'd said but the words could not be called back.

Immediately, her hand dropped from his arm and her eyes grew round with surprise. "You…you were in The Academy?"

Heartsick, he could only nod, watching the disbelief give way to horror and something worse in those beautiful green eyes.

"It was you…" she breathed in amazement as the truth dawned. "You…you were the guard…?"

"I wanted only to protect you," he began frantically, desperate to make her understand.

"Protect me?" Anger appeared now in the mix of emotions in her voice. "You tie me down, blindfold me, rape me and call that 'protection?' How could you do those…those awful things to me when you knew…?" Tears appeared and slid down her cheeks.

The sight of them wrenched at Ston's heart and he wanted nothing more than to take her in his arms and kiss them away.

"If you will listen to me," he begged, leaning toward her and reaching for her hand.

Pulling it away, she stood up. "Get out of here!" she screamed. "Get out of here and never show your cruel, lying face to me again!"

Ston stood, towering over her. "Please. Let me explain…"

"You struck me," she snarled, the realization only breaking then. "You took your whip and struck me. Hard!"

"I did not mean to hurt you," he tried to explain, "only to get your attention. As a small child who refuses to listen but must be made to understand. I would never hurt you…"

"Well, it did hurt!" she shot back. "A lot. You're a mean, bullying, sadistic pervert and I don't ever want to see you again! If you don't get out of here this instant, I'll call the guards and have them lop off your head, here and now. Get out!"

As he backed toward the door, she followed him, cursing and shouting until the door closed behind him and he heard it lock. Shoulders slumped, head drooped to his chest, Ston felt as though his whole life had just been closed off and for the first time since his childhood, he felt the sting of tears behind his eyes.

* * * * *

"Well, Minsee my love," Albre snarled as he slammed shut the small listening port door, "I hope you are satisfied at last."

"But...but I don't understand," she whimpered, looking up at him and sticking the tip of her finger back in her mouth. "This is not how it is supposed to be. How...how could this have happened?"

"It happened because you are dealing with two intelligent, sentient beings," he replied sarcastically, "not game pieces that can be moved around a board to suit your whims."

"But I was only trying to help," she insisted pathetically.

Albre shook his head emphatically. "No, you were meddling, a most undesirable trait in a mate but absolutely unforgivable in a ruler. Beings can not be manipulated and toyed with for your own ends. I warned you this would happen but did you heed me? No. And now you have shattered what might have been if you'd simply been honest. Or even just left things to their own course."

"What am I to do?" Her lower lip quivered and he saw the shine of tears in her eyes. "Help me, Albre," she pleaded. "Please."

Already he could feel his anger ebbing, washed away by the look on Minsee's face. He knew he should let her suffer, but he knew also that he could never do that. Frustration and resignation rose up and ran together like melting wax.

"If I do anything," he replied sternly, "it will only be to help Daria and Ston who should not be made to pay for your selfish silliness. I will be in charge and whatever happens, you must not interfere. Agreed?"

She nodded her head and smiled at him. "I will do whatever you say if only you can make things right again."

"I do not know if I can right this tangle," he sighed, "but I can certainly make it no worse. Come with me and be still."

In a moment they arrived at Daria's closed door, Ston still rooted to the spot in despair. Looking up and seeing them, he straightened his shoulders and raised his head. He started to speak but Albre raised his hand.

Two loud knocks on the door.

"Go away." Daria's voice sounded muffled but still angry.

"It is The Sildor and Counselor Albre," he shouted. "We demand entrance."

Almost instantly, the door swung open and Daria's pale, shaken face appeared. "I'm sorry Sildor, Counselor, I thought…I thought it was someone else. Please, come in." Opening the door wider, she caught sight of Ston and the anger returned.

"The Sildor and her Counselor are most welcome," she growled, "but not you. I told you to go away."

"Ston is with us," Albre told her sharply. "You will admit him also."

With no choice, Daria stood back and the three entered. When the door closed, she opened her mouth but Albre raised his hand and shook his head.

"I have had enough of these games and prattle," he announced. "Therefore, you will speak only when you are spoken to…"

The Sildor started to say something but he just glared at her. "And this includes you too, Minsee. All of you will be silent and attentive to my words."

A glance at the three faces told him that he had their attention at last.

"Now," he started, his voice resuming its normal calm, even tenor, "we will begin with Ston. You admit that you went to The Academy to be with the female?"

"Yes, Counselor," he answered, not realizing that their conversation had been overheard but believing that somehow the Headmaster had discovered his ruse. He'd paid the student Enor a great deal of money so that he could have his place with Daria. They were the same height and build, his face had been covered and he'd been careful to avoid the Headmaster. Perhaps Enor had let the wrong word slip and been found out. He knew Enor would betray him without hesitation to escape the wrath of the Headmaster and The Sildor.

"Even though you know it is forbidden both to go to The Academy uninvited and to interfere in any way with the lessons of a student?"

"Yes."

"Yet you did it anyway? Why?"

Ston glanced at Daria and then back to Albre. "When I first came to attend Daria Evans, I thought her beautiful but cold and hollow as a statue. Her mind had much knowledge but her heart had no warmth, no wisdom. She spoke to her promised mate yet I heard no passion in her voice, felt no blood rising. Aloof and apart, I thought perhaps this is the way of human females. But as I grew to know her, to understand her, I realized that she was not hollow, but only empty, searching, needing to be filled."

His gaze traveled back to her and his eyes seemed to glow from within. "I began to have feelings for the female. Not just because her beauty made my body ache for her, but because I longed to show her all that lacked in her. All that waited for her.

"When I discovered that The Sildor wished her to go into The Academy, I became at once joyful and yet fearful. When she spoke to the male of her great desire to return to him as quickly as possible, I knew her terror of The Academy was great. She believed then that she loved him and he used that, not to calm her spirit and ease her fears, but to force her to do what she did not want to. Not because he believed that she would learn and profit from the experience, but because his greed was greater than his caring.

"I must admit that my motives were not altogether pure. Yes, I wanted to make sure that no harm came to her, even accidentally, and I wanted to share this journey of discovery with her as she moved away from what she was toward what she might become. But also, I wanted to experience the joy of possessing her, even for a little while. To know her body and to feel her joined with mine."

"But...but you let me whip you." Daria ventured, confused at this point. "Why? You didn't have to submit. I...I could have..."

"Do you still not understand the true lesson?" he asked gently. "That the gift of submission is trust. Trust that your partner will serve your needs as his own. Trust that your mind remains in control even if the body is shackled with metal or disability or fear. Trust in yourself that you can endure and prevail.

"In the pool, I watched as you confronted your worst fear — that you did not possess enough strength, enough courage to take care of yourself — and triumph. I knew then that if you could learn to trust yourself, in time you could learn to trust others. When you whipped me, I gave you my trust as my gift. I knew no real harm would come to me because such evil is not in you. You felt only the need to vent the frustration and rage that comes with always feeling trapped. Powerless."

"Whatever your reasons," Albre's voice cut in like a cold knife, "you have willfully and knowingly broken the law of Utan. It is therefore decreed, in the name of The Sildor and the people of Utan, that you be taken from this place immediately to the nearest portal and turned out. I will personally inform your clan of the great shame you have brought upon them and your name will be forever banned among us."

"I understand, Counselor," he replied simply.

"Good, I will summon the guards."

"Wait!" Daria squealed. "I...I don't understand. What's going on? What does 'turned out' mean?"

"It is not your concern," Albre told her harshly. "It is the business of Utan."

"But it is my concern," she answered angrily. "If Ston's to be punished for what he did in The Academy, I want to know. I'm entitled to know. After all, he did it for me."

"Ston will be taken to one of the portals that lead to the surface and he will be turned out."

Daria blinked, as appalled and disgusted as when The Sildor's proposal for her entrance into The Academy had first reached her ears.

"You...you'd send him to the surface?" she gasped.

"It is the punishment for his crime."

"But...but he can't survive out there with no food, no shelter. You're...you're condemning him to die!"

"He condemned himself when he broke the law."

"Sildor," she pleaded turning to the older woman. "Do something! Tell Albre to stop this! It's not fair to do this to Ston for nothing more than wanting to help me."

She glanced at Albre who returned her gaze with stony silence.

"I am sorry, Daria Evans, truly," she whispered, looking down at her feet, "but the law is the law. I can not undo what has been done."

Tears of rage and frustration and something very close to fear welled up in Daria's eyes as she looked from Albre to The Sildor to Ston and back. Surely they wouldn't kill him for something so...so stupid. So trivial.

Albre turned his attention back to Ston. "You are permitted one last request before you are turned out," he intoned flatly. "What is it that you wish?"

"There is nothing that is within your power to grant me," Ston replied quietly, watching as Daria's tears slid silently down her flushed cheeks. All he could think of was how beautiful she was.

"Perhaps if you take a moment to consider," Albre prodded.

"No..." Ston turned his head and saw the older man jerk his head a little in Daria's direction and purse his lips ever so slightly. It took a moment for him to grasp the Counselor's meaning.

"There...there is one thing," he said slowly, looking back at Daria.

"What is it?"

"A good-bye kiss from Daria Evans. Something to warm me against the icy wind."

Their eyes locked and she saw the pleading, the light shining in them. Carefully, he stepped to her, taking her wet, red face gently in his hands and turning it up to him. She felt her eyes close just before their lips met.

The kiss rocked her like none she could ever remember, filled with longing, passion, desire, despair and something so powerful it seemed to melt her body, making her weak in the knees and light in the head. If it hadn't been for his strong, tender hands cradling her head, she knew she would have simply melted into a pool of goo on the floor at his feet.

They parted and her eyelids fluttered open. Just beyond her nose, her whole world seemed taken up with his face and those beautiful, glowing eyes.

"I love you, Daria Evans," he whispered softly. "Remember that always."

Slowly, he released her and turned back to Albre. "I am ready now."

"We will go then."

The Sildor and the Counselor started across the large room, Ston following obediently behind them.

"Wait!" Daria screamed, rushing to where they'd stopped.

"What is it?"

"What Ston did, he did for me. If anyone's to blame for this, it's me. If you turn him out, you'll have to turn me out too." The defiance in her tone surprised even Daria. It certainly didn't match how she felt.

"You do not know what you are saying," Ston told her fearfully. "I did what I did because I love you. I would die now rather than see you hurt."

"I know exactly what I'm saying," she replied, "and if you die, then I do too."

"Do not even think that. Know that without you, there is no life for me anyway. It's better that it end here instead of all the long solar revolutions alone."

"Do you love the male?" Albre asked her without emotion.

Ston looked at her hopefully.

"I...I don't know," she mumbled. "I...I just don't know."

"That is unacceptable," he told her firmly. "Love is or it is not. It is not a question for the mind but for the heart. The male has declared his love for you. He broke our laws and risked death to protect and care for you in The Academy and now he chooses death because it is preferable to living without you. You tell me that you would be turned out to certain death to stand with the male and yet you do not know if you love him or not."

"Sildor," she begged, turning again to the old woman. "Spare Ston's life and I will stay here on Utan and be your Minister of Natural Resources."

"That would be a fool's bargain. I have no doubt that you would honor your word and stay, but it would do me little good to have you serve as a prisoner and that is how you would feel. No. You can serve me only because you wish to."

"There may be a way," Albre said quietly.

Three pairs of anxious eyes focused on the older man.

"You have not answered my question, Daria Evans. Do you truly love the male, Ston?"

She looked up into his face, hope, fear, love all showing in those deep, dark eyes. *Let yourself go,* she heard a voice inside say, *listen to your heart.*

"Yes," she smiled at last. "Yes, I love Ston with all my heart."

"Ston, if the female Daria made the decision to take you to mate, would you agree?"

"I could but dream such a wonderful thing would happen, but yes, I would agree and thank the Creator every day for such a gift."

"And you, Daria Evans, you would take the male Ston to mate?"

"I can't think of anything I want more."

"What about Unitech and the male you are promised to?"

"The only thing I want is right here."

The Sildor grinned and clapped her hands together like a small, delighted child. "It is agreed then," she bubbled. "You and Ston will join in the *Fahn-jul* when the moon is new. That is about three of your Earth weeks. The new moon is also the best time for conceiving female offspring."

"But three weeks isn't enough time," Daria said in shock. "I mean, how can I put together a wedding in only three weeks?"

The other woman waved her hand. "Everything will be taken care of. I have had many *Fahn-juls*. This one will be grand. All Utan will celebrate with you. Now, Ston give Daria a kiss and be away to the mate's quarters."

"Away?" Daria squealed. "What do you mean 'away'? We just got engaged. We have all kinds of things to plan. To talk about."

"On Utan," Ston told her wistfully, "when the date of the *Fahn-jul* is set by the female's clan, the male is sent to the mate's quarters and they are not allowed to see each other or have any contact at all until the ceremony."

"And I will put a guard at your door to make sure that you remember," Albre laughed.

The Sildor leaned over, put her arm around Daria's shoulders and pulled her aside. "Do not worry, Daria Evans. There is much to do to prepare and the time passes quickly. And besides, after three weeks without you, more than his soul will be glad to have you with him once more." She laughed and released Daria.

"Now the kiss. And make it a good one; it will have to last until you meet again."

Chapter Seven

"Daria? It is I, Minsee." The old woman glanced around the outer room but did not see the young human. She motioned to the servants trailing behind her to bring in their burdens and put them on the table.

Just then, the doors to the sleeping chamber opened and Daria looked out, smiling at the sight of her friend.

"I hope I do not disturb you, Daria?"

"Of course not, Minsee," she called cheerfully. "Just finishing up my bath and going over the ceremony. Don't want to make any mistakes tomorrow. Let me put something on and I'll be right out."

By the time she reappeared, Minsee stood at the table, seeing to the last details of the arrangement. Coming up beside her, Daria put her arm around the old woman's waist and pecked her cheek. In the three weeks since she and Ston had become engaged, she and The Sildor had become dear friends, almost inseparable.

"What's all this?"

"It is called, *Lanweh*," Minsee smiled, "another one of Utan's endless rituals, I'm afraid. Please, sit down and I will explain."

Daria took a bite of the pastry on her plate. "Oh, that's wonderful," she gushed.

"The loss of a female to her mate's clan is always a sad time for her clan," the old woman started, picking at the delicacy on her plate but not actually eating any. "Especially in the Time Before. When the female left her clan and went to dwell with her mate, often they traveled far away and the female never saw her clan again. Of course, we lived on the surface then. The land and the distances made travel difficult. Not so much now. The

Lanweh is the traditional time when the female that produced the offspring sits down for one final time, to pass on what wisdom she possesses and enjoy the company of her female offspring before she departs."

She looked at Daria, a mixture of love and pride on her face.

"You were not born of my body but I have come to feel about you as my offspring. Even with all the details of the *Fahn-jul*, you still find time to take care of the mining project. You are all that a female could hope for in an offspring."

Taking the old woman's hand in hers, Daria smiled, fighting back her tears. "I never had a mother or a father," she told The Sildor lovingly, "but I know that if I had, I couldn't love them anymore than I've grown to love you and Albre. I hope that I can someday become the person you believe me to be now."

They hugged, each one taking from the other the shared joy of their companionship.

"And anyway," Daria said brightly when they'd parted again, "I'm not going anywhere really. As soon as Ston and I get back from meeting his clan, in about two weeks, he and I will be living right here in the palace. Between me being Minister of Natural Resources and Ston being Lord Chamberlain of the Royal House, you'll probably get tired of having us underfoot."

"With my own offspring scattered to the winds of Utan, I look forward to having you and Ston under my roof. Especially so that I may soon enjoy your offspring as well."

"Could I ask you a question?" Daria ventured shyly. "It's kind of personal."

"For the *Lanweh,* nothing is too personal. What is it you wish to know?"

"I've...uh...heard that you have...uh...a sort of...well...a harem of husbands."

"That is so."

"About one hundred."

"One hundred and four in your numbers."

"Well uh...I was, uh, wondering...I mean how do you...?"

The Sildor laughed and took a sip of the hot beverage that had been served with the pastry.

"You mean how does one woman satisfy the needs of so many men?"

Feeling the crimson rush to her face, Daria lowered her head and nodded.

"I will tell you a small secret, Daria, but you must promise as a blood oath, never to repeat it. Even to Ston."

"I would never repeat a secret entrusted to me by my ruler and good friend."

"All right then. With two notable exceptions, I have been very fond of all my mates. But those joinings mostly sealed treaties and alliances and trade pacts. Little more than formalities, really. Of course, some joinings provided the royal house and other important clans with offspring. An obligation...duty and nothing more."

"Then you haven't...."

She laughed and shook her head. "No, Daria, I did not enjoy the pleasures of the flesh with all of them. Some came here as strangers until the joining ceremony. For offspring, we mated only at the time for seeding. Offspring come easily to me and it mostly took only one time. Never more than three. When we planted the seed, they went away."

"But I thought that you had a harem, here, in the palace, locked away from the world except for you?"

Another ripple of laugh shook the other woman's body.

"That is the secret, Daria. There is no one in the *karavat*. That is why it is guarded and no one is allowed in. All the mates I have had are gone."

"Except Albre," Daria finished knowingly. "He's your one true love, isn't he?"

The old woman's smile broadened into a happy grin. "My first and he remains so in my heart. Our joining produced the female offspring who will be The Sildor when I pass from this place to the next."

"How many children do you have?"

"Twenty-nine, in your numbers."

"My Goodness," Daria yelped. "That's amazing. On Earth, ten is considered to be a large family."

"Ah, but I have read that human primates incubate for some nine months and generally produce only one offspring at a time. Utanian females can give birth after only six of your months, and many times two and three offspring at once. I had two births of three myself.

"You and Ston will make excellent mates and produce many fine offspring. The night of your *Fahn-jul* would be a good time for you to begin. New moons always produce females."

"Well, I don't know if we'll get started quite that soon," Daria giggled. "I mean, I think we should wait at least until we find out if Ston's clan will accept a female not of your planet or even your kind."

"Ston's clan will welcome you because you are a female and will help insure the clan's survival. But beyond that, you are kind and good and beautiful. Be yourself and all will be well."

"I don't know. I mean, what if they don't like me?"

Minsee sighed and took Daria's hand. "When my youngest female offspring took to mate her first male, I did not meet him until they came here on the eve of their *Fahn-jul*. Upon first sight, I was not impressed. He was small...smaller even than my offspring...with a round face and drooping eyes the color of water when it's filled with dirt. All in all, I could not see why my beautiful, intelligent offspring would settle for such a male when she had the whole planet at her feet.

"But as I watched them, I saw the light in her eyes when she looked on him, heard the sound of her voice when she spoke his name. And I knew by every word and gesture that he, too, adored her. How Albre and I, and you and Ston, feel about each other. How could any clan not love someone who can put this look on the face of one of their own? When my offspring took her mate, I knew her happiness was complete. You will find that there is no greater wish than that for your offspring."

Her voice grew suddenly soft and a sadness settled in her eyes.

"Unfortunately, my offspring's time was too short and she passed from this place while still young. But he filled all her moments, even the last ones, with love and caring, giving her two female offspring of her own to enjoy, even for a little while. When she left, the sun of his world went out, leaving him in a cold darkness. Had it not been for the offspring, I think he would have followed her out of this life much sooner than he did."

A tiny smile reappeared although Daria could still see the terrible pain in the other woman's eyes. "He told me he was blessed that the offspring looked like her and not him. When their time came, he saw them both joyfully into clans of their own and then, he, too, passed from this place to the place where she waited."

The old woman held her hand tightly for a few more moments and then, with what seemed to Daria a great effort, resumed her former cheerful manner.

"It is too joyous an occasion to speak of such sad things," she announced, "so we will put those away and think only of now. Which reminds me..."

Minsee reached into the folds of her gown and produced a small white box that she set on the table in front of Daria. "At the *Lanweh*, it is the custom for the older female to give a small token, a trinket to the departing young female. Something personal so that even should they not meet again, the female's clan will not be forgotten."

"Oh, Minsee, you shouldn't have. Not after everything else you've done for me. The gown. The ceremony. The party."

"This is a trifle. Only something for you to have as a remembrance." She pushed the box toward Daria. "It is an old ritual to humor an old female."

The little lid slid open and Daria gasped with surprise when she saw its contents. Lying on a bed of velvet lay a single perfect, emerald, cut in a pear shape and hanging on a thin, delicate gold chain.

"I found it in my jewel box and it made me think of your eyes," the old woman told her. "I hope you like it."

"Oh Minsee, it's beautiful!" Daria reached in and carefully lifted it out, setting it in the palm of her hand, the chain dripping through her fingers. "It's the most beautiful emerald I've ever seen. It's absolutely, utterly gorgeous. Thank you. Not just for this and for everything else you and Albre have done, but for letting me feel, for the first time, like part of a real family."

Tears choked her and the old woman took her into her arms.

"You must not weep," she whispered, her own voice full of tears. "This is a happy time and it warms two old hearts that you would share it with us. Wear the stone close to your heart and know that is as close as you are to ours."

Daria raised her head and looked into that warm face, so different than the one she'd first seen in the reception room. Or maybe not. Perhaps she'd changed, looking at the world through different eyes.

She held out her hand. "If you'd be so kind as to help me put this on, I promise never to take it off."

The Sildor took the small necklace in her hand and Daria turned her back, sweeping her hair from her neck. Gently, the other woman slipped it around her neck and closed the tiny clasp.

Turning back, Daria fingered the green stone, watching it as it caught the light and seemed to shine with its own fire.

"It goes well with your eyes," Minsee commented happily. "If all your female offspring are as beautiful as you and your males as handsome as Ston, you will be truly blessed."

"On Earth, it is our custom to call our children...our offspring...after favorite family members. Of course I haven't been able to discuss it with Ston yet, but if it's all right with him, I'd like to name our first girl, Minsee and our first boy, Albre."

The tears that had been brimming in the old woman's eyes welled up and spilled over her wrinkled cheeks. It was several moments before she could speak again.

"If the people of Utan raised a monument of gold to us and placed it in the temple of the Creator or sang our praises to the last generation of our kind, Albre and I could not be more honored than to give our names to your offspring. When I tell him, he will no doubt weep with joy also."

"It is we who would be honored."

"So," Minsee chirped, wiping at her face with her gold cloth napkin, "are you ready for the ceremony tomorrow?"

"I hope so," Daria chuckled. "I mean, it's a lot more complicated than a wedding ceremony on Earth."

"Ah, I have investigated this custom of yours," Minsee sniffed scornfully. "You stand up before an official and make promises and those attending throw food at you and you throw flowers at them. A silly ritual if you ask me. Certainly nothing to mark such an important occasion. I think the *Fahn-jul* a better joining."

"I don't know," Daria sighed wistfully. "On Earth, it's considered bad luck for the groom to see the bride before the ceremony only on the actual wedding day. Here, it's been three whole weeks."

A wicked gleam appeared in The Sildor's dark eyes. "A little waiting makes the fruit sweeter. That is what I told Ston only this morning."

"You've seen him?" she asked breathlessly.

"Of course. I am The Sildor. I am free to go wherever I like in my own palace. Besides, I am not joining when the sun reaches the middle of the sky tomorrow."

"Oh, how he is?" Daria asked anxiously. "Is he all right? Did he say anything about me? Does he miss me as much as I miss him?"

"Believe me, he misses you terribly. The mere mention of your name produced…a most positive and very visible reaction. I told you that it would be more than his soul that would be overjoyed to see you. You will find him most anxious to…express how much he has missed you. Especially since your time together in The Academy."

Daria knew exactly how Ston felt. He haunted her thoughts, her dreams. Her skin seemed to ache for his touch, her insides cried for his thick, hot cock to come inside her, fill that gaping, empty hole deep within her. More than once in the last three weeks she'd found herself having to relieve the growing pressure herself. Satisfactory as a safety valve against her own body's needs but nothing compared to what she longed for from him.

One more day.

After three weeks she could last one more day.

Perhaps. But could she last one more night?

* * * * *

"What!" Minsee shouted angrily.

"You heard me," Albre replied quietly. "He is here in the palace. And he wishes to see Daria."

"He cannot see Daria," she shot back. "Daria is preparing for her *Fahn-jul*. She has no time for such nonsense. Send him away."

"I cannot do that and you know it."

"Then I shall have my guards send him away."

"You cannot do that either," he continued, trying to maintain his patience.

"I can do anything I want!" she roared. "I am The Sildor of Utan."

"And he is the one she was promised to. He has come all the way from Earth and demands to see her."

"He has no right to make demands here. He is on Utan, not Earth."

"We must tell Daria he is here. It is for her to decide if she wishes to see him or not."

"What if he has come to take her back? Have you thought of that?" Minsee put a nervous fingertip in her mouth and began to nibble absently.

"That, too, is her decision."

"And what about Ston? Does he not have something to say about this? In a little while, she will take him to mate. Perhaps he does not wish her to see another male before the *Fahn-jul*."

"I will tell Ston and see what his wish is. Then I will tell Daria that the male is here and whatever Ston says. But it will still be her decision."

"Then let us wait until after the ceremony." The anger in her voice faded to anxiety.

Albre glared at her silently.

"It is not right," she pouted, chewing on her finger a bit harder, "or fair. He had his chance and he threw it away. She is promised to Ston now. He can not simply appear out of thin air and take her back. I will not permit it."

"You said that you sent Daria to The Academy because you knew she possessed intelligence but not wisdom. You said she must come to trust herself before we could come to trust her. Well now, we must put that trust to the test. If she goes or if she stays, at least we will know where her heart lies. Is that not an important thing for us to know?"

Minsee's mouth turned down and she sighed heavily. "If we lose her, it will be your fault," she told him, "and I will never forgive you. Ever."

He recognized their long understood signal that she agreed, however reluctantly.

"I will go and see them now," he told her sweetly. "You will stay here in your apartments and finish dressing for the ceremony."

"It will be a ceremony of loss...of mourning," she insisted, still pouting.

"Nevertheless, you *will* stay here until I return with news. Give me your word."

"I am The Sildor. Is that not sufficient?"

He took her in his arms and held her, looking down at her tenderly. "I do not want the word of The Sildor. I want the word of my mate, Minsee, that she will not interfere in this. For political or personal reasons."

Frustrated, she bit her finger a last time. "Very well. You have my word that I will not interfere."

Gently he kissed the tip of her nose and smiled. "It will be well, you will see. Now, I am off to see Ston and Daria. And remember, you gave me your word."

"If he takes her from us," she grumbled as he put his hand on the doorknob, "not only will I turn you out, but I will shut the portal myself."

The door had barely shut behind Albre before Minsee crossed the room and opened the door a little, checking the deserted hallway in both directions. Slipping out, she closed the door softly behind her and headed quickly away.

She had given Albre her word she would not interfere and she would abide by that. But she hadn't said anything about the listening port outside Daria's apartment.

* * * * *

"Does Daria know?" Ston asked calmly.

"Not yet," Albre replied, trying not to be swayed by the pain in the other man's eyes. "I thought it best to tell you first. In case you wished to speak to her before...before the other male. Or to be there when they meet."

"Then you don't know if she even wishes to see him?"

"No."

Ston sighed wearily and gazed into the distance for several moments. Finally he turned back to Albre.

"If she wishes to see the male," he said quietly, his voice sad and resigned, "it is not for me to say she can not. After all, it would profit me little to possess her body if her heart is elsewhere. And only she can say where that is."

"You are sure?"

"No," he smiled thinly. "But there is little I can do about it. We are in her hands now."

* * * * *

"Trout? Here?" Daria felt suddenly dizzy and lightheaded and dropped into a chair just as her knees turned to gelatin.

"He arrived a little while ago," Albre continued quietly. "He is in the anteroom awaiting an audience with Minsee. He says he must see you and that he will not leave until he has."

"Does...he know about the *Fahn-jul*?" she asked tentatively.

Albre shook his head once. "We relayed nothing to Unitech but your resignation. We specified no reason and they asked none. I believe that his arriving on this particular day is only what you would call an unfortunate coincidence. But whatever the reason, he is here and the only question that remains is whether or not you wish to see him."

"I...I don't know."

"Then you must find out and quickly. The time is very short now. You must either take Ston to mate when the sun is at its high point in the sky or you must say that there will be no ceremony. As the female, it is your choice."

"But…but how will I know?" She searched his kind face for an answer.

"This, too, is a question of the heart," he told her gently. "You must listen for the answer inside."

Closing her eyes, Daria tried to calm her anxious mind and still her body. For several long moments she sat perfectly still, trying to empty her conscious mind and tune to the voice inside. After several long moments, she opened her eyes again and smiled up at Albre.

"Yes," she announced. "Tell Trout I'll see him."

* * * * *

"Daria!" he shouted happily, crossing the large outer room of her apartment and grabbing her up in his arms. "Oh God, Daria, you don't know how good it is to see you. How much I've missed you." Bending down to kiss her, she turned her head slightly, slipping out of his grasp and pulling back a step.

"You're looking well, Trout," she said evenly. "Suspension agrees with you."

Slightly perplexed, he put his arms down. He'd expected something else in the way of a greeting.

"You look terrific, Daria," he tried again. "I sure am glad to see you're all right. After…after what happened, I didn't know what…what condition I'd find you in."

"After what happened?" she repeated, cocking her head to one side.

"You know. The business with the sex place." His discomfort and desire to avoid discussing the subject came through to her, loud and clear.

"Oh," she replied casually, "you mean The Academy."

He nodded uncomfortably.

"That was several weeks ago," she continued, still keeping her voice steady. "I thought you'd forgotten."

"All right, Daria," he told her firmly, grabbing her arms just below the shoulders and bringing her close to him. "Let's just stop all this. I know you're hurt and you're angry and you have every right to be. I'm not going to make excuses for what I said. Hell, there isn't anything I could say to excuse it. But if you knew the kind of pressure they had me under to get this contract wrapped up. Our careers...yours and mine...our marriage, our lives together, were on the line. I know it's not much now, but I really did do it for both of us." He looked down at her and smiled...that warm, engaging smile that always melted her heart.

"When I found out that you'd resigned, weren't coming back, I knew why and it tore me apart. That's why I've come here."

"Why *did* you think I'd resigned and decided to stay here?" She gazed up at him, real interest showing in those deep emerald eyes for the first time.

"Let's not talk about that," he tried brushing the comment aside. "Not now, not ever. All that matters is that you come home, with me, now. There's a liner leaving this afternoon. We can be on it and back to Earth in a week. Hennessey says that as soon as you lay that signed contract on his desk, you'll become Vice-President in Charge of New Projects, Mineral Division.

"And I've already told my family that regardless of what they think, you and I are going to be married. We'll plan for a small church wedding this autumn. The fall colors in Vermont are so beautiful, they have to be seen to be believed. Then a honeymoon some place warm. I've put a deposit on an apartment on the seventy-fifth floor of the Alexander Building and my parents have agreed to let us have the guest cottage at their house until we can find a summer place of our own in Vermont. It's going to be wonderful. Just the way we planned."

"We never planned it," she responded quietly, staring up, seeing him clearly for the first time. "You planned it."

"How can you say that?" He seemed genuinely surprised. "I don't know how many times we've talked…"

"You've talked, Trout. But you never listened. I never wanted to live in some great big impersonal glass and titanium box seventy-five stories up. I wanted a little brownstone with my own backyard and a flower garden. And I never wanted to spend my summers in Vermont with your family. At least not all of them. I wanted to travel a little and maybe see some of the things Earth and this great big universe have to offer."

"I don't understand, Daria…"

"No," she agreed sadly, "and I don't think you ever did. You said you knew why I'd resigned and wasn't going back to Earth. Tell me why you think that is."

"Daria…"

"No, tell me," she insisted, her voice rising a notch.

"It's…it's because of what happened in that sex place," he mumbled, looking down at his feet. "You're…you're ashamed and you think…you think you're not good enough now. For Unitech…for me."

The silence between them dragged out so long, he finally looked up. She watched him like some kind of interesting specimen she'd discovered under a rock.

"You know," she began quietly, "loving you was really very hard…took a lot of work. I had to spend every waking moment thinking about you. What you did, what you said, what you thought, what you wanted, what you didn't want. You always made me feel just a little beneath you…like I should always kiss your ass for the privilege of being in your life, even if it was just kind of at the fringes. You played on all my worst fears, my biggest self-doubts to control and manipulate me. You made me feel as if I had a big scarlet "O" for orphan stenciled on my forehead. That just being Daria Evans carried some kind of social and moral stigma that could only be erased by becoming *Mrs. Trout Erdman.* Of course, that could only happen through the condescension of the whole damn Erdman family and then only through the back door.

"But the worst part was I let you convince me to buy into that. I agreed to go to The Academy because I thought once and for all it would show you what kind of sacrifice I'd make for you. How much I truly loved you. In my own blindness and stupidity, I didn't even realize that if you'd loved me...even a little bit...you would never have asked me to do it in the first place."

"Daria..."

"No, Trout, you're right, we should stop all this. True love isn't just caring more about the other person than yourself. It's having that feeling shared and returned by another person who doesn't require perfection. Someone who wants the best for you, even if you don't know yourself what that is. Someone to take care of you and watch over you. Endure physical and emotional pain and even be willing to die for you. Someone who cares as much about giving as they do about taking."

"Come home," he cajoled, seeming not even to have heard her, "back to Earth. If you don't want to work for Unitech, that's fine. You're a bright girl and with this mining coup under your belt, you can go anywhere you want. Hennessey'll be disappointed, sure, but I can step in and carry the ball. I mean, I know almost as much about the project as you do. And if you don't want to live in the Alexander Building, we'll find you a little brownstone. And this sex thing...well, we'll just put it behind us. It will be like it never happened." He wrapped himself around her again.

"When you're back home, among your own kind, you'll forget all about this. You'll be your old self in no time."

She pushed him away.

"Don't you understand, Trout? I don't want to go back to Earth. I don't want to be among 'my own kind.' And most especially, I don't want to be my old self, ever, as long as I live. I'm getting very fond of my new self."

He opened his mouth to respond when they heard a light tap at the door. An instant later it opened and Minsee stepped in, closing it behind her.

"Ah, Daria," she chirped sweetly, "I came to see how your preparations for the *Fahn-jul* progressed." She threw a curious look at the young man. "I had no idea you had a visitor."

Daria didn't believe her for an instant. She knew that Albre would have told Minsee immediately about Trout and his mission to the palace. Still, she welcomed The Sildor's interruption.

"This is The Sildor Minsee," she told Trout, bowing slightly and signaling with a nod of her head that he should do likewise, "ruler of Utan. Sildor, this is Trout Erdman. You've heard me speak of him."

Immediately, Trout slipped into his best customer relations demeanor. Rising from his bow, he beamed that glorious, phony smile at her. "A privilege and an honor, Sildor. I'm surprised to find that such a young, beautiful woman rules over this entire planet."

The Sildor returned the fake grin. "Ah, Trout Erdman." She tipped her head to one side and surveyed him critically. "Strange," she muttered almost to herself. ">From the way Daria spoke of you, I had pictured you much taller. And not so skinny." With a shrug, she turned back to Daria.

"The preparations go well?"

"Yes, Sildor. Everything is fine."

"You have bathed and perfumed?"

"I was just getting ready to when Trout arrived."

"You should hurry then. The *Fahn-jul* must begin at the moment the sun is at the middle of the sky."

"*Fahn-jul*?" Trout looked questioningly between the two women.

"You have not told your friend of the ceremony?" Minsee raised an eyebrow and Daria struggled not to laugh out loud.

"I was just getting to it."

"Then you will permit me?"

"Of course."

"Today Daria takes to mate the Lord Chamberlain of my household, Ston. They are a most extraordinary pair. Their offspring will bring much pride to both our people."

Trout's mouth fell open and Daria could only picture a fish, suddenly plucked from the water, gasping in the air. Unable to hold back any longer, a small chuckle escaped her.

"You're...you're getting married?" he choked.

"Yes, Trout. In a very few hours, as a matter of fact."

"I would, of course, invite you to stay for the ceremony," Minsee told him, trying to muster up some semblance of regret, "but I am afraid all the arrangements have been made. Besides, I would not have thought you would want to be there, considering that the contract has been canceled."

Trout turned white and Daria could almost smell fish frying.

"Canceled?" he repeated, the panic in his voice almost swamping the word.

"Certainly. I thought you knew. We sent the communication about a week ago in your time. Did you not receive it?"

"I...I left on the liner eight days ago."

"Ah, well, in suspension you would have had no way of knowing." Daria could see the obvious enjoyment Minsee got from tormenting Trout even as she pretended to be totally ignorant of her game.

"But...but why? I mean...I thought..." Helplessly he looked first at Daria and then back at The Sildor.

"There is in the contract...what is the term?" She wrinkled her brow. "I am sorry. My knowledge of your language leaves much to be desired. But my Minister of Natural Resources will know." Turning her head, she grinned at the younger woman.

"Minister Daria," she asked. "What is the contract term I seek?"

"Morals clause," she replied, no longer making any pretense at seriousness.

"Ah, yes. Morals clause. A very wise and useful addition. It says that if anyone in your company does something of an immoral or dishonest nature, the contract is broken."

"I...I don't understand."

She looked at him like a small boy not grasping an easily understood school lesson. "You are the representative of Unitech. You gave your fellow worker and promised mate to strangers for their sexual use, whatever that might have entailed, for the purpose of securing a contract that would make you rich. The people of Utan can not do business with such a person or with a company that would have such a person working for them. In fact, that is exactly what I told Unitech when I canceled the contract.

"And I have made sure that my Minister of Natural Resources had such a morals clause placed in the contract we are negotiating with Galactic Enterprises for the mining rights to the northern hemisphere.

"She is most remarkable. In the midst of the preparations for her *Fahn-jul*, she has managed to negotiate a better price for the *pluronium* than Unitech offered. It will be most interesting to see what she accomplishes when she can focus her whole attention on the project."

"My God, Daria!" he yelped like a puppy who'd just been stepped on, "do you realize what you've done! What am I going to do? Hennessey'll have my head on a platter."

A malicious gleam appeared in Minsee's eyes and Daria knew The Sildor pictured just that image in her mind. Trout's head served on one of her beautiful gold platters, perhaps in a bed of fresh green lettuce, surrounded by a lei of tomato slices.

"Perhaps another time," she murmured wistfully to herself. "Daria, your meeting is concluded?"

Daria looked into Trout's mystified, anguished face one last time. "Yes, Sildor," she said quietly, not taking her eyes off him. "We're quite finished."

"Then I must help Daria attend to these last preparations. Since you will not able to join us for the ceremony, and I know you are anxious to return to Earth, I will have my guards escort you to the liner and wait to see you safely away."

With that, she raised her hands, clapping them together twice, very loudly. Immediately the doors flew open and four large soldiers, sabers drawn, appeared.

Minsee's smile continued to ooze syrupy sweetness. "I wish you a safe and pleasant journey. Good-bye, Trout Erdman."

He looked desperately at Daria.

"Good-bye, Trout," she smiled.

The guards made a square around him and hustled him out, closing the doors behind them.

"And now," Minsee grinned gleefully, "we must hurry if we are to have you ready for your mate on time."

Chapter Eight

"Well, how do I look?" Daria made a slow twirl. The dress shone a beautiful dark gold, almost the color of her hair, which had been left to hang around her face in soft, silky waves. Cut high at the neck with long, tapered sleeves, the dress fell to the floor, clinging to her, especially across the bust where the material in back had been tightened and bunched up, before it cascaded down her back and formed a small train behind her. Only the emerald necklace adorned her.

Albre smiled like a proud father. "If not for the fact that you are as offspring to me and that Minsee would kill us both, I would throw myself at your feet and beg you to take me to mate as well."

She reached up and pecked him lightly on the cheek. "Thank you. Coming from such a handsome, distinguished man, I take that as a very great compliment. If I didn't love Ston very much…and Minsee would kill us both, I would be honored to have such a man as you for my mate."

"You warm an old heart," he told her, running his fingertip gently along her cheek. "And not just because of your kind falsehood, but because Minsee and I have come truly to love you. I feel the same tug of loss and joy at giving you to Ston that I felt when I surrendered my other female offspring to their mates. When Minsee told me that you wished to give our names to your offspring, we wept. Tears of great happiness and honor and loss."

"You're not losing me," she assured him. "Ston and I will be living here in the palace. You and Minsee will see me every day."

"But you will no longer be truly ours. You will belong to Ston and soon we hope, to your offspring. It is the way of all living things. But you will not understand until you give your first female offspring away."

He sighed once more.

"Now it is time for us to go. We will walk slowly and not take the most direct route to the *Fahn-jul* chamber. That will give us a few more moments."

Taking his arm, Daria and Albre left her apartment and began the long walk to where the ceremony would be held.

"May I ask you a question?" she ventured, looking up at him shyly.

"Of course."

"It's…sort of the other side of a question I asked Minsee before. It's very personal."

"Did Minsee give you an answer?"

She nodded.

"If Minsee could answer such a personal question, then I too will attempt an answer."

"Minsee told me that she has a hundred and four mates."

"That would be about right," he answered matter of factly.

"And some twenty-nine offspring."

"Yes."

"Well…how did that make you feel? I mean, I've never seen her with any of her other mates but it's obvious that you two love each other deeply and have since childhood. I can't imagine…I mean…well…sharing someone…" Words failed her as they had when she'd tried to talk to Minsee. "I want to understand this…this way that Utanians have of looking at love and sex and life because it's how Ston looks at them and how I'll have to adjust my life. I need your help in understanding the male view."

"I suppose it must seem very…different than what you've known," he replied slowly, keeping his gaze straight ahead, "but you must understand that even though our kinds look the same, our evolution has been along a different path."

He glanced at her then, patted her arm and flashed a quick smile. Turning his eyes back to the front, he continued.

"Even before the ice came, Utanians struggled for survival. We were nomadic hunters mostly, living in small clans. The survival of the clan depended on healthy females and offspring, difficult to do even when times were relatively good. But when a clan did not have enough of either, they found themselves forced to seek females from outside clans.

"In those days, the clans lived scattered over the surface, contact between them infrequent and for the most part, violent. Settlements and trade would come long into the future. So, when a young male would come of age and desire to mate and produce offspring, he had few choices. He might fight other males for an available female in his own clan, but often he literally had to ride down on another clan and 'take' a mate. Many times, the…more romantic elements of courtship gave way to the necessity of the moment, if you understand my meaning?"

Daria nodded, entranced by Albre's words.

"If the male could escape the wrath of the other clan and return to his own, he might find he then had to fight other males for his prize. But if he could drag her, often spitting and howling to the elder of the clan, the chieftain would tie her right arm…usually so she could not use it as a weapon…and his left arm…leaving his right free to defend himself and his female…and declare them joined. Then the male would carry her to his place where she would claw, bite and scratch to repel his advances. The rope would be used to keep her from running away until she resigned herself to her new life or became too heavy with offspring to try and escape. I know that it sounds harsh now, but the clans survived. And it benefited the race as well. Only the strongest, most determined males prevailed to mate and reproduce."

Albre glanced at her again.

"Perhaps not a romantic picture, but even from such humble beginnings, much love came forth. Later, when we became more settled, what you would no doubt call, more civilized, we traded our females as we did other precious, necessary goods...to make peace, to form alliances. Whatever must be done, we sacrificed to insure that our people, our planet would continue.

"When the ice and then Gul-Shad's Death came, many thought that we would cease. Only those who held on—who refused to surrender—survived and produced offspring. And these offspring came into the world with the fire of communal good burning in them. So the remaining women began the process of taking many mates. We wished all clans to be helped and that the best parts of all of them be mixed together to create who we are now. Minsee is the most powerful woman on the planet...she is looked up to by all our people, male and female. It is for her to show the way."

"She called it 'duty,' and nothing more," Daria finished, a small glimmer of understanding lighting a corner of her brain.

"A most accurate description," he agreed solemnly.

"But still," she pressed, eager to turn the glimmer into the sunshine of knowledge, "how do you bear it? Seeing her swelled with offspring and knowing...knowing..."

"That another male has seen her naked flesh? Known the pleasures of that flesh? Left his seed within her?" The tone of his voice hadn't changed but Daria sensed the immense pain he must be feeling.

"Yes."

"I bear it," he answered simply, "because it is necessary that I do. And I know in my heart that Minsee's body is but the shell, the vessel. Any male she permits may know it. But I have her heart, her soul, that which makes her special and which no other male may know because we are joined in more than ritual or the making of offspring."

He paused then and turned to face her, love and pride and pain in his eyes, covered by a sheen of unshed tears.

"We are joined in our love. That is something apart from all else and which makes her mine alone, regardless of other mates or offspring. It is our gift from the Creator and which nothing may ever steal or even diminish because it is a part of us. It makes us one."

The sun rose brilliantly over the horizon of her mind, filling a brand new, unexplored landscape with beautiful, radiant light.

Like everything else since she'd come to this strange place, she'd been wrong even about something as seemingly trivial as sex. On Utan, it had an entirely different function, a different meaning than on Earth. Their biology, their evolution, their history had all been so very much removed from hers. In her arrogance—that word again—she'd believed that simply reading about them would tell her what she needed to know. Another illuminating, painful lesson in her own ignorance.

Lesson.

The Academy.

The place where Utanians came as they approached maturity, not to learn about vibrators or whips or to lose their virginity. Submission taught them the acceptance of duty, the pain and pleasure that life would bring them. Domination taught them that power must be used for the good of everyone and not just the selfish desires of a few. And it taught them trust. In themselves and in the mates they would choose.

With this knowledge, they could go forward and find love. They could have multiple mates and offspring, but still know that special bond that comes only when two people are, as Albre had said so beautifully, 'joined in love.'

"Thank you," she whispered, her voice raspy with emotion. "Thank you for giving this gift to me. I...I think I understand a little. A beginning at least."

"I am pleased that I could help you along your journey."

She chuckled and he looked down at her quizzically.

"I just thought of the story Minsee told me about how you and she came to be mated."

"The one where she tricked me into falling back in love with her after I had fallen out to pursue other females?" he asked shrewdly.

Daria nodded.

The older man laughed. "I will tell you another story Daria, but you must promise never to tell Minsee. Agreed?"

"Agreed."

"As you know, my male parent was Headmaster of The Academy for Minsee's female parent, the last Sildor. I was a mere babe when Minsee was born and we grew up in the palace almost as clan. Except that I can not remember a moment in my life that I did not love her. I never thought of any other female. But she scorned me and spurned me and refused my attentions. As she came to maturity and the time for her to choose a mate, I went to The Sildor and pleaded with her to command Minsee to join with me. I told her that if she took another mate, I would die. She told me that Minsee had a mind of her own and would not obey such a command. She would not take any mate but of her own choosing. Certainly not one chosen for her.

"But she did tell me that Minsee only wanted what she could not have. If I wanted her affection, I would have to force myself to stop trying to woo her and turn my mind to other females. She said that I would have to trust Minsee. If she truly had feelings for me, she would seek me out. If not…well, then I should seek a mate elsewhere.

"So, as much as I hated it, I ceased attending Minsee and began to attend other females at court. To my horror, Minsee behaved as if she had forgotten my existence. Only when The Sildor summoned me and told me that Minsee had begged her to take me to mate, did I understand she loved me too."

"It sounds like a comedy of errors," Daria giggled. "And all this time, she's thought that she tricked you."

"And it has cost me dearly," he added. "Even now she believes in her skill at these silly games. Although I think you and Ston may have finally put an end to her continual meddling. At least I hope."

They walked the short distance remaining in comfortable silence.

"Well," Albre told her as they paused, "we are at the doors of the chamber. You remember all that is required of you?"

"I hope so," she grinned.

"Then we will proceed." He let go of her arm momentarily and pushed on the huge wooden door. As they swung open, Albre took her fingertips in his hand and with great solemnity, began to walk slowly forward on the thick, wide deep blue carpet.

Nervously, her eyes swept the giant hall. *My God*, she thought, *there must be three hundred people here and all of them staring at me!*

And then she saw a familiar face, standing above the crowd, a tissue clutched in a pale blue paw, waving slightly. Beside Analet stood Benwa, smiling and nodding to her. The sight of her friend seemed to calm Daria and she focused again straight ahead.

Absolute quiet; no music, no laughter, no whispers. Only all those eyes trained on her every move. She felt her mouth go dry and her palms get damp. As if to reassure her, Albre gently squeezed her fingers.

Ahead of them, the carpet ran up six wide steps to three large, high-backed wooden chairs, not quite as large as Minsee's in the reception hall. The chairs on the left and middle stood empty but The Sildor sat in the right hand one, her face as blank and impassive at that first meeting.

Slowly, they made their way, Albre helping her up the steps and making sure she was seated before he too sat down. Another heartbeat and Minsee nodded ever so slightly. As one, the assembled crowd sat down also.

Voh appeared between the bottom of the steps and the first row of spectators, some twenty feet away, Daria guessed.

Dressed all in crimson with gold braid dripping from his shoulders and chest, she thought he looked like a beautiful, showy bird.

"Since the female is not of Utan, we will be speaking the ceremony in her language. Any of you who do not understand, please turn on your translation units now."

Murmurs and rustlings rippled through the crowd as people adjusted their translation units and settled back into respectful silence.

"As it was from the beginning," he intoned gravely. "As it was in the Time Before, we are gathered in this place for *Fahn-jul*. Today, the human female, Daria Evans, Minister of Natural Resources, takes to mate the Utanian male, Ston, Lord Chamberlain to The Sildor."

He moved away to the left and another man shuffled slowly up to take his place. Silver haired, wrinkled, stoop shouldered and dressed all in black, he seemed to Daria the epitome of age. Turning toward them, he bowed to The Sildor, to Daria and to Albre who in turn acknowledged him with a movement of their own heads.

Taking a breath, he turned back to the assembly.

"As elder to the household of The Sildor," he began in a surprisingly strong tenor voice, "it is my duty to perform this joining. Who speaks for the female?"

Albre stood up and moved quickly down the steps.

"I do," he announced crisply. "Daria Evans is not of our clan or even our kind. But she has been accepted into The Sildor's household and has become as one of our own offspring." It seemed to Daria that he stood a bit taller, sounded a bit more imperious than usual.

"And where is the male?"

Again, the doors at the back of the huge room swung open and Ston began striding purposefully, but to Daria's mind, entirely too slowly, toward them.

Ston walked toward them, dressed in a soldier's regalia, a breast plate of some dull, brass-looking material covering his chest and stomach, a short 'skirt' of some kind not quite coming to his knees and thick high-topped brown boots on his feet. Over his shoulder hung a bow and a quiver of arrows. At his side hung a long scabbard the color of his breastplate, the hilt of his sword a bright gold. In his right hand, he carried a large sack.

Stopping in front of the elder, he bowed and then to The Sildor and Albre.

Immediately, Daria looked down, remembering that in this part of the ritual, neither she nor Ston could look at each other.

Still, the sight of him coming toward her had made her pulse quicken and the room grow instantly hot. She wondered if he wanted her as badly as she wanted him.

"I am Ston," he announced boldly, the sound of his voice raising goose flesh and setting a fire between her legs, "from the clan Mucchay. I have come for the female, Daria Evans."

"You love the female?"

"More than my own life."

"You are prepared to become her mate?"

"Yes, elder."

"Is it the wish of the female that you become her mate?"

"Yes, elder."

"She has told you this?"

"Yes, elder."

"And you, Albre, she has spoken of this with you as well?"

"She has told me that she is willing," he replied simply.

Oh Lord, Daria thought, the fire spreading through her body with each passing moment, *why did everything in Utanian culture have to be steeped in so much damned ritual? Why couldn't they just say 'I do' so they could get down to the business of doing it?*

"As head of her clan," the old man continued, "what do you say?"

"I say," Albre's voice suddenly dripped disdain, "that the words of a male, hungry for the body of a female, are of little worth. Especially not in comparison to the loss of a female offspring to her clan."

"What, beyond your words, are you prepared to show the female's clan that you are worthy to take her from them?"

At last the ritual allowed her to look up.

Ston had just set down his sack and opened the top.

"I make these promises to the female and her clan," he responded seriously.

Carefully, he reached into the bag and produced a small, round loaf of dark brown, peasant bread which he set on a clean white cloth at the elder's feet. "This is my promise that the female will never know hunger."

Next, he produced a small bundle of twigs and solar glass used for starting fires. "This is my promise that the female will never know cold."

A rock about the size of Ston's hand and a handful of thatch appeared. "This is my promise that the female will always have shelter."

A length of animal skin came next. "This is my promise that the female need never fear anything, even the largest, fiercest Balmeer."

He slid his bow and quiver off and laid them beside the skin. "This is my promise that I will serve Utan as is my duty and that no dishonor will ever come to the female, her clan or our offspring."

Finally, he took a small dagger from his belt, held out his left index finger and made a swift pass across the tip. Instantly, a drop of vermilion bloomed. "This is my promise that I will love the female as long as blood or breath of life run in this body and that I would gladly sacrifice them for the female."

Daria looked at the gifts as they appeared, one by one, suddenly moved by the importance of what they represented. She'd read the ceremony and knew her part in it; knew that this ritual stretched back thousands and thousands of years. But not until this moment had she truly understood what the promises represented. What Ston and all the other males down through the ages had actually been saying.

These were mere tokens, symbols now. But once, there had been a real Balmeer to be slain and skinned. A real house to be built and firewood to be gathered. Real promises made and kept.

She realized keenly these promises stood for something far and away more significant than rings and rice.

Love and lust rose up and Daria was seized with the urge to race down the steps and into Ston's arms. But the ritual must be finished, not just for their sake but for Albre and Minsee as well. Any breach would reflect on them and she'd only just begun to understand the true importance of family.

"This seems evidence of the male's promises," the elder told Albre.

"It is better than mere words," he agreed non-committally. "However, it is for the female to decide if it is enough."

Again Daria felt all those eyes upon her, including Ston who now stood at the bottom of the steps, awaiting her answer.

"This is a very solemn, very dignified occasion," Minsee had told her in the days before the ceremony. "You must be careful and deliberate in your movements, as if contemplating each moment whether or not you will actually take this male to mate." She'd grinned then and tapped Daria playfully. "It's good to make them suffer a tiny bit more with the uncertainty. You want them to feel as if they've won a prize of great value, not gotten a free gift."

Slowly, Daria rose and with a last, quick sidelong glance at Minsee, she slowly descended the steps, stopping finally beside Albre. His expression did not change, but she saw the joy in his eyes as she bowed her head to him and then the elder.

Quietly, she stepped to where the bread lay. Picking it up, she tore a large piece off and set the loaf back. Next, she picked up a twig and the lighter and placed them carefully on the rock and thatch. Picking up the Balmeer skin, she draped it like a stole across her shoulders, feeling for an instant that same rush of hot excitement and sexual power as in The Academy. Taking another step toward Ston and using the fingers of her left hand to hold on to both the bread and the stole, she bent down and picked an arrow out of his quiver.

Finally, they stood face to face, the longing and the love and the need she felt, mirrored in his deep eyes. She wanted desperately to reach up and kiss those inviting lips and at the thought, a ripple of electricity ran through her.

It's almost over, she told herself. *Almost.*

Taking the arrow, she broke it and dropped it between them.

The crucial time had come. The moment that everyone, including Ston had been waiting for. She had acknowledged all his promises except the most important, food. Food was life itself. If she accepted his bread, if she told him in front of everyone that she loved and trusted him to provide her with life sustaining food, the commitment would be made.

In slow motion, she put the bread to her mouth and took a bite, holding the other piece out to him. Relief and gratitude joined the other emotions swirling in the dark depths of his eyes as he moved his mouth to her fingers, taking up the offered bread.

Silently, Ston put his left hand on her right and they turned together back to the elder. Out of the corner of her eye, she thought she saw Albre flash a quick smile, but it vanished as quickly as it had appeared.

"By taking the bread of the male," he announced solemnly, "the female has agreed to take him as mate." He held out a thin, withered hand and Ston produced a pouch from his waist. Opening it carefully, he shook the contents into the old man's palm.

A beautiful gold cord, at least two feet long and as big around as her thumb appeared, uncoiling from the bag like a living thing, its body radiant with diamonds, rubies, emeralds and sapphires, all gleaming like the markings of some rich, exotic snake. Holding it up for everyone to see, a collective gasp of wonder and the buzz of excited conversation erupted in the assembled crowd.

"Silence," he ordered sharply. Immediately, the noise stopped.

Twice he wrapped the cord around their arms, leaving the 'tails' to hang over. Pressing his hand on the cord he raised his voice and his eyes toward the ceiling.

"By these acts, the female Daria Evans, and the male Ston, have committed to this joining. Being the elder of this household, I proclaim that with the binding cord, they are joined now from this moment to the end of their lives. It is the wish of those who gather here that you, the Creator of all things may bless this joining with long life, much joy and many offspring."

How Daria longed to hear the words, "you may kiss the bride." The feel of Ston's skin on hers had only increased the fire inside, turning it to a raging inferno that must be satisfied or kill her. But she knew the ritual would continue.

Albre stepped forward, his eyes shining with delight but his voice as sharp as a razor. "You have made many promises this day," he told Ston, "not just to the female who would have you as mate but to The Sildor and to me. Remember them and hold them dear in your heart because we will. A hurt to our offspring, no matter how slight, will be a hurt to us and to all our clan. It will be repaid a hundred times over."

"You and The Sildor and all your clan may rest well," Ston answered, keeping his voice solemn and respectful. "My life now is to make the female greet each day with rejoicing and thanksgiving for this joining. To protect her from harm or unhappiness, I would gladly surrender my life."

With a single nod, Albre looked at Daria and his voice softened to melted butter. "Your parting brings us much sadness," he told her tenderly, "even as your new life brings us joy. But know that this is your place too and that we are your people, your clan. You are welcome and loved always."

Tears blurred Daria's vision and she closed her eyes as they fell. She felt Ston's other hand cover hers and she heard Minsee's voice close in front of her.

"To celebrate this happy occasion," she said in a calm, even tone, "there will be a feast in the Great Hall. Food, drink, music and good cheer. It is the wish of The Sildor that all of you who have witnessed this joining should present yourself and share in our joy."

As she opened her eyes, Daria saw Albre put his fingers on Minsee's arm and they began the journey down the carpet and out of the room. A few steps behind them, the elder followed. Ston smiled at her and they took their place, walking slowly behind the elder. Voh came after them, making sure that none of the crowd left their seats until the wedding party had departed the room.

"I love you," Daria whispered as they made their way down the hall.

"I love you, too," Ston replied.

"After three weeks of being apart," she grinned, "you better."

He returned her grin. "I will do my best," he assured her.

Chapter Nine

"Ston," she breathed in his ear, "I want you…now."

He tried to concentrate on the flight path of his vehicle but the feel of her so close, the warmth of her breath on his cheek, the scent of her aroused musk…

"I must attend the vehicle," he swallowed, trying to keep his mind and his hands focused ahead.

The tip of her tongue wiggled in his ear, sending shock waves of heat through his body. Her lips brushed along his cheek, settling finally like a butterfly on his lips. "The vehicle's on auto-pilot," she whispered. "You haven't touched the steering mechanism for half an hour at least." The tips of her fingers ran lightly along the sensitive flesh of his other ear.

"Nevertheless," he managed to croak, "I…I must keep watch."

"The vehicle will find its way to wherever we're going," she insisted in hot, breathless pants. "Come lie down and make love to me as you promised. Living these last weeks without you, going through the endless ritual of joining and then the party… Mid-way through, I thought seriously about ripping off your clothes and taking you on the dance floor."

"We have been patient this long," he growled, hardly able to bear the swelling of his cock in his tight garments. "We can endure a few moments more."

They had changed from their ceremonial dress to comfortable traveling clothes. Playfully, Daria ran her hand down his chest and stomach, and rested lightly on the bulge in his lap. "Are you sure about that?" she asked wickedly.

Swallowing hard, he moved her hand. "Yes," his voice raspy with need. "If you will only stop tormenting me."

"What about you tormenting me?" she responded in a throaty growl of her own and moving her hand back to his lap. "There you are with that great, big, lovely cock of yours, dying to get inside me and you won't share. You just keep saying, 'patience,' 'patience.' Well I don't think you've got any more patience than I have." She rubbed her palm against his lap, feeling the heat and hardness of him through the thin fabric.

"Unless," she pretended to pout, "you don't really want to make love with me."

He turned to face her, his tongue running over his dry lips, those eyes filled with a need and desire at least to at least match her own.

"Every moment apart while we waited for *Fahn-jul* tortured me worse than death. I could not eat because even the sweetest fruit could not compare to the taste of your breasts, your treasure. Nor could I drink because I had tasted the juices of your passion and even *Fal-Trank* paled. Your scent filled my mind as it had my nostrils that first time I massaged you. When the night breezes blew across my body, I could feel your touch, your lips on my flesh and it screamed for you.

"No matter how many times I tried to relieve the pressure in my cock, it refused to be satisfied, crying out that only the softness, the richness of your body would ease the ache. The want of you became a pain that colored my life and made the solar rotations seem like solar revolutions. You surrounded me and yet I could not be with you."

"Then why are we waiting? Pull over and give us what we both need. Both want." She pressed her lips against his, twining her fingers in his hair and scooting almost on to his lap. Unfortunately, she couldn't quite fit between his chest and the steering mechanism.

"Please," he whimpered, his pleadings mixed with their growing passion. "A little while longer. We are almost there."

"I don't understand," she breathed, pulling her face just far enough from his to speak. "You told me that your clan is in the far western part of the planet. That even if we left the vehicle on auto-pilot all night, we still wouldn't get there until late tomorrow afternoon."

"That is right."

"Then why don't you just come back here and get comfortable? I know you want me as much as I want you. Just a quickie so that I can get through until we stop. Please."

"We cannot join here," he insisted, trying not to be dissuaded by her lips and breasts pressed against him.

"Why not? You and I have had lots of sex. Lots of pulse racing, heart pounding, white-hot sex in some pretty strange places. What's one more going to matter?"

"Because…" he fought the fire now racing through his own blood. "Because this will be the first joining since we have become mates. This must be a special joining in a special place so that all the moments of our life, even to the end, we will remember it and be glad."

"Any place, any sex," she panted, "would be special with you. I'm so hot for you now I can't stand it. Here, see what just the sight, the touch, the taste of you does to me." She took his hand and dragged it slowly over her breasts. He knew she hadn't put on any undergarments and he could feel her nipples, hard and erect as his cock, straining to him. As his hand passed over them, he felt her tremble.

"And here." She hiked up her dress, exposing her soft curls and slit of pussy. He let his hand be guided between her legs and felt her sweet wetness. The scent of her rose up like the heady aroma of a thousand rare flowers. His cock screamed to be released from its cloth prison and driven into her.

"Please," he begged pitifully. "I will ask nothing more of you all the moments of our life if you will grant me this. I would not ask if…if it were not important. Please do not push me any further."

Daria looked into those beautiful eyes and the look she saw there made her stop. Obviously he wanted her as much as she wanted him, but she saw something else, something that overshadowed even the physical need.

"Tell me, what could possibly be so important that you'd pass up making mad, passionate love to a woman who wants you more than anything else in the world?"

"I will explain everything. As soon as we reach our destination."

"Now."

"It will make no sense to you if I try to explain now. When we get where we are going, everything will be made clear. For now, you must simply believe and trust me. And know also that I will make up ten-fold for any inconvenience you are suffering now."

Daria made a face and pulled away. "Inconvenience does not begin to cover the situation."

They rode along in silence, the landscape desolate and deserted, growing dim in the twilight. It had been hours since they'd left the city and she hadn't seen any signs of life for some time. Looking out the port at the land slipping by under the vehicle, she wondered where they could possibly be going in such a lonely place.

Night had just fallen when she felt the vehicle begin to slow and descend. Outside, she could see nothing but empty, unbroken darkness. A few moments later, the vehicle glided to a smooth landing and stopped, its engines shutting down automatically and the interior lights coming on.

"Where are we?" she asked.

"Come with me," he told her getting up from his seat.

"Come with you, where?" Combined with her physical frustration and weariness after the long ride, this game, whatever he intended, had grown thin and she didn't want to play anymore.

"Come with me and I'll show you," he replied patiently.

"I'm not getting out of this seat, much less this vehicle until you tell me where we are, where we're going and what the hell is going on."

Squatting down in front of her, Ston took her hand and pushed a few stray hairs off her forehead. "A few moments more," he cajoled. "I promise."

Sighing in frustration and resignation, Daria rose and followed him to the back of the vehicle. From the luggage compartment he took a large, soft-sided duffel bag and a smaller box, which she recognized as a food container.

"Put on your coat," he said, handing her a bulky jacket. "There are gloves in the pocket. And cover your head with the hood. It will be cold when we get outside." He reached in, drew out his own jacket and began to put it on. Seeing no other choice, Daria followed his example.

When they had their coats and gloves on, he handed the small container to her, hefted the duffel bag over his shoulder and reached into the compartment a final time, pulling back a large lantern. Flipping it on, he turned out the interior light and opened the door. A blast of cold air immediately engulfed them. Stepping down into the darkness, he adjusted his burden slightly and put out his hand to help Daria down.

Clutching the container, she grabbed his hand and alighted into the pool of light provided by the lantern.

"It is this way," Ston told her, waving the lantern to his left. "Not far now. Down this path a little. But be careful and hold my hand. The ground is uneven."

Daria tightened her grip on his fingers as they set off into the darkness. Above her, a canopy of stars in unfamiliar constellations, twinkled down on them like the lights of some distant city. *Wherever this was leading*, she thought angrily, *had better be warm and have a soft bed.*

"There," he said excitedly, stopping suddenly and pointing the lantern into the dark.

She squinted into the darkness and finally spied a small light, glittering like one of the stars, except it hung too low and too near. But at least it finally marked the journey's end.

After a few more minutes, they crossed a last, small open space and entered a portal, the darkness around them broken only by a few tiny lights of some sort twinkling feebly above them.

"Where are we?" she asked, surprised by the hollow reverberation of her voice. "I can't see anything."

"Shhh," he hushed, pulling her further along.

The lantern cut a bright path ahead of them but Daria could see nothing but patches of black walls that looked like stone and though now out of the wind, the place still felt cold and dank.

"Here we are," Ston announced happily, dropping his pack on the ground with a thud.

"And where exactly is 'here?'" Daria grumbled, her voice tired and cranky.

"Let me get some light and I will show you."

Rummaging in the duffel bag, he produced two more lanterns, bigger than the ones he held. In a moment, they blazed to life illuminating the area around them.

"It's a cave!" Daria shrieked, her head spinning in all directions, unable to comprehend why her husband of only a few hours would bring her to such a place.

She turned on him like an enraged Balmeer. "It's awful!" she screamed. "How could you…why would you bring me to such a horrible place on our wedding night! Take me back to the palace! Now, this moment!"

He took a step toward her and put out his arms but she batted them away.

"I can't believe you'd do such a mean, hateful thing!" she continued, her voice reaching fever pitch and breaking up into sobs.

Gently he enveloped her, pressing her to him. "It is all right," he soothed. "You are tired and this is not what you expected. Let me explain and if you still wish to return, we will do so. But please, hear me out first."

"Whatever it is, it can't be worth staying in this awful place," she sniffled.

"Please."

Wiping her wet face on his shirt, she looked up at him and he could see her determination to listen but only so she could escape.

"Come and sit down here while I make a fire."

"I don't want you taking time to build a fire," she responded coldly. "I just want you to spit out whatever it is you have to say so we can get the hell out of here."

Guiding her gently, he sat her down on a small wooden platform and went to a small circle of stones between the lanterns. From the duffel bag, he took a package of 'Instant Fire,' which he laid in the stones. A pull on the tab and the package burst into flames and almost immediately the warmth of the fire seemed to find her.

"Long ago," he began as he watched the fire expand and grow into a cheerful blaze, "in the Time Before, there lived a male named Galvar. A hunter and a warrior, he lived off the land, taking what he needed. Not a violent man, but a man living in violent times. While still almost a child, he was the only one to escape the murder of his clan by a band of outlaws so he set off by himself."

"This is all very interesting," she interrupted, "but it's not getting me back to the palace."

"You promised you would listen," he reminded her, squatting on his haunches and warming himself.

"All right, but just get on with it."

"Galvar grew to be a great warrior, much feared and respected by the other clans. He did not make war and only used his weapons to defend his property or to take what he

Elizabeth Stewart

needed. In time, other males without clans allied themselves with him. And eventually, the time came when he wished to take a mate and begin producing his own offspring."

"So he rode into some clan site, grabbed up the first female he saw and rode away into the sunset," Daria added sourly.

Ston only sighed and looked at her.

"He decided that he would make peace with one of the clans and settle his own people. But first, he would seek out a mate for his heart and not just his bed. So he traveled far, riding peacefully among the clans until he found Hanrah in the western country. She was called the most beautiful female on the planet, wise and with the gift of knowing the future. The stories say that as a small child, she told her father, head of the clan, that her mate would come out of the rising sun, strong and bold but with a gentle heart. And it is said that when they first gazed upon each other, their hearts were sealed."

"That's very nice, but it still doesn't explain this cave." The fire burned warmly now and the shadows it cast danced merrily on the smooth black walls.

"After they joined, they set off back toward his people so that he could lead them to their new home. But a huge storm came up, bringing with it a howling wind that blew out their fire and a biting cold that pierced their bodies like arrows. He covered her with his cloak and held her tightly, but he could feel the life seeping slowly from her small, delicate body because she had not lived in the elements as he had.

"By the time night came, he knew that Hanrah would not survive without help. So he called upon the Creator. He declared Hanrah the most beautiful, most precious thing he possessed. That without her, his life would be of no value and would be better ended. 'I will strike you a bargain,' he said. 'Spare Hanrah and return her safely to her clan and I will gladly surrender my own life.'

The Creator, touched greatly by Galvar's plea, sent a sign to him. Making a small spark of light in the great darkness, he spoke to Galvar's heart. 'Follow the light,' he instructed and Galvar heeded the voice. Picking Hanrah up, he carried her until they came to this cave. Using stones from the floor, he made a sort of wall at the entrance to shield them from the wind and the Balmeers and then he carried her in here, to the main chamber. With some sticks he found, he made a fire and set her close to warm her.

"Searching through the cave with a torch he made from a burning stick, he found first a spring of cold, clear water and in the very back, the body of a she-Draak, a large creature which sleeps when the planet is cold. She had been dead many solar rotations and only her bones and warm coat remained. Giving thanks to the Creator and the Draak, he cut her skin from her bones and brought it to where Hanrah lay. They ate what remained of their joining celebration food and drank water from the spring.

"Finally, wrapped in the soft, warm skin of the Draak, Galvar and Hanrah joined as mates. They gave each other great joy many times that night and slept at last in each other's arms. In the morning, they found that the storm had passed and they continued their journey. From their night of passion came the first of their many offspring, a female, from whom my clan comes. Every solar revolution, they came and spent the night again in this cave, reliving each time the passion of the first joining. They said that each time renewed them even as it left a little of them here.

"As their offspring grew and took mates of their own, it became the custom for them to spend their first joining here, in this place of joy and refuge. Truly they had long life, much joy and many offspring. And since that beginning, my clan has considered it sacred, the place where all joinings should begin."

"But...but this can't possibly be the same place," Daria questioned softly, now completely caught up in the story. "I mean, that must have happened when your people lived on the surface and we're still underground. Aren't we?"

"Unfortunately, yes," he sighed. "We could not bring the cave underground so we did what we could. We created this cave, exactly as it had been on the surface, taking the rocks, twigs, dirt...even the crystals from the ceiling...and moved them here. Of course, now we have lanterns and ready-made fire and the spring is fed from an underground reservoir and the Draak's coat, although exact down to its molecules, was created in a replication device, but the essence of the story, the joining, remains the same. Now, do you wish to leave?"

"Did you really think I would?" she smiled.

"Not if it meant putting off our joining any longer."

They laughed. "Okay. Why don't you take a lantern and go find us some spring water and a Draak's coat and I'll see what's in the food container. But hurry. I'm absolutely ravenous."

* * * * *

"You are warm enough?" Ston asked, curling himself around her back and pressing his cock against her ass.

"Hmmm. Between this heavenly soft Draak's skin and your hard body, I'm positively hot." She ran her fingers along the velvety soft, pale gray nap of the pelt that covered their naked bodies. "It feels so luxurious. I can't believe any real animal ever had a coat this wonderful."

"In the Time Before, the animal was greatly prized because of its size and because killing it was difficult. I have read that some stood twice the height of a grown male and that a single carcass could feed a clan of twenty through the cold time. But they were vicious when disturbed and feared nothing. Even the Balmeer packs avoided them."

"I'm glad we have air pads, though," she remarked. "And pillows. I don't think I would have relished making love on the cold, dirty ground. I guess I'm just not hardy pioneer stock at heart."

Ston laughed. "It would not have been so bad," he teased. "In the back of the cave grows much moss and other such vegetation clinging to the walls. I would have gathered enough to make you a soft bed and then laid part of the pelt on it and wrapped us in the rest."

"Yes, well, if it's all the same to you, I prefer nice clean air beds and pillows."

She felt his erection press against her ass, hard and hot as rigid steel fresh from the tempering forge. "What would you like for our first joining?" she asked tenderly.

His lips touched her neck and shoulders, dropping kisses soft and light as rose petals on her skin. Reaching around her, his large hand cupped her left breast, his thumb and forefinger bringing her nipple to attention.

"I wish to taste the warm, wet flesh of your treasure and the sweet flavor of your passion. I have dreamed and hungered for you since that first time in The Academy."

Moving to his side, he rolled her flat on her back, exposing her to him. The sight of her pale flesh lit only by the flickering fire and a single lantern by the head of their makeshift bed, caused him to quiver with anticipation and his cock to throb with aching need.

Gently, he reached down and put his mouth on her tender pink nipple, sucking and nipping and dancing his tongue quickly over it. She rewarded him with little moans of pleasure as her body squirmed under him. Not wanting her other breast to feel ignored, he moved his head and brought that nipple to erect as well.

As her soft moans became louder, he bent down to the soft blonde curls that covered her like a pale blanket, just barely hiding the pink slit of her pussy. Easing himself down, he tenderly parted her lips and revealed her swollen, pink clitoris, glistening like a small, delicate pink berry, ripe for the plucking.

Covering it with his mouth, he sucked a little, bouncing the tip of his tongue quickly up and down and then sweeping the flat expanse of it over and around, like licking dew from a sweet melon.

"Oh…oh…Dear God…" she moaned, her eyes closed, her back arched slightly.

He knew she needed to come and soon. Their bodies verged on eruption. When they had both released, they would be able to take their time and enjoy each other's bodies at a more leisurely pace. Right now, nothing mattered but ending their mutual torment.

Under him, her squirming had become writhing, her moans escalating in pitch along with her passion. His own body seemed to be on fire, fueled by the feel, the taste, the smell of her.

Sweeping his tongue from the engorged tip of her pussy, across the opening and down as far as possible before returning. Short, dart-like flicks peppered the most sensitive part of her, causing her body to tremble. Sucking started to bring her juices flowing.

With a final wail of ecstasy, he felt the shudder of release flood through her and out into his waiting, hungry mouth. Frantically, he swallowed and slurped, anxious to catch every precious drop of her.

Daria could never remember any orgasm like this. The universe, time itself, seemed to have stopped, catching her at the pinnacle of physical explosion and keeping her suspended in this incredible state of exhilaration. Rushes and waves of pleasure washed over and through her, each one more wonderful than the last, each one sending her higher.

After what seemed hours, the shuddering stopped and she became aware of herself again. And the fact that this overwhelming release had not dimmed her passion, drawn her into exhaustion. Instead, it seemed just to have whetted her appetite.

Ston gave her pussy a last little peck and looked up at her, not needing to ask about her satisfaction.

"Come here," she demanded, reaching her arms for him.

Obediently, he moved to her, their lips meeting, parting to let their hungry tongues explore and exchange sensations. As he settled, he felt her hand reach down to his enormous, pulsing cock and guide it inside her.

"Oh," he muttered as her soft wetness enveloped him, sending his already racing pulse even quicker, his burning temperature to the flash point.

"You feel so good," she mumbled, easily matching herself to his rhythm. "I've missed you so much. Thought about this moment…"

Raising his head, he looked into her face, saw his passion, desire, love reflected in her dreamy, half-closed eyes. "You are so beautiful…you make me feel as I have never felt… Being apart from you…"

He couldn't talk, couldn't think, anymore. Only the building excitement rushing through his body as she squeezed and pulled and gently surrounded him, pulling him toward the edge — only that mattered.

Her fingers dug into his hard, muscled ass, pulling on him as she ground her hips beneath him, trying to take him deeper, more fully into her.

A small tremor shivered through her body as she came again, the thought of bringing her a second round of pleasure, making him glow almost as much as his own physical pleasure.

"Oh!"

Something between a cry and a shriek escaped her, filling the cavern and echoing as she crested again, the convulsing of her body pushing him into his own release. For a moment, they froze, melded together in their own supernova of white-hot pleasure. Explosions of pure sensation jolted through them, exploding and drifting gently down like fragments of a rainbow.

Together, they collapsed in a tangled heap of arms and legs, enjoying the satisfied silence as they tried to catch their breath and return their hearts to normal. Quietly, Ston slipped out of her, turning on his side and pulling her to him.

"I hope you found that worth the delay," he chuckled, feasting on her naked body with his dark, sparkling eyes.

"Not bad," she teased playfully.

"The first or the second?" he retorted.

"Hmmm, tough call. I'll let you know after I've had a bigger sampling. Say, five or six."

"So, this is the insatiable monster I created in The Academy?" He laughed again and planted a peck on the tip of her nose. "You will kill me yet, female."

"Ah, but as we say on my planet, 'what a way to go.'"

He frowned then, the sparkle going out of his eyes. "I have been thinking much about your planet," he told her, the serious tone of his voice bringing her to attention.

"What about Earth?" She searched his face, his eyes, worried now that there might be some kind of problem.

"You have given up much to take me as mate. Your job, which meant much to you."

"Not as much as you do," she assured him. "Not even as important as being Minister of Natural Resources to The Sildor of Utan."

"But important, nonetheless. You have given up your planet and the society of your own kind to live among strangers on a world half a galaxy from Earth. You have adopted our dress and our language…"

"Well, trying to adopt your language."

"Trying then. You have adopted our ways and our customs. It is a great deal to sacrifice."

"Not if you love someone," she tried to explain, her anxiety continuing to grow. "And I love you. On Earth, and I hate to keep bringing it up, we say, 'whither thou goest.' It means, wherever you are, that's where I am."

"Well, I have decided that you have given up enough. I love you and wish only your happiness. Therefore, I have decided that I will adopt some of your Earth ways and customs so that you will not feel so cut off from that which is familiar."

"That really isn't necessary…"

"No," he shook his head firmly. "I have considered it much and that is my decision."

"Well then, what customs do you want to adopt?"

"As we settle into our lives, you will decide which customs are dear to you and that you wish to keep. For now, I have decided that we should adopt your custom of each female taking only one mate."

Daria laughed, relieved to grasp what he'd been talking about.

"You mean I should give up the chance for twenty-four other males?" she giggled. "What about my duty to the survival of Utan?"

"The survival of Utan is not your duty," he pouted, "but I promise you enough offspring so that you will feel you have made your fair contribution. And I remember your disgust at the thought of many mates."

"Yes, but that was before my enlightenment in The Academy. A good measure of which, by the way, I owe to you."

"I do not wish to share you," he whimpered like a small boy. "The thought that some other male might look upon your naked body, bring you pleasure, give you offspring, is awful enough. But that some other male might turn your heart from me…"

For the first time, Daria saw anguish in her mate's eyes, his whole body tense with the weight of profound misery.

"I know that for a male of Utan to feel such selfishness is a betrayal of all that we as a people have stood for. The need for our people to survive. But you are the treasure of my life and to surrender even a tiny part of that treasure to another male is more than I could bear. Even The Sildor would understand, though, if you wished to keep this human custom of a single mate, and I could walk among my people with pride instead of shame."

Suddenly, she understood what he was really saying. He'd been raised in a culture of communal welfare. No Utanian male kept a female to himself. It went against everything Ston had been taught, lived, was. And yet now, for the love of her, he was willing to forsake everything.

Looking into his eyes, she knew that the pain must be unbearable for him. He was asking her to help him absolve himself of his heinous crime of selfishness by insisting that he follow her custom of one mate to compensate for all she had 'given up' for him.

Daria took him in her arms and he buried his face between her breasts.

"There will never be anyone else, my love," she cooed softly, stroking his hair. "I promise you. And I hold that promise as dear as the promises you made to me at our *Fahn-jul*."

He looked up at her then, the light returned to his eyes. "I love you," he whispered.

"I love you, too."

They shared a long, passionate kiss, filled completely by their love, knowing they were joined in spirit as well as body.

"I have one more surprise for you," he told her softly. "Lie on your back and watch the top of the cave."

"I don't know if I can stay awake for another 'surprise,' she giggled.

"It is not that surprise," he answered playfully, reaching over and turning off the lantern.

Instead of the expected total darkness, Daria watched in amazement as the whole ceiling, as far as she could see, lit up in soft colors of blue and red and green and yellow.

"Oh, Ston!" she breathed, her eyes scanning the scene, "it's gorgeous! I've never seen anything like it! What is it?"

She felt him shrug beside her. "It is the crystals in the ceiling glowing. No one knows why, not even the scientists. There are no other crystals on Utan like these and they glow only here. If you take them away, they become only cold rock. But my clan believes it is the Creator's gift to all who come here in love and find joy."

"I don't understand."

"When Galvar and Hanrah had finished with their joinings and prepared to sleep, she noticed a small glow of red over the spot where they had made their bed. Galvar took a torch and raised it. He saw the roof of the cave covered with crystals. Like tiny blocks of ice, is how Hanrah is said to have described them.

"They thought perhaps it was the light they had seen which guided them first to the safety of the cave and saved their lives. But as time passed and they came to the cave each solar revolution, they noticed that more and more crystals seemed to glow, always after their joining and they came to understand that a part of them, the power of their love was taken up and kept by the crystals. As their offspring and their offspring's offspring came to this place, the power grew and grew, taking up from the lovers and giving back the blessings of that love to others."

He put his arms around her and pulled her to him.

"Somewhere, up there, we have left a small part of ourselves, our love. As we will do each solar revolution when we return to mark this time. And a thousand solar revolutions from now, when our bones are dust and our memory slipped from the minds of our clan, a part of us, our love, will remain here to be shared by other lovers."

Together, they lay wrapped in each other's arms, bathed in the soft glow of the warm rainbow above them.

In a little while, she heard the deep, even rhythm of his breathing and she knew that he'd fallen asleep. She could feel it settling quietly over her too.

Gently, so as not to wake him, she turned on her side, pulled the Draak skin up to her chin and closed her eyes. Immediately, she felt Ston's arm adjusting her body to him, his cock resting snugly in the crease between her cheeks, his right arm loosely draped over her. She had never felt so warm, safe and loved.

Tomorrow, they would continue their journey and arrive at Ston's clan. A prickle of anxiety tickled the hairs on the back of her neck like a cold breeze. Perhaps they wouldn't like her. Wouldn't accept her.

In two weeks they would return to the palace and she would accept the awesome responsibility, not just of negotiating this first mining contract with Galactic Enterprises, but the management and oversight of all the vast, untapped resources of Utan. Not to mention establishing and preserving those places and resources of importance to the Utanian people that would need to be protected, not just for the now but for the Time After, when the glaciers melted and people returned to the surface. A time so far in the future, she couldn't even imagine it.

The cold breeze blew over her neck again, accompanied this time by a hard knot in her stomach.

Accept and trust.

The words popped into her head almost as if someone had spoken them.

She had no control over the feelings of Ston's clan and must accept their judgment of her. But she did have control over her reactions and she could always trust that her actions would make her welcome, thanks to her lessons at The Academy.

Likewise, she had no control over the natural resources or how those who came after her would manage them. She must accept the limits of her authority and knowledge. But she could trust herself to make the best decisions she could, lay the foundations that would hopefully create a sound base on which to build.

Accept and trust.

And love.

She had made these promises to herself and to Ston when she'd agreed to take up her life with him. To accept him as he was, to trust that he would honor his promises and to love him for all the days of her life, no matter how long or short.

The knot melted and the cold breeze on her neck died away.

And anyway, she thought dreamily, *I always have my* gorlach.

THE END

About the author:

Elizabeth ("Liz") Stewart has been writing since the age of three. Her professional credits include press releases, newspaper articles and columns, short stories and a screenplay. Published novels are in such diverse genre as mystery, contemporary romantic suspense, paranormal, horror and futuristic romantica.

Elizabeth Stewart welcomes mail from readers. You can write to her c/o Ellora's Cave Publishing at P.O. Box 787, Hudson, Ohio 44236-0787.

Also by ELIZABETH STEWART:

- Stray Thoughts

Why an electronic book?

We live in the Information Age—an exciting time in the history of human civilization in which technology rules supreme and continues to progress in leaps and bounds every minute of every hour of every day. For a multitude of reasons, more and more avid literary fans are opting to purchase e-books instead of paperbacks. The question to those not yet initiated to the world of electronic reading is simply: *why?*

1. *Price.* An electronic title at Ellora's Cave Publishing runs anywhere from 40-75% less than the cover price of the <u>exact same title</u> in paperback format. Why? Cold mathematics. It is less expensive to publish an e-book than it is to publish a paperback, so the savings are passed along to the consumer.

2. *Space.* Running out of room to house your paperback books? That is one worry you will never have with electronic novels. For a low one-time cost, you can purchase a handheld computer designed specifically for e-reading purposes. Many e-readers are larger than the average handheld, giving you plenty of screen room. Better yet, hundreds of titles can be stored within your new library—a single microchip. (Please note that Ellora's Cave does not endorse any specific brands. You can check our website at www.ellorascave.com for customer recommendations we make available to new consumers.)

3. *Mobility.* Because your new library now consists of only a microchip, your entire cache of books can be taken with you wherever you go.

4. *Personal preferences are accounted for.* Are the words you are currently reading too small? Too large? Too...**ANNOYING**? Paperback books cannot be modified according to personal preferences, but e-books can.

5. *Innovation.* The way you read a book is not the only advancement the Information Age has gifted the literary community with. There is also the factor of what you can read. Ellora's Cave Publishing will be introducing a new line of interactive titles that are available in e-book format only.

6. *Instant gratification.* Is it the middle of the night and all the bookstores are closed? Are you tired of waiting days—sometimes weeks—for online and offline bookstores to ship the novels you bought? Ellora's Cave Publishing sells instantaneous downloads 24 hours a day, 7 days a week, 365 days a year. Our e-book delivery system is 100% automated, meaning your order is filled as soon as you pay for it.

Those are a few of the top reasons why electronic novels are displacing paperbacks for many an avid reader. As always, Ellora's Cave Publishing welcomes your questions and comments. We invite you to email us at service@ellorascave.com or write to us directly at: P.O. Box 787, Hudson, Ohio 44236-0787.

9 781843 605645